THE FIREDRAKE

THE
FIREDRAKE

Cecelia Holland

Atheneum   New York

1966

To Miss Susan Harris

Prefatory Note

The name "Laeghaire" is the Gaelic spelling of Lear, as in *King Lear*. It may be pronounced that way, although a speaker of Gaelic would undoubtedly correct it.

The historical details of the story are as close to truth as possible. The major exception is the events of October 1066, prior to the occupation of the town of Hastings. I have rearranged the facts here to suit purposes of plot and characterization. I ask the reader's pardon for these and any other inaccuracies.

The greatest inaccuracy a writer of historical fiction can commit is to assume the inevitability of events. I ask the reader to approach the events of this tale not as accomplished facts, but as the unfolding of the continual, unforeseeable present. The decisions of the dark and violent eleventh century were no more inevitable and no less agonizing than the decisions of the dark and violent twentieth century.

Cecelia Holland

THE FIREDRAKE

In the trees it had been very dark. Here in the clearing the sun still shone a little. He turned in the saddle and looked back. He could see only a little way into the forest. The trail wound back down the slope and vanished into the deep heavy darkness.

He moved the black horse a little farther from the trees and dismounted. The grass was thick and high. The spur of the rock would make good shelter. He lifted the reins over the head of the black horse and let them trail. He went slowly to the rock spur. The rock lifted in a great arched crest. He thought the ground was level beyond it. But when he rounded the rock he saw that the ground fell sharply away, sweeping back down to the forest. He had not realized how high he had come, following the ancient trail.

He was tired. He stood a moment, not thinking. He lifted one hand and thrust back the hood of his cloak. He looked around. He saw the fire bed at once. It was crowded up to the rock and heaped with black ash and stubs of wood. He started a little. His hands rose, and he turned and looked all around. He could see everything from here, all the clearing; there were only the two horses, grazing, the lead line drooping between them. The brown stallion lifted his head once, nosed at his shoulder, and lowered his head again to the grass. Laeghaire relaxed slowly and went down to the fire bed.

It had been used before the rain, some three or four days ago. He kicked idly at the heap of rubble. Gypsies, he thought. Heinrich's knights would not have come so far so quickly. He wandered around the clearing. The ground was rough under his feet. The clearing tilted like a tent to the crest of the rock. Near the edge of the forest on the north side there was a flat space. Here the grass was still crushed down from the weight of horses. He found the hole a picket pin had made. Gypsies, he thought. He shrugged.

His heel scraped on metal. He knelt and probed at the ground with his forefinger. It was a bit shank. He weighed it in his hands. The shank was long and curved back sharply. He rose and flung it into the trees. Thuringians, after all. He went back to his horses. The black horse lifted his head. Laeghaire pulled off the saddle and bridle and dumped them in the lee of the rock. He took the waterskin from the saddle and turned. The black horse was right behind him. He unlaced the skin and gave the horse water. The horse raised his head. The water dripped from the fine hairs around his muzzle. The horse butted at Laeghaire. Laeghaire shoved him away. The horse laid back his ears and snapped at Laeghaire's hand. Suddenly he wheeled and galloped off, leaning into the curve of the slope. Laeghaire went to the brown stallion and led him to the rock spur. He unpacked him and hobbled him. The black horse trotted back and began to graze.

Laeghaire ate a little dried meat and drank some water. He gave the brown stallion grain. While the stallion ate, Laeghaire stayed by him, keeping the black away. The black stood watching curiously. Laeghaire took the empty nosebag and put it down and made a fire. He sat by it and leaned against the rock. It had become very dark. There was no moon. The stars were small and sharp. He burrowed into his cloak. He was not tired for sleeping. He thought of the Thuringians who had stayed by a fire in almost the same place, tethering their horses down by the forest. He wondered if they had spoken of him. He wondered who they had been. They would be ahead of him now. Probably there were more behind him. He had followed the old trail too faithfully. He took a mouthful of water and held it on his tongue. Finally he swallowed it. They would surely not expect him to stay on the old trail now, not with the fire and the bit for good evidence of their passing.

He dozed. Several times he woke up, stood, and looked around. Before dawn he harnessed the horses. He had thought a long time in the night. He left the horses, packed and ready, and went down to the forest. He found the bit shank on the even pine-needle floor of the forest. He knocked the dirt from it and looked at it. The broken edge showed uneven knife cuts. He put the shank in his pack when he returned to the horses.

He left the old trail and rode southwest, picking his way through the tall slender trees. The ground was fairly open. He made good speed. The horses moved quietly over the soft thick ground. Toward noon he found another trail, much newer than the one he had followed to the clearing, that ran south. He turned along it. It was marked with cart wheel ruts; the more he followed it, the wider and clearer it became. He camped by it that night and slept well. He rode on along the trail. In the dusk of that day he came from the forest onto a plain. He camped on the edge of the plain. The horses grazed in the wild grass. He thought about the Thuringians. He wondered which of them had left the bit shank. They were heavy-armed, broad-faced men, as strong as the Slavs. They did not talk deeply. He remembered their faces, lit up by firelight, in the camps they had made campaigning. They talked of women and the loot they would have and how strong they were. He wondered how many of them hunted him. Their faces in the firelight had had pits of shadow for eyes.

He thought about the bit shank the next day, riding on. Once he reined in and looked for the shank in his packs. He studied it while he rode. It was like any other Thuringian bit. It was like the bit the black horse wore. He put the shank back.

The plain stretched out on all sides. On it many

farmers worked. He saw men in the fields and carts and mules. He stayed away from them. The grain was half cut down. The stubble stuck up out of the dark earth. He stayed away from the men, who turned and watched him pass and bent back to their harvesting. The women carried slings on their backs to put the ripe grain in. Hay wains stood in the middle of the fields. Laeghaire moved steadily along, never changing his course.

This was rich country. He rode for days in the fields, and always he saw the harvesters; once he crossed a deep river valley, and in the valley he crossed a road so worn with wheel ruts that the brown stallion stumbled to his knees on it. Finally he came to the end of the farmland. The plain continued but the farmland stopped. The fields of stubble and mown hay stopped and wild grass grew up. The plain sloped steadily higher. He saw no men. In the twilight he rode to a little rise and looked all around. The grass shivered under the wind and the darkening sky closed down over him. He saw a tree far down the plain. The first stars came out. He relaxed himself into his saddle. His legs felt as if iron rods were bound to his knees. He shifted his weight a little and rode on to the base of the rise to camp.

The next day he saw a fortress, far away, and found a road. The road led to the fort. All day long he rode before he came to the fortress. It lay on a river valley, where the river had worn deep into the plain. One side of the fortress was against the plain, and the other lay hard on the valley's edge. He saw men on the wall of the fort. It was a small fort, but the wall was high.

He reined in. The brown stallion came up to the end of the rope, his head raised. His eyes turned steadily on the fortress. Laeghaire slouched into the saddle. He let the rein slide between his fingers. The black horse moved two steps to the side. He pushed against the bit. Laeghaire thought, I can ride around that wall and go into the valley. These men would ask him questions. The stallion tugged at the rope, and the wind lifted his mane.

Laeghaire shrugged. He drew the rein through his fingers and rode straight to the fortress gate. Men dug around the outside of the wall, repairing the earthwork there. He rode by them without looking at them. He rode straight to the gate.

"Who goes?"

"No enemy of yours. I want a bed. Food, for myself and my horses."

"Are you knight?"

"Dubbed and spurred."

"Are you alone?"

"Yes."

"God's peace to you."

Laeghaire sank down into the saddle. He took his feet out of the stirrups. He decided it was worth the risk if he could sleep lying down for once.

The gate opened. The man on the wall shouted something in a German dialect. Laeghaire decided he was repeating Laeghaire's answers. He kicked his feet into the stirrups and started forward.

A man walked through the gate. "Hold in," he said. He spoke Latin also. "Who are you?"

In the pause the man's eyes narrowed.

"I am Laeghaire from Tralee. Laeghaire of the Long Road."

The man said nothing. He looked Laeghaire up and down. He turned suddenly.

"Wilfried."

Wilfried appeared on the wall.

"How long ago did the knights from Thuringia come by?"

"Two days, my lord."

The man looked at Laeghaire. He looked only as high as Laeghaire's breastbone. "Wilfried will take care of you."

Laeghaire rode by him. He rode through the gate. In the courtyard he glanced around, elaborating his ease. He dismounted slowly.

The lord came up behind him. "The boy will take your horses," he said. He gestured. A small ragged child stood beside him.

"No matter," Laeghaire said. "I can do it."

"The boy is very capable."

"I always tend my horses myself."

The lord turned abruptly and went off. Laeghaire took the reins and started toward the stable. The boy fell in beside him. It felt good to be walking. The boy jogged beside him. The boy ran ahead to open the door to the little stable. Laeghaire put the horses in the nearest corner. He tugged at the harness straps. The boy ran off and came back with water in a bucket. He swung himself up over a beam and sat, looking down.

Laeghaire put the pack under the manger. He fed the stallion his grain. The boy kicked his heels in the air. Laeghaire unsaddled the black horse. He drew his sword and scabbard out of the pack and buckled the belt around his waist.

An older boy came into the stable and approached them. He said, in fair Latin, "My lord is in the hall, if you will come, sir."

Laeghaire knelt and opened the pack. He took out the little sack of coins. He looked at the boy on the beam. The boy grinned suddenly. Laeghaire hung the sack from his belt, near the hilt of his sword. He followed the page away. At the door he turned and looked back. The stableboy was down under the manger, rifling through the pack. Laeghaire went out after the page.

* * *

He left that place the next morning and for a week saw nothing but the open plain. Finally he came to some fields, full of harvesters. He was far from the travelers' road. The people in the fields looked up to see him pass and looked harder when they saw that he was not of their country. He stopped for water. The people spoke only a dialect. He made signs with his hands. He watered both horses well and filled his waterskin. The children came out of the fields to stand and look at him. A woman came boldly up and fingered the heavy carved leather of his rein. She pointed to it and her brows rose.

"Ireland," he said.

She shook her head.

He rode on. These people knew nothing beyond their fields. He was safe here. The Thuringians would not have come so far south. Such safety no man wanted, to be shut off. He smiled over that. He was still uneasy about the Thuringians. Another thing occurred to him. He had sent word by the merchants that he would be in Flanders by Christmas. He was unsure of it now. It had seemed time enough, back at Pentecost. Now he rode a wide circle, and he was far from the landmarks he knew. He supposed that if he rode west he would reach the river, and he could ride along it to the ford. But he had no idea how far it was to the river. Perhaps the river ended north of here. He cursed Heinrich again.

He came on another fortress and asked lodging. The man on the wall spoke no Latin. He motioned that Laeghaire should wait. After a moment another man appeared on the wall.

"God be with you," the man said.

"And with you also. I want food and bedding for myself and my horses."

"Come in. We have room and we welcome travelers."

He rode in through an old-fashioned gate. The gate was worked by hand. Two heavyset men stood by the ropes.

The man who had spoken to him greeted him with enthusiasm. "We have few travelers here—perhaps one or two a year. We are far from the road."

Laeghaire muttered something.

"I'll show you where to put your horses. Where are you from?"

"Thuringia."

The little man nodded merrily. He trotted beside Laeghaire. Laeghaire took the horses into the barn and put them up. The little man talked to him all the time. "I am lord of this castle. Those are my fields out there, also. Not much—but they support us. I have nearly one hundred serfs. My liege lord is the lord of Swabia."

"I speak High German," Laeghaire said.

"Good. Come along and I'll show you your quarters."

They went up to the keep and climbed the stairs. The little man opened a door. The vast room was empty. It smelled of long moldering. "Modest, but it's all we have. Do you mind?"

"I'm pleased with anything. This is very nice."

"And you'll dine with us? Good. I'll send a boy up to fetch you. Where are you bound?"

"Flanders."

"Ah, such a distance. Your master has some great dealings with the Flemish lord, I suppose."

"I have no master. I left the service of the Duke some time ago."

The little man looked around. Presently he sat on the floor.

"Are you then in the service of the Flemish lord?"

"I hope so, but I won't know until I get there."

The little man frowned. "That is a great uncertainty."

"Yes."

"Are you Thuringian?"

"Irish."

"Irish?"

"From Ireland. An island west of England."

"You are a far-traveled man."

"Well, yes."

"I— Have you told me your name? I have a poor memory."

"Laeghaire. Laeghaire from Tralee."

"Tralee must be a fortress in Ireland."

"A village. There is a monastery there."

"You're obviously a knight."

"Yes."

"Why were you in Thuringia? If you don't mind. I'm sorry if I am too bold. Perhaps you are on some secret business."

"I was paid to be in Thuringia."

"Hunh." The little man rose. "I'll send the boy. Good day to you, Sir Laeghaire."

"Good day to you, my lord."

The door closed softly.

Laeghaire spat. He went to the high window. He looked out over a courtyard and the wall and the fields. The mountains grew up behind the fields. Perhaps, if Guillaume had no work for him in Flanders, he would go back to Ireland. He squinted slightly; the sun was just beyond those mountains. He thought of his brothers and his father. He was full of a sudden hunger to hear Gaelic. He turned from the window.

At supper, the little man was gay and full of questions. "How will you travel to Flanders, Sir Laeghaire?"

"West to the river, then north to the ford. There is a ford by Worms."

"Have you traveled much in Germany?"

"Only in Thuringia and around there, my lord."

The little man leaned back and shouted for more beer.

The hall servants were taking away the platters. The beer came in a keg. The little man broke the top himself. His wife stood up. The little man nodded to her, and she left, silently, with her women.

"You'll cross the river at Worms?" the little man said. He poured beer into Laeghaire's cup. The foam spouted up and poured off onto the table.

"Yes."

A young man, the lord's son, lifted his head. He had not spoken at all before. "There is a better ford, much farther south, and you could travel through France."

Laeghaire drank deeply of the beer. "You grow good hops, my lord. You, sir, why should I travel through France?"

"Don't listen to him," the little man said. He put a cup of beer before his son and cuffed him lightly. "He's traveled a little, on the errands of my lord, and he thinks he knows the world."

"Nevertheless," the young man said, "if I were an Irishman named Laeghaire, just come out of Thuringia, I would hardly stay very long in Germany."

"Wolfram—"

"No," Laeghaire said. "Let him talk. What have you heard of me?"

"Only that the Thuringian Duke has set his knights on you. They say you robbed him."

"They say lies, then. He robbed me."

Wolfram shrugged. "I only say what I have heard, sir. That's what I have heard."

"You should learn to keep your mouth shut until you're sure of what you say. Are you a dog carrying lice from one man's barn to the next?"

"I—" Wolfram bit his lips. He glanced at the little man. The little man stood, his eyes flying from his son to Laeghaire and back again.

"You carry lies like an old woman," Laeghaire said.

"And if I give you a tale, you'll parade it back to the court of Swabia and pour it into their ears."

Wolfram looked at his hands. His neck flushed.

"He owed me a small matter of fifty marks," Laeghaire said. He looked quickly at the little man and back to Wolfram. He tapped his forefinger on the table. "Three years' worth, he owed me. He wouldn't pay it. So I took it. Ask those knights."

"They spoke well of you," Wolfram said hastily.

"Oh?"

"They said you were a better fighter than all of them together."

"Who said this?"

"I don't know all their names. What does it matter?"

"Give me a name, boy."

"Lorenz."

"Ah." Laeghaire sank back onto the bench and picked up his cup. "If you should . . . chance on Lorenz again, tell him his bit's in good hands."

"Is this code?" the little man said.

"He'll know."

"Code."

"Have you been to Spain?" Wolfram asked.

"No. The Spanish hire no knights."

"Why?"

Laeghaire wiped the foam from his upper lip. "Do you hire knights?"

Wolfram laughed. "I should like to go to Spain."

"Perhaps you will."

"No," the little man said. "He'll stay here, he'll inherit my lands, like a good son."

"You're fortunate, then," Laeghaire said. "To be heir."

"Do you have brothers?"

"I had when I left Ireland. If they are still alive, I don't know."

"How many?" the little man asked.

"Two." Laeghaire grinned. The little man reached across the table and took his empty cup and went to fill it. "We have Viking blood," Laeghaire said, "and Ireland wouldn't have held the three of us when we were younger. My father knew it."

"Ah." The little man slid the cup back to him. "You should have taken orders, then." He climbed onto the table.

"I was four years in a monastery."

"Oh? Why did you leave?"

"My mother died. I dislike monks."

The little man frowned. He snapped his fingers. A hound jumped onto the table beside him. The man toyed with the dog's ears.

"The Devil's work. You ought to have stayed."

Laeghaire shrugged.

"No offense meant, of course."

"And none taken."

"I can't know the circumstances. Perhaps you were forced." The little man patted the hound. "Still, more and more men are leaving the land. A terrible thing. Terrible."

Laeghaire grinned at Wolfram.

"Only gypsies and traders travel. It's a wicked life."

"Father," Wolfram said.

"A wicked life."

"If you will forgive me, my lords," Laeghaire said. "I'm very tired."

"Of course. Forgive us for keeping you. But it's so seldom we have guests, we want to hear everything at once. Don't we, Wolfram?"

"Yes."

"How long will you be staying?"

"I'll leave in the morning," Laeghaire said.

"Oh, but you mustn't. You should stay a while."

"I have to be in Flanders by Christmas."

"Christmas is a long way away."

"It's a long road."

"One day won't matter. Stay another day."

Laeghaire thought of the long ride and of the Thuringians; Heinrich's knights had come a long way and were all around him. Here he might be safe for a while. He shrugged. "A day, then."

"Good." The little man folded his hands. "We hear Mass in the chapel. I'll send a boy for you."

They were treating him better than a high lord, Laeghaire thought. He pulled the cover over him and straightened his spine. The moonlight struck in through the window. If he rose and looked out that window it would be richly silver beyond, past the wall. The mountains down there. South. In Ireland it was the sea. Wolfram might be sitting by his window now, looking at those mountains. Moonlight did strange things to eyes. Like looking at someone in profile. The eyes were like glass. Wolfram might be there, staring straight out at the mountains, with eyes full of the light from the moon, all clear and wild. Blind men stare that way. He shifted his hips over a ridge in the pallet. Blind men and prophets. But if he had been Wolfram, he would have challenged him, sitting there insulting him, calling him a dog and an old woman. Perhaps Germans didn't think those were insults.

When I was Wolfram's age I would have challenged me and killed me. In my father's house? There are many mansions.

Mass. He had not heard the Mass for a long time. The forest was no place to hear a Mass. Trolls, the women said. Witches. Dwarfs. Christ stopped at the edge of the forest. He rolled over. He shut the moon out with his arms. The cover was thick. He slept.

After Mass, Wolfram sought him out where he sat mending harness. Wolfram sat down beside him and watched. Laeghaire threaded a thong through a hole in the strap and looked up.

"Good morning, my lord."

"You're going to Flanders."

"Yes."

"Why?"

"I know the captain of the Count of Flanders' guard, and he'll give me a place, if they fight this season."

"I'd think it more exciting to go wandering to places you've never been."

"For a young man, yes."

"You're young."

"Who are you to tell me I'm young? I was younger than you when I left Ireland, and I haven't been five Christmases in the same place since."

"Still, it would be terribly exciting."

"Not alone."

"Then take me with you."

"Hah. So you've been a little while with the Count of Swabia, and you think you'd like to go elsewhere. Not with me, boy."

"But you said you disliked being alone."

"I never said so. You misunderstood me."

Wolfram bit his lips. "Then let me ride with you just to Flanders. I'll set out for myself after that."

"No."

"Why?"

"You would slow me down. Go out alone, if you want."

"How can I leave? My father—"

Laeghaire spat. Wolfram stopped speaking. He dug at the dirt with the heel of his boot.

"It's a hard life, and your father knows it. All I've got is my horses and my armor. You'd be a fool to throw off what you have here."

"What do I have here? A patch of dirt, a stupid fortress no bigger than a count's cattle shed—"

"It's better than what I have."

"You have your reputation."

"Who knows my reputation? Nobody but a handful of landless knights."

"The Count of Swabia knows you."

"This is foolish."

"Then take me with you."

"I don't want to talk about this."

"If you won't take me with you, I'll go alone."

"Then go alone. You'll come back, in a year at the most, all penitent, and they'll have you back and marry you off, and you'll live happily ever after."

"I won't come back until I've made a name and found myself a bigger domain than this—this—clump."

"And rescued a princess and married her and been dubbed the champion of all Christendom. You'll come back poor and happy you're done with it. It's a bad life, boy."

"Then why do you keep on?"

"A man has to live. I'm tired of talking to you; go away."

Wolfram left. Laeghaire straightened the harness and hung it from a peg. The horse boys were lying in the sun by the water trough, talking. Laeghaire went over and dipped up a handful of water to drink. He nudged one of the boys with his toe. "Fetch out my black horse."

The boy leaped up and trotted toward the stable. Laeghaire sat on the edge of the trough. He splashed water at a flock of chickens pecking corn from the ground. The other horse boy sat up and watched him. Laeghaire saw a deep scuff on his boot and frowned at it.

The boy said something in dialect. Laeghaire shook his head. "Slower."

The boy grinned. He spoke slowly, with long gaps between the words. "I don't speak good High German. That black horse is very nice."

"Thanks."

"Someday I am going to learn High German."

"You don't have to speak as slowly as that."

The boy laughed. "All right." His hair fell into his eyes.

The black horse came out, shaking his head and kicking. The boy clung lightly to the lead rope. The horse dragged him a little. The boy kept easily free of the moving hoofs. Laeghaire stood up and put his hand out. The black horse came to him. He took the rope and let it hang. He bent and lifted one forehoof. He tested the shoe and took out his dagger. He cleaned the hoof.

"What's the country like, to the west?"

The boys sat and looked at each other. The one who had brought the horse cleared his throat and said slowly, "It's very bad. There are wicked men in the forest. The river is not far, though."

"Are there fortresses?"

"No," the other boy said. He hooked his elbow into the other one's ribs. "The outlaws are too strong. Not so slow, Willi. He can understand it."

"What kind of outlaws?"

"Oh, just wicked men," Willi said.

The other boy said, "Some say they are knights who've left their lands."

Laeghaire, working now on a hind hoof, glanced over at him. "My deepest thanks."

"But they are wicked men," Willi said. "You're good.

I heard Wolfram tell his father the lord."

Laeghaire snorted. "How far is it to the river?"

"Not far."

"How far is not far?"

They looked at one another, grinned, blushed, and turned back. "Just not far."

"Two days, three days?"

"We've never gone to the river."

Wolfram, when Laeghaire asked him, said, "It might take you four days, it might take you ten, or you might not get there ever."

"Willi said there were outlaws."

"Willi?"

"The horse boy."

"Oh. I've never known their names. I'm never here. They're just children from the village. Serfs."

"I suppose there are few travelers over the way from here to the river."

"Well, there are never people through here in large groups. But the road to Champagne goes just a bit north of where you'll be going. The people will speak High German, if that's what you mean."

"That's what I mean, my lord."

When he left, it was false dawn; he rode out before anyone else was awake, except the horse boys. They followed him to the gate and said good-by to him.

He rode due west. The sun was just coming up. The mist was rising. A thousand rainbows ran over the top edge of the mist. Suddenly the mist wasn't there any more. The ground and the forest ahead were sharper than before. The air was damp and chilly. He shivered.

Almost as soon as he was in the forest, the land broke up, crushed into sharp hills. The trees enveloped everything. The sun came through the trees only in thin shafts. He rode down a steep slope and from the bottom he looked up and saw the jagged outlines of the mountains.

There was no trail. The darkness of the forest made him uneasy. He led the brown stallion close to him and worked along the higher ridges. The slopes were steep, and he often dismounted to lead the horses down. The rocks shouldered up out of the ground with moss clinging to them. Pine needles lay four fingers thick around them. The horses left no prints on the earth.

His mind kept returning to Wolfram. Always before he had been able to shut out thoughts that irritated him. Now Wolfram plagued his mind. Wolfram was half courtier and half little boy wanting to leave home. Wolfram itched in his mind. He decided that Wolfram would not like this plunging down slopes.

He dismounted and led the horses down a steep shoulder of the mountain. At the foot of the slope the black horse stumbled. The stallion flung up his head and snorted. He was frisky from resting. He arched his neck and bucked. Suddenly he lunged. The rope flew from Laeghaire's hand. The stallion wheeled and galloped out onto the valley floor. Laeghaire vaulted into the saddle and raced after him. The stallion heard him coming and laid back his ears and galloped harder. He ran beyond the edge of the rocks and thorny brush onto the open flat. Laeghaire laughed at him. The black was faster. The valley floor was narrow. The stallion swerved north, running with a heavy driving action, flailing twigs and dry brush out of his way. His great hoofs tore at the ground. Laeghaire caught up to him and reached out to get the rope. He saw the first farmland. He caught the rope and sat back in the saddle. The black horse stopped fast and Laeghaire wrestled the stallion to a halt. He studied the farm. If there were outlaws here, there should be no farms.

He rode down the fields. They were full of wild wheat. He could see no sign of men. Near the slope stood the shell of a hut, burned hollow. Perhaps the farmers had been killed. He rode through the wheat. He saw a place where deer had lain down in the ripe wheat. The seeding grain lay crushed in a wide circle, littered with droppings. Poppies grew up through the yellow grain. He saw no fences, no more huts. But the whole valley was full of wild wheat.

A stream ran along the edge of the valley. He watered the horses and drank a mouthful of water and rode along the stream. The valley twisted. It was very narrow, and the slopes were steep. Ahead, it bent, and he rode around the bend and saw huts, gathered in a little cluster by the stream. A fence of peeled tree trunks stood along the north side of the cluster of huts.

He drew up and looked for a way to climb the slope. It was steep to the right, and on the left it was like a cliff. He drew the horses toward the left. He heard a horn down by the huts. He spurred the black horse. Beside him the brown stallion thrust his head forward and lengthened his stride. They swung around the huts. Men ran from them and raced to stop him. Laeghaire headed the horses straight for the running men. He drew the brown stallion closer. A man caught at his rein. Laeghaire leaned forward to club him down with his fist. They were all before him. They jumped for him. He dropped his rein over his saddle pommel. With his fist he knocked down a man who clawed for him.

The brown stallion stopped and reared. Laeghaire beat at him with the rope end. They broke through the line of outlaws. The outlaws fled. Laeghaire slapped the stallion on the rump. He caught his rein. He did not lessen his speed. The horses splashed across the stream. The water rose in sheets from their hoofs. On the other side was a little meadow and the rock face of the slope. The trees grew down close around the rock. Laeghaire made for that, for the shelter. He looked over his shoulder. The outlaws were coming after him. They ran close to the brush-choked ground and disappeared sometimes into the high grass.

In the lee of the cliff he dragged the horses to a halt. He drew the stallion to him, hand over hand on the rope. The stallion protested. He snapped at Laeghaire's knee. Laeghaire kicked him in the head. He moved his shield under the lashings of the pack and drew out his bow and the quiver. He nocked an arrow and waited. The outlaws were chasing him fearlessly.

He counted eight or nine. They kept ducking into the high grass. He aimed at the nearest and shot him down. He shot a second crossing the water and a third before the others understood and retreated. They halted only long enough to pull one man out of the stream.

He loosened the pack enough to get at his sword. If he took his shield out, he knew, the whole pack would come loose and dump his mail and clothes and money onto the ground. He held the sword in his hand. They were talking, out there, in a little group. One of them set off at a loping run for the huts. Laeghaire shot at the group, but his arrow fell far short.

They charged him again, in a wide separated line, dropping often into the grass. He shot three arrows. One hit, but the other two went wide; they were cleverer now. He unslung the bow and dropped it. They burst toward him, running fast. He spurred the black horse. The stallion ran beside him. The men closed in on him. They raised shortswords and axes. They seemed very far below him. One man lunged against him, heavy shoulder down to throw the horse, his sword raised like a shield. Laeghaire brought his sword hard across the man's wrist. He spun the black horse away and clubbed down at a black-bearded man. The man turned the blade on the haft of his ax. Laeghaire turned the horse on his haunches, striking at the man. The horse wheeled in quarter-turns. The man could not dodge back. The horse swung after him. Laeghaire beat and beat at the black beard. Always the ax haft got in the way. Laeghaire swung the horse in the other direction and caught two men right in front of him and ran them down in two jumps. He headed toward the brown stallion, who was bucking excitedly just beyond the outlaws. The brown stallion charged him. Laeghaire wheeled out of the way and the stallion galloped on by. The men were confused. They turned and ran. Laeghaire chased them as far as the stream. He reined in there. The brown stallion darted in small rushes in the meadow. Two men lay still in the meadow.

Laeghaire stood in his stirrups and leaned over to look at the black horse's legs. Fighting foot soldiers was dangerous. He remembered once when a Slav had slipped past him and gutted his horse in a single knife thrust. The black horse's legs were all right. He looked up. The outlaws had regrouped.

The man who had gone back to the village rode out with horses on a leading rope. He had eight horses besides his, but they needed only three now. Laeghaire rode over to look at the men lying in the meadow. One was awake. He looked up at Laeghaire. He lay flat on his back. The black horse stamped his feet. Dust spurted over the man's hand. Laeghaire rode past him. The other man was dead or badly wounded.

He turned and saw them charging. Their horses were shaggy little ponies. He held the black horse a moment. He rammed the spurs down. The black horse charged straight for the line of outlaws. They spread out, trying to circle him. The black horse ran into one of the shaggy ponies and took it cleanly off its feet. Laeghaire turned him back into the line. They scattered before him. He shot by one man and leaned back and swung full-arm. The man's breath went out of him in a scream.

The others attacked him. He would not let them catch

him in the middle. He charged at one man, veered away to charge the other. He swept one out of the saddle and the other, the blackbeard, whirled and galloped off. Laeghaire rode back to the rock face. He held the sword across his saddlebows. Two of the outlaws staggered to their feet and walked across the stream. Their horses were down by the stream, looking at the brown stallion.

They made a respectful line, the outlaws, just across the stream. Only one of them was mounted. Laeghaire put his left hand on the blade of the sword.

"Who are you?" the blackbeard said.

"Nothing for your ears. I have nothing you'd want."

"Horses."

"Stand aside. I'm riding."

"Are you a knight?"

"Yes."

"I also. By my knightly word, you will not be harmed. Stay a while."

"You filthy troll. If you're a knight, I'm a god. I'm riding. Stand aside."

He glanced around for the stallion. His bow lay on the ground near him. He looked at the outlaws a moment, rode to the bow, and dismounted. They seemed to strain, but they stood still. He picked up the bow, walked to the stallion, and thrust the bow through the packing harness. He hauled the harness tight. He picked up the sword scabbard and mounted. He sheathed his sword. He took the lead rope and rode by the outlaws. He rode at a fast lope down the valley. The outlaws made no move.

When he was far away from them, he stopped and buckled the scabbard on. He thought, They'll come after me. Let them try. He judged he had killed three and wounded at least three more. They would not be forgetting him. They would be more wary of travelers. He breathed deeply of the fine clear air.

* * *

He saw nothing more of the outlaws. The riding was slow and hard. He spent much time climbing slopes beside the horses. His grain was almost gone. Wolfram still sat heavy in his mind. The memory of Wolfram was soothed by the men Laeghaire had killed. He wondered about that. He would be thinking and his mind would suddenly wince from something, and he would think of the fighting and be happier. He wondered. His mind was very full. He did not remember having thought so heavily before. Perhaps, he thought, I'm old now. I suppose a man's old when the inside of his head bothers him. Soon it's Ireland for me, and a place by my brother's home fires, and long tales of my travels for the children, and the neighbors speaking of my wicked youth.

I would sooner live with Murrough, he thought. Murrough fights long wars, or so they say. He remembered the man he had met in Aachen that one summer, who had spoken of Murrough MacMalah's wars with Connaught. Murrough, he had said, fought the kings, even the kings' King; they called him the new Cuchulain of the South of Ireland. And he had been surprised a moment, to learn that Laeghaire was Murrough's brother.

"You hardly look like him."

"He looks like our father, Malachi; did you hear of him in Ireland?"

"They say Malachi sits under the eaves and tells tales to his sons' children. They say he's a little mad."

"Ah, he's old."

"And Shane, your other brother, he is a lawful man, and keeps the peace with everyone."

"Well, Shane was the middle of us, and he was always peaceful."

He remembered the Gaelic words like things from a dream.

He rode down a valley and turned a twisting corner, and there before him was the river. There were huts by it. He rode past them, not caring to find more outlaws. There was no ford here. He rode north. He left the huts behind. After a while, he tried the horses down the bank into the river. The brown stallion refused entirely. Laeghaire dropped the rope and rode the black horse into the river. Almost immediately the water was to his knees. The horse edged forward a little, his head low. He turned and plunged back to the bank, and Laeghaire did not stop him.

He was hungry, and he took his bow from his pack. He rode close to the bank, looking in the mud for tracks of deer come down to the water. He rode like that for a long time. He heard screaming and shouting and looked up. A little hut lay over by the last straggling edge of a long narrow meadow. He rode by it and saw that a village stood on the far boundary of the meadow. He rode back to the single hut.

He drew rein and watched the hut. The brown stallion's ears pricked up. Laeghaire crooked his right leg over his saddle pommel and waited. He grinned at the stallion.

The door burst open. A shaggy old man came part way through, dragging something by a rope. He struggled farther out. The other end of the rope was tied around the wrists of a girl. Laeghaire frowned. She was far too young to be the old man's wife, and now he did not understand.

Her hair was long and tangled. It was very pale, like wheat flour. She fought with a good young strength. Her shift was torn and her body was bruised and filthy. Laeghaire stopped trying to understand. He saw her face once, when she writhed toward him. Her face was scratched and dirty. Her eyes were black, blacker than the bruises.

The old man suddenly struck her on the side of the head. She staggered. The old man hit her again, cunningly, in the stomach. She lay on the ground gagging.

"Good morning, stranger," he said.

"Sir," Laeghaire said.

"Sir, then. May I help you, my lord?"

Laeghaire saw that he still held the bow. He turned and thrust it through the lashings of the pack. "Is there a ford here?"

"Two days' ride, they tell me."

"North?"

"Yes."

"What's the matter with her?"

"She won't marry. He's a good solid boy, too, and the only one in the village not related to her. The lord wants her to marry, sir, but she won't. I thought I'd beat some sense into her."

The girl lifted her head. She snarled something in dialect.

The old man shrugged. "She's very impudent. The lord wants her to marry, for good reason, as who would not? And it's the lord's right." He kicked the girl.

Laeghaire shifted in the saddle. He looked at the girl. She was breathing heavily. Her hands lay together, bound by the rope. The dust settled over her. Laeghaire felt for his wallet. He took it from his belt and opened it. He took a silver coin from it and put the wallet slowly away on his belt.

"Who is your lord?"

"Johan von Mark."

Laeghaire held the silver in his hand. "Give this to your lord, then."

"But that's just one, sir."

Laeghaire turned his eyes toward him. "So it is. And how's Johan von Mark to know you got any?"

The old man thought. "She is my only daughter."

"Many men have many daughters."

"The lord—"

Laeghaire tossed the mark into the dirt. The old man considered it. He went to it and picked it up. "This is good silver," he said.

He turned and patted the girl. Laeghaire threw his leg across the saddle and dismounted. He lifted the girl to her feet. She turned and struck at him with her bound hands. He slapped her. She reeled away from him. He followed her. She tried to stand and he slapped her again. She lay on the ground. She looked up at him. Her mouth bled.

The old man said something in dialect. Laeghaire understood only that she deserved what she got. Laeghaire bent down and picked her up. He carried her to the brown stallion and put her in front of the packs. He tied her on with the rope around her wrists. He mounted the black.

"Her name is Hilde," the old man said, "for her yellow hair."

"It fits her. But it was for the black eyes I bought her."

The old man laughed. Laeghaire rode off. He looked at the girl once, looking a long time at her. She kept her face turned away from him.

He wondered why he had done that. A woman would slow him down. With a woman on his hands he could hardly fight well. Perhaps Guillaume wouldn't give him a place if he had a woman with him. A bad bargain.

She said nothing all the rest of the day. He made a camp at sunset, down by the river. While he made the fire, she watched him with her strange black eyes.

"Do you speak High German?" he said.

"A little."

"Go down to the water and wash yourself."

"Why?"

"Because you are dirty."

"All right."

"And don't try to run away."

"Why?"

"Because I'll catch you and beat you. Go on."

She held out her hands. He had forgotten. He cut the ropes with his dagger. She went silently. He heard her low murmur at the water; he thought she was cold. He undid his pack. In with his mail he had two surcoats. He took one and went after her. She was standing naked in the water, hip deep, splashing water slowly over her arms. She ignored him. He sat down with the surcoat over his knees. He had not had a woman since Thuringia. He watched her. He saw her blushing, even in the twilight.

"What will you do with me?" she said.

"What you would expect."

"Please take me home."

"To marry some pig of a villager and spend the rest of your life working the fields and having children like a sow? Marry him and spend your first night with a lord?"

"Is it better to spend it with a man I don't know?"

Laeghaire spat into the water. "You'll know me soon enough. My name is Laeghaire—Laeghaire of the Long Road."

"Are you from Swabia?"

"Ireland."

"Is that in Germany?"

"It's a country. An island west of England."

"And where is England?"

"Come out of the water. You're turning blue."

"No."

"I won't hurt you. Come out."

A bad bargain, he thought.

She came out of the water. He stood up. He turned her around. She was bruised all over. He put his hand on her breast. She shook under his hand. Her mouth twisted. He sighed. "All right," he said. He put the sur-coat on over her head. He took her by the hand and led her back to the fire.

He had shot a deer on the way, and he cooked part of it, ignoring her. She sat across the fire from him, her long damp hair curling in the heat. He thought of taking her back. He took the venison from the fire and cut meat for her.

They ate in silence. She was wrapped in the surcoat as if in a blanket. She smelled like the running water of the river. He stood up to put more wood on the fire. He passed by her to get the wood. She drew a little away from him. He came back with the wood and put it piece by piece into the fire. The glow lit up her hands and the ends of her pale curling hair. She turned her face toward him. She was crying. He held out his hands. She came clumsily into his arms. She put her face against his shoul-der. She cried in great shuddering wails. He rocked her. He felt like a fool. He shut his eyes. He rocked back and forth. Her hands pulled lightly at him.

He got up and brought his cloak and wrapped it around them. He turned her face toward him and kissed her. She was frightened. He could feel her trembling un-der him. She had stopped crying. In the light of the fire he saw her eyes, wide and black, staring past him into the sky.

She rode on the stallion, among the packs. They crossed the river four days later and rode up the western bank. That night they camped in the trees.

"Where are we going?" she said.

"To Flanders."

"Do you live there? Have you got land and a castle?"

"I have a friend who is captain of the Count of Flan-ders' guard. He may give me a place in it."

"And me?"

He shrugged.

"Where were you before?"

"Thuringia."

"Do you live there?"

"No." He poked at the fire with a stick. "I was captain of the Duke of Thuringia's army."

"Where do you live?"

"Nowhere."

"Nobody lives nowhere."

"Then I am nobody."

She made a face. He laughed at her, and she smiled.

"Do you have a wife?" she said.

"No."

"Good."

"I won't marry you, I've told you that, and why. It is better this way."

"Have you had other women?"

"Of course."

"Did you have one in Thuringia?"

"Three or four."

"You're very wicked."

"Yes."

Now she laughed. "What were they like?"

He shrugged. "Thuringians. All but one."

"What was she?"

"A Slav."

"A pagan?"

"Yes."

"How could you do that?"

"The same way you and I do it."

"Hunh."

"Was she beautiful?"

"No."

"Did you love her?"

"No."

"That's awful."

He thought quickly of the Slavic girl's long body, long arms, long entwining legs, her deep arched back, and the glint of her eyes in the dark.

"Where will we live in Flanders?"

"In the castle of the Count of Flanders in Ghent."

"What is Ghent?"

"A village."

"How long will it take us to get there?"

"Why do you ask so many questions?"

"Because you know the answers."

He laughed. "Well, we'll be there in time for Christmas. Now don't ask me any more questions. I feel sleepy."

"Would you be sleepy if I came over there?"

"Probably not."

They rode on to Worms, and there he found a friend of his, Joffre, who ran an inn. He saw Laeghaire and called to him and drew him aside. He looked at the girl, who was watering the horses.

"The Duke of Thuringia is hunting you high and low," Joffre said.

"Tell me something new. I didn't think he'd send so far west, though."

"Here he'd have trouble. This is an imperial city, you know. He can't just take you. I'd thought you'd want to know. What did you do?"

"He refused to pay me, so I took it."

"Ah, so. I'd heard the other half. Now it makes sense. Do you want a bed?"

"Yes."

"Who's the woman?"

"I got her in the south."

Joffre made a shrug with his eyebrows. "Is she a bother? Do you want me to take her?"

"I paid good silver for her."

Joffre made another gesture. "I'll give you a mark."

Laeghaire turned to look at her. She sat on the brown stallion. Her long bare legs thrust down over the stallion's shoulders. Her hair hung around her. He thought of the black eyes staring past him into the sky.

"She's worth more than a mark."

"Two, then."

"No, she's no trouble."

"You're sure?"

"Yes."

"You and your damned honor." Joffre patted his belly. "Now, listen. The news that the Duke was hunting you got around pretty quick. Just a few days ago I got a message by one of the traders who come through here. Ben Abram, you know him. Anyway, it was from Guillaume, the Flemish Count's captain. He said if you came by I was to tell you that he'll make a place for you in the army."

"The army or the guard?"

"Small difference. The army, he wrote. He may have meant the guard."

"The guard is just by the court. The army—I had the idea that Baldwin's army was all raised by knights' fees."

"He said it would be for a long time."

"Who knows? Let me see the letter."

Joffre went inside. He came back with a big leather pouch. From it he took a smaller pouch, and gave that to Laeghaire. The letter was in a very monkish hand. Laeghaire put it back into the leather pouch and called to Hilde. Joffre stood by watching. Laeghaire went up to the sleeping room. Hilde sat down on the bed. He went to the window and took out the letter and read it in the light from the window. He looked up and saw Hilde combing her hair, with her eyes fixed on him.

"What does that say?"

"That we have to be in Flanders by Allhallows."

"Then you will be fighting for the Count?"

"Yes."

"Good."

Two pack boys brought up the packs. Laeghaire stood by the window and watched them. Allhallows was only a few days away. He turned back to lean out the window. It was barely noon. The wind from the river smelled of fish. A fish vendor had put up her stall almost under this window. A fishhawk was sitting on the eave of the inn across the way. Laeghaire wondered if the fishhawk would have the daring to steal a fish.

"How do you know that man?"

"Who? Joffre? He owns the inn here."

"I know that."

"I stayed here once. When I had been wounded."

"Oh."

He went to the pack and got his sword and cleaned it. There was a bit of rust by the throat. He rested the tip of the sword on the floor and poured a drop of oil on the cloth. He rubbed at the rust spot, bracing the hilt on his hip.

Allhallows they spent near Aachen, and did not come into Ghent until four days later. The autumn rain blew in on the wind from the sea. In Ghent Laeghaire found an inn and left Hilde there, with instructions to the innkeeper. He left the brown stallion, too, but put on his sword. The rain was light but it bothered him, and he had some trouble finding his way to the gate of the castle.

"Who comes there?" a man called in Flemish.

"I seek Guillaume of Bruges."

"Who are you?"

"Laeghaire of the Long Road."

The front gate opened. "Come in out of the rain," the

man said. "But no farther than here. I'll find Sir Guillaume."

Laeghaire set his wet saddle under the stone arch of the gate. His cloak smelled foully of wet wool. He thrust back the hood. He could not see beyond the edge of the courtyard for the slanting rain. A light glimmered up there somewhere. The black horse pulled at the bit.

Laeghaire heard footsteps and slipped his hand under his cloak. The man who had given him entrance said, "There, in the archway, sir."

"Wait here."

That was Guillaume. Laeghaire relaxed. The man came, swaddled in a cloak, out of the smothering rain. He looked at Laeghaire.

"A man in Worms gave me a letter," Laeghaire said.

"By the Holy, it is you. Come down from there; how can I see you when you sit up over my head?"

Laeghaire dismounted. Guillaume clapped him on the shoulder. "Hunh. You've changed since I saw you last."

"Nine years sit on a man," Laeghaire said. "But you're the same—do you still drink your wine with water in it?" He poked at Guillaume's belly. "You're soft."

"You impudent whelp. Remember if you will who's older here. Nine years? Is it that long?"

"The year the Count's daughter married the Duke of Normandy. Have you forgotten?"

"Forgotten? Never. Come in. The hall's warmer. Leopuild, come back to your post. Nine years. But I recognized you." Guillaume put the edge of his cloak over his head. "Foul weather. Follow me. You're late."

"Four days."

They went to the stable. Guillaume lit a torch. He looked at the black horse.

"Is that your war-horse?"

"Of course not. I left him by an inn."

"Oh. And you weren't sure of your reception."

"I had reasons."

"Let the boy do that." Guillaume took him by the arm and pulled him away from the horse. "Come up to the hall. The Count's drinking. He's a good fellow. And important, too."

"No, wait a minute. I had my reasons, as I said. I have a woman with me."

Guillaume spread his hands. "No matter. Is she proud? She can work in the kitchen. Keep her out of mischief."

"Good."

"Now will you come? I left a good drink of wine."

"No wonder you've gotten soft."

"Hunh. I've been hearing about you. This way. Now left. They talk of you almost in the same breath with Harald Hardraada."

"Just almost?"

"By the Holy, you're insolent."

"Tell me about this place you have for me."

Guillaume had his hand on a door latch, but he turned and his hand dropped.

"The Count, you know, is not a young man, and he dislikes warring."

"I know."

"But he's bound by his alliance to the Norman Duke, and the Norman Duke is wildly fond of warring. He wants to fight against Maine soon—perhaps in the next year—now that Count Herbert is dead. Some business of a mutual pact. The Count has no desire to go, but he must send men, and these men must have a captain."

"He doesn't trust William?"

"No man with a good head on his shoulders trusts the lord William. Not that he would attack the Count, his own father-in-law, but he's poor in the way of men and money and he does like to fight. He might use the Count's men as his own, to fight somebody the Count would not like to have his men fighting—do you understand me? Especially since the Count is the regent-guardian for the King. You know?"

"I can see the difficulties."

"So. The Count asked me to go as captain. But I—as you say you've noticed—am getting old for such things, and I like to have the court nearby, and plenty of wine. I told him I would find him a man."

"Why me?"

"Because I heard in the summer that you'd finally left the service of that German pig. I knew you'd be by Worms. Your reputation is quite remarkable, especially when I remember the scrawny wild brat you were nine years ago."

Laeghaire smiled. "I was coming here anyway," he said.

"We're all lucky," Guillaume said. He opened the door and they came into a great roofed hall, where the platters from a supper still stood on the table. The Count sat talking to his Countess. Half a dozen servants and some women of the Countess stood and sat around them. A harper played in the corner. A little group of young men was in the far end of the room, talking and drinking. Guillaume bowed casually in that direction and led off toward the Count.

The room was very rich. Laeghaire thought it much more magnificent than the Thuringian great hall. It was not a warrior's hall. He guessed that the tapestries were the work of the women of the Flemish Court. He paused a moment and looked into the eyes of the Count of Flanders and he knelt.

"My lord," Guillaume said, "I've found you a captain for the army."

"So I see. Bid him rise."

"Rise," Guillaume said. Laeghaire stood up.

The Count looked him over at his leisure, and turned to Guillaume. "A strong healthy-looking fellow. Who is he?"

"Laeghaire from Tralee, my lord."

"Yes. Indeed." The Count turned to the Countess. "My dear lady, I ask your permission to speak at some length with this man. You may retire if you wish."

"If I might take the harper, my lord."

"Stay." Baldwin turned back to Laeghaire. "You are Irish?"

"Yes, my lord."

"A wandering knight? Not a thing to give me confidence in you. Where have you wandered here from?"

"Thuringia, my lord."

"Whom did you serve there?"

"The Duke, my lord."

"In what capacity?"

"Captain of the army."

"And whom did you fight?"

"Slavs and Germans, my lord."

"And is the lord of Thuringia too old to do his own captaining?"

"Too fat, my lord."

The women laughed.

"Too fat?"

"There is hardly a horse in Germany can carry him, and he complains that long marches make him sick."

"A poor lord."

"But clever."

"I said he was a poor lord, and you contradict me. I find you most insolent."

"Do you, my lord?"

The Count wheeled on Guillaume. "What kind of knight is this? Insolent, disrespectful—"

"He's young, my lord."

"How old are you?"

"Thirty-three, my lord."

"A guess. Sheer guesswork. You are too young. Far too insolent."

"As you wish, my lord."

The Count banged his fist on the arm of his chair. "Rascal, uncouth, unknightly rascal."

"My lord."

"By God, Sir Guillaume, he's just the sort to send to my son-in-law. He will set William back on his heels. You, what's your name again?"

"Laeghaire of the Long Road."

"You know what I want of you."

"Yes, my lord."

"Good. Now, listen to me. William is a rogue, a pious, bad-tempered, ambitious, good-for-nothing rogue."

"Then he is well fitted for the work of this world, my lord."

"I refuse to answer that. My sweet and godly daughter dotes on him. Sir Guillaume will show you your duties. Raise me some five hundred men and take them to Rouen, or wherever he wants to gather, sometime soon. Speak for them and for me, on instructions I will give you. Can you use a bow?"

"Yes."

"Then you can occupy your empty time with training archers for this army."

"He has a woman with him," Guillaume said.

"A woman? Is she his wife?"

"No. Is she, Laeghaire?"

"No."

The Count frowned. "This may prove difficult. But it is easily avoided. Give her a place in the kitchens. You see, Sir Laeghaire, my son-in-law is most incredibly pious. Being a bastard himself. Now, go with Sir Guillaume. He will give you a closet. Guillaume, you know better than I. Now leave me to my music."

Guillaume went off through a little door, and Laeghaire followed. Guillaume turned in the corridor. "By God," he said, "I thought he was going to hug you. He loves men who have pride. He loves William, too—don't you be misled. I'll send a man to fetch up the woman."

"First show me where we sleep. I'm dead tired."

"This way. The Duke will come north to discuss his plans. He's supposed to come over Christmas. I won't give you any lists until then. Unless you want to be able to spit facts and figures at him. Here."

The room was a little closet on the west side, close to the wall. Laeghaire nodded. Guillaume went out. Laeghaire sat on the pallet. He thought over the whole of what had happened. It was strange how men tried to test other men, and how they amused themselves and made themselves feel important. The Count amused him. He thought of what the Count had said about the Duke of Normandy. He sounded like a wild boar, like old Malachi.

The Count reminded him a little of the Duke of Thuringia, but he supposed that was only because neither of them led his own army. It was better for him that way, of course. A lot of lords were happier playing courtier than living off the land on a prolonged raid or risking an arrow in the belly during a charge. He remembered Heinrich's merry little explanation of why he preferred to let a stranger lead his army.

"A lord is the anointed of God, and he should not waste his sacred flesh in such dangerous and unhealthy pursuits. Bring me that wine."

"On the contrary," Heinrich's bishop-brother had said. "The lord is anointed of God for the specific purpose of fighting for God against the heathen."

"And Christians too, my lord Arnulf?" Laeghaire had said.

"And to punish evildoers."

"You just say that to justify your own fighting," Heinrich had said. "I for one do not intend to waste my sacred flesh on the battlefield, when I can pay the Irishman one mark a month to do it for me. I'd be doing him out of his way of living, anyhow."

Heinrich's brother was a good man, a strong-armed priest, who had taken Laeghaire's part in the quarrel. Before fighting, he would hold Mass in the fortress chapel. Most priests made a Mass uncomfortable, but Arnulf's Masses were short, strong and simple. Laeghaire would stand in the fourth or fifth row, behind the lords he commanded, and admire Arnulf's logic. Arnulf swung a lusty ax, too.

The door opened and Hilde came in, carrying part of the packs, followed by a stableboy with the rest. She directed the boy imperiously. Laeghaire grinned. He was glad he had brought her. He watched her unpack and arrange his mail and helmet in the oak chest, hang his bow and quiver from pegs, lean his shield against the wall. She left for a moment and was soon back with a broom. She swept the floor.

"Busy little housewoman," he said. "Did you hear that you're to work in the kitchens?"

"Yes. I think I shall be happy to be among women again."

"Well, I don't know if you'll be able to talk to them for a while. Flemish isn't exactly like German."

"That man spoke some Flemish to me and I understood some of it."

"You'll learn."

She leaned on the broom, like a warrior leaning on his lance. "I like it here."

"We'll be here a while."

He asked for the lists of the knights' fees owed to Baldwin, and Guillaume gave them to him. Baldwin held a good six hundred fees, plus the services of lords in his domains who held other fees. There were horses to be bought, besides, to carry packs and haul siege engines, if William of Normandy should decide for them. Laeghaire put all these lists on the table in his room. The sun ran over the paper, and the paper, thin-shaved, curled up into the sunlight, so that the curled edge made a shadow over the top three lines of script.

Guillaume had left him six fresh quills with badly cut nibs. He sat down on the bench and took out his dagger and cut new ones. It was cold out. The sun was cold. Dust floated in the stream of sunlight. He put down the quills and leaned against the wall. This is stupid, he thought; he drew up his knees and leaned his forearms on them, and thought, Now I'll have to think of a reason for thinking it. I don't know what's going on.

His hands hung from his wrists, limp fingers. The second knuckle on his right hand was much bigger than the second knuckle on his left hand. The tendon was broad and flat, like a worm.

Somebody knocked on the door. He put one foot down. "Come in."

It was the Count. He advanced a little into the room and looked around. "So he gave you the lists."

"Yes."

"Well." Baldwin moved straight to the bed and sat down on it. "I think it's a great gift you can read. Do you speak French?"

"Only a little. I was once in Burgundy, but their language is a little different."

"Speak some Burgundian."

"What shall I say?"

"Say anything."

Laeghaire recited the first two lines of a Burgundian song.

"A pity. You must learn good French. What did you say?"

Laeghaire told him.

"Oh. No, don't start for those lists, you'll hurt your eyes and not get anywhere. Tell me, where have you been, besides Flanders and Germany?"

"Burgundy, as I said, but only for a little while, I think about a year or a little more. When I left Ireland I went to England and was in the Houseguard of Wessex."

"What? Wessex? Under Earl Godwin?"

"Yes."

"His son married my sister." Baldwin tapped his teeth with his fingernails. "Complications arise."

"Why, my lord?"

"Nothing. You'll learn. And where after England?"

"A while in Wales, two or three years here—"

"Where?"

"In Bruges."

"I never saw you."

"I was in the princess' guard."

"And then?"

"After Burgundy, Thuringia, and then I left Thuringia, and now I'm here."

"Of course, that's how you knew Guillaume. Well, you've traveled far. I suppose you'll want to go back to Ireland."

"Sometime, maybe."

"Have you kin?"

"My father and my brothers."

"Are they still alive?"

"I don't know."

"How did you learn to read and write?"

"I was four years in a monastery."

"You're very precise with your times."

"It's my life, my lord."

"Your tongue will make trouble for you someday. Why did you leave the monastery?"

"My lord, why this inquisition?"

"I'm merely curious."

"There is nothing in my life to be curious about."

"For me, there is. I've rarely gone out of my own domains."

"Everything is the same, everywhere."

"Perhaps. Thank you for your answering."

Laeghaire lifted his head and looked at Baldwin. He turned his head away.

"I'll tell you about this situation—in Maine."

"Good."

"Anjou and Normandy have always fought over Maine. The father of this King used to think that if either of them ever won Maine, he'd be lost."

"And you don't believe it."

"Why do you say that?"

"You're regent for the little King, aren't you?"

"William will take Maine. But I know how his ambitions go, and to be King of France isn't one of them. Besides, nobody can really hold Maine."

"Oh."

"The Count of Anjou's dead, and the family is fighting over who will be the new Count. So William will take Maine. He had an agreement with the old Count of Maine, Herbert, that if Herbert died without an heir, William's son Robert would be Count. Herbert died last spring."

"Unexpectedly, of course."

Baldwin frowned. "I know what you think."

"Is it so?"

"I don't know. I told you, my daughter's husband is a

rogue beyond all accounting."

"A sweet rogue, too, incredibly pious, you said."

"He needs Maine."

Laeghaire put his shoulders against the wall and wiggled into a comfortable position. "I'm listening."

"By God, I don't have to excuse him to you or explain him to you. You are paid to act in my behalf, on my orders, and what he thinks or wants is nothing for you to consider."

"My lord. Such an outburst."

Baldwin stood up. He went to the window and looked out. The sight of his pretty town, all peaceful beyond this castle wall, must have comforted him. Laeghaire watched him look at the bright roofs of the houses by the canals.

"He has had a hard life," Baldwin said. "He is a rogue, and pious, and madly fond of fighting, but when he was young he spent most of his life running from his enemies. He's always had to fight, if only for his own protection. That kind of life can turn a man into a wild dog."

Baldwin turned suddenly. Laeghaire watched the shadow on the lists of knights' fees.

"As you say, it doesn't concern me."

"I'm uncertain about Herbert. He was a young man. There's a chance that William . . . did what you suspect. But that agreement was eight years old. And there are other parties in Maine. Geoffrey of Mayenne, for one. The strongest of them. He and that damned Walter of the Vexin are like hand and glove, and Walter's always wanted to be Count of Maine, or Count of anyplace he could fight William from. Now he's claimed the title and Mayenne is backing him. Walter married Herbert's aunt. Walter hates William, and William hates Walter more than any man alive, and the chances are not good that Walter will be alive much longer."

"God, I hate these politics. These damned feuds."

"I thought you should know. Anyway, my daughter and William are coming here for Christmas. He'll want to talk about it."

"All right."

"He'll undoubtedly want to hunt. Do you hunt?"

"I have."

"Do you enjoy it?"

Laeghaire shrugged.

"You'll have to come with us sometime."

Laeghaire shrugged again.

"Thank you," Baldwin said. He went out the door.

All toward Christmas, the Count's household prepared for the Duke's visit. They had animals slaughtered and hung up in the kitchens, and every day the wagons of the merchants jammed the courtyard. Guillaume and the Flemish constable went out one day to look over the hunting.

Finally the Duke appeared, with his entourage and a small guard of knights. In wealthy Ghent, the little train of armored men made a bad showing. In the gray of the armor only the cart that bore the Duchess was colorful. The cart was covered with red and yellow cloth and hung with ribbons. Laeghaire watched from the wall. The guard was drawn up on the wall to meet their lord's son-in-law. Laeghaire stood a little apart from them. He leaned his forearms on the wall and watched the train coming slowly to the gate. He heard a sound behind him and turned and saw Hilde scrambling up the ladder. She ran over and stood beside him, glowing.

"I have something to tell you later," she said, and giggled.

The Count had gone out to greet the Duke of Normandy. They rode together in the vanguard. The Count wore a long fur cloak and a surcoat worked in brilliant colors. His little band of court officers was brightly dressed. The man who rode beside the Count looked strange among them. He wore a plain white surcoat and a wool cloak. His hair was bright red. His horse was a hand taller than the Count's, and he himself was a big man, so that he loomed over the Count and all the court officers. His face was solemn and he carried his helmet in the crook of his arm. When they had come a little nearer, Laeghaire saw that his cloak had a hood on it lined with fur.

"Is that the Duke of Normandy?" Hilde asked.

"Yes."

"Why isn't he richly dressed?"

"Because he's poor."

"Johan von Mark dressed better than that. All fur and gold and little jewels in his baldric. I don't like this one."

"Why?"

"He frightens me. He looks—"

He waited for her to finish, but she didn't. She clasped her arms together and leaned over the wall.

The train was almost to the archway. Laeghaire saw the greatsword's hilt thrusting up past the Duke's thigh. He saw the heavy fist on the rein and the studs on the gloves. "He looks like a prophet."

"What?"

"Like Jeremiah."

"Oh, no. He would have a gentle face."

The train went through the arch into the courtyard. Page boys ran out to hold the horses. The Norman knights rode big heavy-headed horses. They bore themselves arrogantly. They reminded him of Irish kernes: hard hands and the mouths taut under the helmets.

"They are cousins of mine," he said.

"Oh? How do you know?"

"Distant cousins. They are descendants of Vikings, and so am I."

The Count handed the Duchess of Normandy down from her cart. Hilde gasped. "She's tiny. Look at her."

"I've seen her before."

He went to the ladder and climbed down. The Duke and the rest were walking toward the door. The Duke was drawing off his gloves, his head bent toward the Count. Laeghaire turned and helped Hilde down from the ladder. He let her and himself in through a little side door. She turned toward him.

"Shall I tell you my surprise now?"

"The surprise? Oh. Tell me."

"No, I shan't. You aren't interested."

He sighed. "Tell me. I'm desperately interested."

"Laeghaire—"

He caught her by her long braid and pulled her to him. He kissed her. "I'm interested. Tell me."

She put her hands on his chest. "I'm going to have a baby."

He stepped back. "What?"

"Aren't you happy?"

He took her back into his arms and kissed her again. "Yes. I'm happy. When?"

She sighed with her head against his chest. "I told Lisabet in the kitchen about some things, and that I was sick in the mornings—you didn't know because you always get up and go down to feed your horses or something—and she said I was going to have a baby, but I don't know when. She said maybe in the beginning of the summer but she couldn't be sure. I want it to be a boy."

"So do I. And I don't go down to feed my horses, as you very well—"

"Ssssh. We have to have a name for him."

"He hasn't even been born yet. We can't name him yet."

"He'll have black hair like yours and he'll be big like you. So big I'll walk around like this with him."

She walked around like that, still within his arms.

"No you won't." He caught her back again.

"And he'll have blue eyes."

"No, black. I like your eyes."

"Blue."

"Black."

She looked up at him. She smiled. "You are happy. I have to go back to the kitchen. Good-by."

"Be careful."

"I love you, Laeghaire."

"That's good."

She turned and ran off, but she ran only a few steps, and began to walk, gingerly. He laughed at her. She turned her head and smiled at him.

At supper the Norman knights sat along one side of the great table, and the Flemish court officers on the other, with the Flemish guard. Duke William sat with his Duchess at one end, and the Count and Countess at the other. Hilde served the sauces, smiling at Laeghaire whenever she caught his eye. Lisabet, directing the service of the supper, snapped at her once, so that she came down chastised and pouting.

Laeghaire sat opposite a Norman knight who kept talking to the man on his left. From their glances and nods, Laeghaire knew they were talking about him. He threw a bone to the dogs and reached for another piece of meat. The Norman said, "You, sir. What office do you hold here?"

"No office. Why, what office do you hold in Normandy, sir?"

The other Norman laughed and spoke in French.

"I am a knight in the service of the Duke of Normandy," the first man said. "More than which I need not say. Are you a mere hanger-on? I would swear to have seen you before, sir, but I know it was not here."

"Why, then, sir, you might be forsworn, because I would offer my own word that I have never had the honor to see you before, and if so, why it should matter, I can't say."

The Count laughed. "By God, sir knight. You've done wonders; I've never heard so long a sentence from him before."

Laeghaire bit off a piece of meat and swallowed it. He reached for his wine. "Then I'm finished for the night, my lord."

"Your accent is not Flemish," the Norman said.

"Nor, sir, am I a member of that fortunate breed."

The Duke said suddenly, "Néel, hold your tongue."

The knight said, "Yes, my lord."

"I'll have no fighting between our knights," the Duke said to Baldwin. "And this stranger of yours seems to have no temper for talking."

"Sir Laeghaire," Baldwin said, "you may consider yourself chastised."

"From your lips, my honored lord."

The Duke watched Laeghaire for a while. Laeghaire felt his stare. He ate, pretending not to know. He glanced over at last and saw that the Duke was leaning back and looking elsewhere. A page jumped to take his platter and fill his cup again.

"I meant to talk to you about Maine," the Duke said abruptly.

"I know. It seems to me to be an unpromising enterprise, and I wish you would give it up." Baldwin sat back. He signed to his steward.

"I have implored him to do so, my lord," the Duchess said. "But he sees his own way, may the good Lord help him."

"Don't speak of me as if I weren't here," the Duke said. He tapped his cup, and a page boy filled it from a long-necked ewer. "We'll talk of it later, my lord, when you're not playing Regent of France. You ought to have been south for the hunting this summer. It was magnificent."

"I'm a little old to be galloping through the woods on one of your hunts, my lord. And it's a young man's sport anyway. We hawked a little, but not much."

"Bear," the Duke said. "Nor finer hunting have I ever had."

"Crossbows?"

"Boar spears."

"That calls for a steady horse."

"On foot. No horse I own would go near a bear."

"Have you ever hunted bear?" Baldwin said. He looked at Laeghaire.

"Once. By necessity."

"Necessity?" the Duke said.

"Yes, my lord. The bear was hunting me."

In the general laughter the Duke merely smiled, and his eyes rested on Laeghaire in a flat hard stare.

"We'll have a hunt soon," Baldwin said. "Christmas hunting can be most amusing. Sir Guillaume, you have one planned, don't you?"

"For the day after tomorrow, my lord."

"Not too strenuous, I hope," the Duchess said.

"Hardly. Hares, and we'll have to trust to the snow."

"That's good sport," the Duchess said. "But I'm afraid my lord won't enjoy it."

With good reason, Laeghaire thought. He glanced at the door to the kitchens.

"It's slow. Hares make slow hunting in any weather." The Duke turned his weight a little.

"We'll hunt wolves later," Baldwin said. "Or you will. I'll give you a party and you can go trampling in the snow after the vicious brutes. It's not for me. Here's the dessert. Did you bring your harper with you, my lord?"

"He's sick."

"A shame." Baldwin turned toward the steward and nodded. The steward left. "The finest harper in this world, I'll swear. Irish, like you, Sir Laeghaire."

Néel's head turned and his eyes fixed on Laeghaire. Néel had just remembered where he had seen Laeghaire.

"A shame," the Duke said. "I should have brought him. You could have told me what his songs mean, the ones in Gaelic."

"An Irish ollamh speaks a language nobody but another ollamh can understand, my lord."

"Hunh. You complicated islanders."

Baldwin's harper came in, drew up his stool from the corner, and sat. He played. The cakes and pies and puddings came in the hands of the little pages. Laeghaire got a piece of wine cake. He pushed at it with his fingers and broke off a bit. He chewed it slowly, looking at Néel. Finally Néel turned, and Laeghaire stared at him a moment without blinking, and swallowed the cake.

The Count and Countess and the Duchess hunted the next day and the day following, after hare. The Duke of Normandy did not go. On the second day Laeghaire went up to the main gate to fix the gate rope. He saw the Duke, two knights attending, in conversation with Guillaume. Laeghaire went up the ladder to the top of the gate.

The Duke and Guillaume were speaking French. Laeghaire could hardly see them. He looked at the rope. The gate was raised. He could see nothing wrong with the rope. One of the sheaves was turned off its base. He lowered the gate. The spindle turned freely, and the rope reeled off more slack than necessary. He pulled the slack off the sheaf and straightened it.

"Good morning, Irish," the Duke said.

"My lord." Laeghaire turned. The two knights were right behind the Duke. One of them was Néel. For a moment nobody said anything. Laeghaire turned back to the sheaf and undid the ropes that held it. He wound them around it again to hold it steady. He took the spindle wheel and wound up the slack.

The Duke said something in French. Laeghaire glanced up. "I don't speak French," he said. He found a frayed place in the rope. He could splice it. He took his dagger and cut the rope above and below the fray.

"Perhaps you speak Saxon," the Duke said in Saxon.

Laeghaire glanced up again. "Nor that"—he gestured —"either."

The Duke turned to the knights and said something in French. They turned and went off. Laeghaire looked by the Duke to Néel. Néel kept his head turned. The knights went down the ladder.

The Duke sat on the rampart, swinging his legs. "Hares make bad sport," he said.

"I don't like to hunt very much."

Laeghaire unraveled the rope ends and worked them together.

"How did it get frayed down that far?" the Duke said. "That should never leave the spindle."

Laeghaire pushed the spindle with his foot. It spun. "When they release it, a lot of extra rope comes off. Maybe it twists itself. Or gets caught in the sheaf."

"We'll hunt wolves next week."

"That's better."

"Are you coming?"

"I don't like to hunt."

"Where are you from? In Ireland."

"Kerry. The southern part."

"Is that where you learned rope tricks?"

Laeghaire put his foot on the bight of the rope and pulled the splice tight. "I learned it in Germany, my lord."

"Are you part of the force the Count's sending me?"

"Yes, my lord."

The Duke got up and went off down the rampart. Laeghaire wound up the slack of the rope. He saw the Duke walk across the courtyard. He met his knights by the outer stair. Laeghaire turned and took hold of the spindle wheel. He raised the gate. It was heavy. The rope strained. He kept one eye on the sheaf. It held. He locked the spindle and went down.

All that week he knew the Duke was watching him. He told Hilde. She stopped and turned toward him.

"I told you he was bad."

"There's no harm in just watching."

He mentioned it also to Guillaume, and Guillaume laughed.

"Ever since he was a boy, he's been careful. You don't fit. You worry him. He wants to know how you fit. He's a very tidy man. When he's figured you out, he'll forget you. Don't worry."

On Christmas Eve they hunted wolf. The Count told Laeghaire to come. The snow was fresh. In the forest it was drifted deep under the trees. The wolfhounds caught a track almost at once. The riders shouted and dashed off after the hounds. From their belling the scent was hot. After only a few yards, two horses fell into drifts and threw their riders. Laeghaire reined in a moment. The knights were wading in the snow. Laeghaire turned and followed the hunt. The hounds sounded far away. He did not try to catch up to the others. He could barely hear them. The forest was dim.

I don't know the ground, he thought. He drew rein. The black horse stamped and tossed his head. The cold settled down around them. He heard them shout, up ahead.

He followed them slowly. He saw another knight coming toward him, leading his horse. The knight passed without looking up. Laeghaire rode on. The horse's tracks were marked in blood.

He could not hear them at all, except for the hounds' occasional belling. He followed the track. It came out on the edge of a wide field. The track led straight across it. The sun glittered on the snow.

He let the rein slip. The horse stood still. The snow was drifted deep against the trees and the grass stuck up through it on parts of the field. The wind moved in the snow. He tasted it in his lungs.

"Poor wolf," he said. He took the bow from his shoulder and slung it on the saddle. He turned and rode back into the forest. He rode west, slowly, and he stopped now and then. Once a branch snapped under the weight of the snow on it. The horse shied violently. Laeghaire drew him in and laughed.

In the late afternoon he flushed a deer by a stream. He dismounted and drank, and tethered the horse. He took the bow and climbed a tree. The black horse stood warily below him. All around him the thin branches laced together. A twig almost touched his face. There was a bud on it. He tore it off the twig and took it apart, seeing how the curled little leaves were attached to the stem.

He should marry Hilde. He wondered if the baby would be a boy. He thought it would be pleasant to have a son, to teach and talk to. He would teach him Gaelic. Hilde would not learn Gaelic; it was too different from German. He would teach him to say Gaelic poems and he would tell him the old stories. In time he would take him to Ireland. Murrough and Shane would come down out of the Kerry hills and they would sit and talk, and

Laeghaire would have great stories to tell, and the boy would be proud because Laeghaire was his father.

He leaned back into the branches, against the trunk. The horse was standing with his head up. Laeghaire took the bow and an arrow. Six deer came down the trail, their heads raised, toward the stream. He strung the bow and nocked an arrow. The stag was a giant, with huge arched shoulders and a sprawling rack. Laeghaire aimed just below his withers. Stag meat was tough. He chose a small doe that came just after the stag. The stag saw the horse; his ears raised like flags. Laeghaire shot. The doe leaped violently. The stag bolted, dashing across the stream. The others raced after him. The wounded doe tried to follow and dropped. Laeghaire could see the fletching on the arrow in her side.

He came at her carefully. When he reached her she was dead. He slit her belly and butchered out meat from her breast. He cut out her tongue. He made a fire close to the stream and brought the horse closer to it. He cooked the meat. It was dark before he ate. He got up and got water from the stream. He sat and ate the tongue.

He looked up and saw the lamps of a wolf's eyes, just beyond the firelight. Just behind them another pair winked on and off and on again. He stabbed out a coal from his fire and flung it awkwardly from the tip of the dagger. The eyes darted off. He saw them once more. Finally he heard the wolves tearing at the carcass of the doe.

When he was done eating, he took a torch from the fire and led the horse to drink. When he stamped out the fire, the wolves looked at him. He could hear them, gnawing at the doe. He mounted and rode off and they ignored him. He passed close by them. One of them lifted his head and stared. Laeghaire held the torch out. The wolf flattened his ears against his head. Laeghaire spurred the horse.

* * *

Christmas passed. On Twelfth Night the Count had a great banquet for all his lords, honoring the Duke and Duchess. After it, the lords and ladies danced and chattered and made a great display of themselves. The knights drank.

The knights all gathered at one end of the room. The Flemings were loud and made jokes. One big Norman stood up on the table and picked up a keg and tried to drain it. Most of it he spilled over himself. One of his friends took him by the sleeve and pulled him down.

Laeghaire shouldered two squires out of his way and lifted another keg from the floor to the table. He sat on the table beside it and broke it open. The knights cheered. They were gathered tight around the table. They thrust out their cups. The Normans bellowed to be first. One of the Flemings turned and said something in French, and everybody laughed.

Laeghaire dipped out his cupful and tasted it. "German beer," he said. "Good enough."

"Let's salute the Count of Flanders," a Fleming said.

"All right, Josse, but then we'll have to tipple to the lord of Normandy too." The big Norman shoved Josse. "All right, everybody up."

They all filled their cups, some more than once.

"To my lord the Count Baldwin of Flanders."

They drank. They cheered.

"Now." The Norman took a step forward and sat down abruptly. "Somebody help me up."

The knights around him laughed. Josse dipped out beer and poured it over the Norman's head. "I dub thee Rohan of Rouen." Two knights hauled Rohan of Rouen up by the armpits. Laeghaire crossed his legs under him. He took Rohan of Rouen's cup, filled it, and carefully twined the Norman's fingers around it.

"To my lord the Duke of Normandy."

They all drank. They splashed beer on each other and shoved and pushed. They linked arms and sang part of a song.

"Néel." Rohan of Rouen draped an arm across Néel's shoulders. "I'll welcome you to our little group. We're all comrades here, see?" A shout made him stop. "No fighting. No insults. Here. Have some wine."

"It's beer, you stupid lout," some Fleming shouted.

"Beer, wine, it's all the same, makes a man lose his head. Here. Drink." He held the cup to Néel's chin. "You hear that pretty music? Maybe we should dance. Drink."

Néel drank. Beer ran down his chin. He wiped his face. He looked straight at Laeghaire, sitting on the table.

"You're wanted, Irish."

"Awwwww." Rohan squeezed his arm closer around Néel's neck. "You're going to take him. And just when we were having so much fun." He let go with a shove, and Néel wobbled. His hand slid toward his belt. Somebody behind him pushed him, and his hand fell naturally by his side. He looked at Laeghaire. "Coming, Irish?"

"I'm coming."

Laeghaire swung his legs over the table and slid off. He went through the crowd after Néel. Néel was waiting just beyond the knights.

"You've grown," Néel said.

"Have I?"

"Why did you pretend not to know Saxon?"

"I've forgotten it."

"You knew he was speaking it."

"Shut up," Laeghaire said, smiling.

Néel glanced at the dancing lords and ladies and went on, walking fast. They went out a side door. Laeghaire slammed the door behind him. The music and noise cut off abruptly. He followed Néel down the corridor. Néel turned down another corridor and knocked on a door there.

The door opened. Guillaume stood aside to let them in. The Count sat by the fire. The Duke was on his feet. He glanced at Laeghaire.

Néel stood aside. Laeghaire stepped by him. "You sent for me, my lord."

"Yes. My lord Duke, may I present Sir Laeghaire from Tralee, who will command my forces."

"I thought as much," the Duke said.

"I have told my lord the Duke that I believe we can raise five hundred men for him by Easter."

Laeghaire nodded. He could see Néel out of the corner of his eye.

"Five hundred knights?" the Duke said,

"Yes."

"I'll need them before Easter. By Sexagesima. I will want you ready by Septuagesima."

"Of course, my lord," Baldwin said.

"Do you speak French?" the Duke said to Laeghaire.

"No."

"Learn." He turned back to the Count. "I have other things to talk to you about."

Laeghaire glanced at Guillaume. Guillaume said, "My lord?"

"Leave."

"The Irishman may stay," the Duke said over his shoulder.

Guillaume and Néel went out. Laeghaire shut the door.

The Duke went to a chair and sat down. "I wanted to ask you about my . . . claim."

Laeghaire put his back against the wall by the door and relaxed his weight.

"To England," the Count said.

Laeghaire straightened up. He looked at the Duke's profile.

"You're surprised, Irishman." The Duke turned in the chair.

"Yes."

"Why?"

Laeghaire shrugged. He set his teeth together.

"I've always wanted England. I have a strong claim. The old King's named me his heir. I'll take her. It may be the only thing I'll ever get without fighting for it."

"As you will, my lord."

"Do you know England?"

"I'm an Irishman, my lord."

"Answer my question. I have no interest in Ireland."

"I am duly comforted, my lord."

"Your comfort is no concern of mine."

"For which I am tempted to thank God."

The Duke stood up. He looked at Baldwin. "Your taste in commanders amazes me." His head swung toward Laeghaire. "You are an insolent cur dog, and you'll keep your mouth prudently shut when you're near me, sir, or put something in it to justify your boldness."

"Then I'll take the second choice, my lord. I like the liberty of speaking."

The Duke said, "Get out."

Laeghaire stared at him. He turned and looked at Baldwin. "Have I your leave to go, my lord?"

"Go, Sir Laeghaire," Baldwin said.

Laeghaire smiled. He bowed his head once to Baldwin, once to the Duke, turned, and went out the door. He went down to the main corridor. He stopped and leaned against the wall and laughed.

After Christmas he sent out the summonses to the knights. The knight Josse, who held land just south of Ghent, stayed, by the Count's order, to help him. The squires of the Count's court began their final training, and the Count announced that they would all be knighted on Septuagesima. Josse Laeghaire put to oversee the squires until he had all his summonses sent.

Hilde was making Laeghaire a new surcoat. She had got the cloth from the Countess herself. She showed the surcoat to Laeghaire and said that she would ask the Bishop to bless its specially.

"The Bishop has better things to do," he said.

"But it will only take a few minutes."

"Still—"

"I've already asked him."

"All right, if it will make you happy."

"I'll pray over it, too."

He went by her. He leaned over and patted her stomach. "Pray over him, too. Maybe from you it would do some good."

The squires practiced in a field outside the town. Josse and the master of squires had them practicing all day long. Laeghaire visited the field often. One day he had a mock fight with the best of them. He unseated the squire with some difficulty.

"They need experience," Josse said.

"If they don't learn fast when they get to Maine, they'll have their heads caved in."

The knights began to gather long before Septuagesima. They became bored and unruly and needed watching. Laeghaire kept them playing games. They raced and had mock fights. One of them tried to rape a woman of the town. Laeghaire fined him five guilders and made him ride a mule wrong end to through the camp, with his spurs draped over the mule's ears. After that none of the knights disobeyed him. He gave them all the wine and food they wanted and they were happy.

The Count had him choose a squire from the pages. He took the younger son of a lord from the north, who had no money. The boy's name was Karl. He took Laeghaire's horses to the smith and had them shod, and cleaned his mail and weapons. Sometimes he went with Laeghaire to the squires' field and watched them practice.

"My father says I'll have to wait until all my brothers are knighted and my sisters are married before I can be knighted," Karl said.

"That's the problem with being younger."

"My father says that in the old days things were better. Everything is different now, he says. Everything's corrupted and strange."

"People always say that."

"I think he's a liar," Karl said.

Laeghaire turned to look at him. He laughed.

"What's the matter?"

"Everybody's a liar. Honor thy father and thy mother. How old are you?"

"Pretty old."

"You look at those squires. They're doing the same things your father did when he was a squire. When your sons are squires they'll do the same things. Nothing changes. Everything has always been corrupted and strange."

"That's what the Bishop said at Mass the day before yesterday."

"Exactly."

"Except for the 'corrupted and strange' part."

"Be quiet."

On Septuagesima the Count knighted all the squires. They feasted all day long. At nightfall, when everybody was dead-drunk, a messenger from the Duke of Normandy arrived and said that the Flemish troops were to be at Rouen by Sexagesima. The Count told the messenger it was not possible and that he should tell his master that they would be at Rouen in some ten or twelve days. The messenger left.

On the following day they all rested, and the day after that, at dawn, they all gathered to hear Mass. The Bishop was an old man and spoke slowly. Laeghaire, in his new surcoat, stood in the third rank of the army and was bored. He dared not shift his feet, because his helmet rested against them. He leaned on his sword but that cramped him. They would all notice if he made a single sound. He counted the rings in the sleeve of the mail of the man in front of him. That was confusing. The rings were all alike and his eyes kept juggling them. He concentrated on it. He wished this Bishop were like Arnulf, who fought wars himself and knew what he was talking about.

Now, I should bend my head and listen carefully, and believe that God will stretch down His hand and shield me when a Mainard knight comes charging at me or a crossbowman pulls the trigger. He arched his back carefully, hardly moving.

"Trust in God," the Bishop said. His voice rang hollowly in the church vault. His words came clearly down from the high altar. "If you but trust in God, His holy love will protect you. The man who falters in his belief is as a man who mistrusts his sword, and will not fight with it, so that when he must, he hesitates and is doomed."

On the other hand, a man can always get another sword. Arnulf had used an ax. Laeghaire rested his palms on the crossbars of his sword.

"Let God and the righteousness of your cause be your protection. Fight boldly, that all may know your faith in the Most High. Then will the weak in spirit shrink from you, and the poor in soul flee from you, and your faith will carry all before you on the field of battle."

Laeghaire stared past the ranks of heads into the depths of shadow by the high altar. The torches wavered in the faint draft. The shadows leaped up behind the Bishop, like angels come down to support him. He was a very holy man, this Bishop, and his nose arched like a cart wheel from his face.

"Have faith, and no man can win against you."

The prelates of the Mainards would say as much to their people. And the shadows were only insignificant flutterings of the torch flames.

"Let us pray."

They crossed themselves and knelt. Their voices came confidently to fill the church hall. Laeghaire made his voice a little louder than usual.

Finally it was over. They stood while the Bishop blessed them and sprinkled holy water over them. They all put on their helmets. The tawny, dark, red, brown heads vanished under the dull gray of the helmets. Behind the nosepieces of the helmets their eyes were in shadow and a man could not tell what color they were, and sometimes not recognize a man he had known for years. They filed out and in the courtyard gathered to be exhorted by the Count.

The Count appeared on the upper balcony. Behind Laeghaire somebody said, "He can say all he wants, he's not going."

Laeghaire turned. "Shut up."

"Sorry, my lord."

The army cheered the Count heartily all through his little speech. The Count asked God's especial blessing on Laeghaire. The army cheered that, too. The Count took the banner of the Flemings and carried it to the rail of the balcony. Laeghaire went and mounted the brown stallion. He rode to the stair and took the banner.

"God be with you," the Count said. "You are well followed."

"Yes, my lord."

He rode to Josse, who would carry the banner, and nodded to Lodovic, his hornbearer. At the horn's blast the army marched out to get their horses. Hilde was in the corner of the courtyard. She came to him. She wore a new cloak, one made for the Countess which had displeased her by its bright color. She looked younger in it. Her hair hung in a pale braid over the bright cloth.

"Be careful," she said.

He dismounted. "I will."

"When you come back, he'll be born."

"Yes."

"Laeghaire."

"You be careful," he said.

"I love you."

"I know." He kissed her and mounted. He rode out through the gate. He turned and looked back. She was watching him. He waved. She smiled at him.

Karl brought him the black horse. He dismounted and changed his gear. The army was assembled. He was glad they had no foot soldiers. He mounted the black. Karl fell in beside him. They rode down to meet the rest of the Flemings. The banner snapped and wrinkled against the sky.

When they reached Rouen, the place was full of knights and archers and men-at-arms, and they had to find a camp outside the wall. Laeghaire presented himself in the anteroom of the castle. A man leaving, the Archbishop Maurilius, told him the Duke would see him in a moment. He was surprised that he could see the Duke so quickly. He waited, after the Archbishop left. The door opened and a knight came in.

"Good afternoon."

"Good afternoon," Laeghaire said.

The knight looked him up and down. "Are you waiting for the Duke?"

"Yes."

"And you are—"

"Laeghaire from Tralee. I have five hundred Flemings down by the river.

"Ah. Yes. He should be out at any moment."

"I know. The Archbishop just told me."

"Oh?"

The knight went into the office, unannounced. He came out almost at once with the Duke. The Duke looked at Laeghaire.

"You made good speed," he said.

"Yes."

"May I present Sir William Fitz-Osbern, Lord Steward of Normandy. This is the Flemish commander, Laeghaire of the Long Road."

"We have met, my lord," Fitz-Osbern said.

"Good. Get that map. Come with me, Sir Laeghaire."

Laeghaire followed him. The Duke turned. "Néel of Saint-Saëns says you were in England. He says he saw you."

"He might have."

"Why did you deny you spoke Saxon?"

"You surprised me, I guess."

"You do speak it."

"Yes."

"You could be valuable to me." The Duke held a dagger in his hands. "When I go to claim England."

"That might be years from now, when I won't be around."

The Duke looked up from the knife. "It might."

Fitz-Osbern came in with the map.

"We leave within the week," the Duke said. "I have

already sent part of my men to the Vexin. Under the Montgomerys and d'Avranches. You and I and Fitz-Osbern will invade straight into Maine. Le Mans we must take. First we must take the land between the border and the city. Mayenne and Walter are here, in Mayenne. I don't think they'll come to meet us. They'll fall back to Le Mans. I want them to. These villages here are your responsibility." He swept the land between Le Mans and the northeastern border of Maine. "Small, with only two fortresses near them. Take them and occupy them."

"Yes, my lord," Laeghaire said.

The Duke studied him. He glanced at the map again. "I'll give you scouts. I'll send them to your camp tomorrow. How is your French?"

"Not very good."

"You'll learn." He smiled suddenly. "You're least obnoxious when you keep your mouth shut. I'll expect you here in three days, in the afternoon, with the rest of my captains."

"Yes, my lord. Thank you." He turned and went out.

Josse was waiting for him in the courtyard. They mounted and went down through the town. Josse said, "Did he receive you well?"

"Why shouldn't he?"

"There was some talk of disagreement between you."

"Who told you that?"

"I just heard it."

"He received me well."

"He's a strange man. Did you meet anyone?"

"Fitz-Osbern. And the Archbishop."

"The Archbishop isn't the important one. Of the priests. The Duke's half brother Odo and the Prior of Bec, Lanfranc—they run things, I've heard. We hear a lot about Normans, in Flanders. Priests are very strong here, I've heard. Very strong."

Laeghaire said nothing.

"Although no man's really close to him. They say not even Fitz-Osbern and his half brothers know his mind completely."

They were in the middle of Rouen, full of knights and townspeople. The dust was thick.

"He is one of God's chosen," Josse said. "Or else one of the Devil's." He looked around and crossed himself. "No normal man has his success at everything."

"He looks like a prophet."

"Yes." Josse nodded. "That's good. He wasn't made to plod along in the dust like the rest of us."

"Your vision is very slightly offensive."

"I didn't mean to include you, sir. I hope you don't—"

"It was a joke, Josse."

"Good."

"Why should it matter to you what I think, anyway?"

"Of course it matters," Josse said. "Are you thirsty? There's an inn down there."

"All right. Why?"

"Why what?"

"Why does it matter?"

"Because, at the risk of seeming preacherly, we all are responsible for what other men think of what we say, because everything a man says has some effect on every other man. That's why lies are so dangerous, more dangerous even than murders, because they delude."

"More dangerous than heresy?"

"Why, heresy is lying, isn't it?"

"I don't know."

"Are you joking with me again, sir?"

"Yes. I'm sorry. It was a bad joke."

"All lying is heresy, anyway," Josse said.

They went into the innyard. Laeghaire dismounted.

"That was very well put," Laeghaire said slowly. "Very well put."

"Thank you, sir."

The inn was mobbed with fighting men. It was stifling. They sat down at a bench. Josse shouted for wine. Laeghaire rested his forearms on his knees. He shifted a little so that his sword rested more comfortably. He wished he had not come in here; it was crammed. He wondered if his son would ask him awkward questions.

Josse brought wine in cups. Laeghaire took his and raised it. He set it down again on the bench. Néel was sitting across the room. Laeghaire looked down and saw an empty wine cask on the floor nearby. He hooked it with his foot, rolled it to him, and smashed in one side with his heel.

Néel turned at the noise and saw him. He stood and came over. Laeghaire stretched out his legs before him.

"So you came after all," Néel said.

"I hear you've been telling tales about me to the Duke."

"I told him you spoke Saxon."

"Did he ask you?"

"No."

"Who gave you license to meddle in my life?"

Néel darkened. "Who gave you license to talk that way to me?"

"I'll talk that way to any man who takes liberties with me."

"Get up and face me, you—"

"It would give me great pleasure. Here or outside?"

The others were dead-still, listening. Néel glanced around at them.

"Outside. There's more room."

He turned and went out. Josse caught Laeghaire's arm. "Are you mad, sir? You'll have them all down on us."

"He suggested it."

"That—" Josse glanced around. The other men were pushing out into the innyard to watch. Their voices rose in a high excitement.

"Well," Josse said, "you've got the right one. They don't seem to like him. Good luck."

"Thanks, Josse."

Josse grinned. "It's your business, I suppose."

Laeghaire went outside. The knights had made a circle. Néel stood alone in it. He had his sword out. The crushing wall of knights parted to let Laeghaire into the circle. He took off his cloak and threw it aside and drew his sword.

"He's got reach over you, Néel," someone shouted. "He'll take your ears off with that long arm."

Néel snorted. He held his sword in both hands, took a deep breath, and charged. Laeghaire dodged away from him. He came up almost against the wall of men. He feinted to draw Néel off and ducked by him into the middle of the circle. He held his sword low. Néel followed him hard. He drew Laeghaire a little off balance and leaped in, swinging at shoulder level. Laeghaire parried the blow. He felt the sting of the meeting swords even through his heavy gloves. He disengaged his blade and struck at Néel's body, stepping into the blow. He missed and almost fell. He avoided Néel's lunge only by throwing himself to one side. He rocked to get his balance and parried two heavy strokes. He felt the men behind him like a wall.

"Get back. Give me room or it's your ears."

Néel flailed at him. Laeghaire circled him. He crouched. He weaved back and forth. Néel was panting. His mouth was open.

"Christ," Laeghaire said. "I'll kill you, Norman."

Néel struck out, almost tentatively, and Laeghaire caught his blade on his own and held it and pushed him. Néel staggered back and Laeghaire followed, battering at him. Néel moved back rapidly, groping with his feet. His sword was high against Laeghaire's. Laeghaire clubbed at him. The clanging of the swords filled his ears with a roar. He held the sword two-handed and smashed it at Néel. Néel just met his blows. Laeghaire wanted to smash his head apart. He saw the sweat like blood on Néel's face. Néel ducked under a blow, trying to get past. Laeghaire swung backhanded. He felt the sword crash into Néel's body. His own stomach contracted like a good fist. Néel screamed. Laeghaire wheeled toward him. Néel wobbled back. He dropped his sword. The blood leaped from him. He fell and lay in the dust.

The watching knights were silent. One of them came forward and looked at Néel. "He's done. He won't be going to Maine."

The others withdrew slowly into the inn. Laeghaire went after, wiping his sword. He saw two men carrying Néel upstairs. He picked up his untouched wine and drank it.

"God's ears," a Norman said. "I'm glad you're on our side. You're Flemish, aren't you?"

"Irish."

"Irish? Irish?" A man shoved his way through the others. "I thought I recognized that berserker's swinging. Laeghaire. Laeghaire of the Long Road. By God."

"Who's that?"

"Tell me you don't remember me." The big man stood in front of him. The others were watching.

"Jehan."

"Yes. Jehan. Here, bring me some wine, somebody."

"It's a long way from Burgundy, Jehan. What are you—"

"I took up the knight-errant's trade, having learned of it in good places." He turned to the others. "You screaming bastards, we have, fighting for the side of right, God and William of Normandy, the greatest sword-fighter in all Christendom. I use an ax myself."

The knights decided to be pleased. They cheered and pressed in around Laeghaire. They drank a toast to him and to William of Normandy.

"I told you," Laeghaire said to Josse. "These are cousins of mine."

"You never told me, sir."

"Cousins, Irish?" Jehan roared.

"Not you. Only Normans. It's Viking blood; it makes all men cousins."

"Let's drink to that."

They all drank. They sat on the benches and tables. Laeghaire wanted to go. He couldn't. He thought, Pay the price. Kill a man, you must drink with his friends. Somebody gave him more wine. Josse swallowed his the wrong way and Jehan pounded on his back.

"When we take Maine," a Norman said, "I want this Irishman right next to me." He grasped Laeghaire by the wrist and raised his arm. "And we'll have every woman between the border and Le Mans."

"Drink to that," Laeghaire said.

"And the rest of you can wait in line."

The other knights shouted him down. Josse sat nervously by Laeghaire. They switched from Latin to French, and the Normans laughed at Laeghaire's difficulties with it. Laeighaire and Jehan spoke Burgundian for a while. They drank all through it, all through the rest of the afternoon. By evening some knights came down to say that the lord Duke had heard them and wanted them to disperse. They tied up the knights and put them in the empty wine casks, but the effort of this sobered them up a little, and they thought it timely to go back to their camps.

Karl held the head of the brown stallion, patting him and talking to him. Laeghaire had one of the great hoofs in his lap. He shaped the outer wall of the hoof, clenching his teeth. It was hard to hold the dagger right. He put down the stallion's hoof and stepped back. Karl led the horse in a little circle.

"That's better," Karl said. "Whoa, now, my beautiful."

"I have to trim it some more. Hold him right there."

He bent and caught hold of the stallion's fetlock. The horse set himself. Laeghaire drove his weight against the horse's shoulder. The stallion jumped sideways, trying to rear, and Laeghaire wrestled up the hoof and held it against his knee. The stallion stood braced. Laeghaire swore gently in Gaelic.

"Perhaps you should hobble him," Karl said.

"He'd hurt himself. He's stupid. Hah." He put down the hoof and went to the anvil. The shoe was red as a cherry in the fire. He took it out with the tongs and set it on the anvil. "Great ugly brute," he said to the horse. He took a spike and made the holes and threw the shoe into a bucket of water. The steam blew up like smoke.

"Does your head still hurt?" Karl said.

"Yes."

Karl stroked the stallion's face. "He's a beauty." The stallion put his ears forward to hear. When Laeghaire took the sweating shoe out of the bucket and came toward him, the horse pinned his ears back and snorted.

"He's an infernal misbegotten dog of a horse foaled in the dark of the moon from a sow mated with a banshee."

Laeghaire got the hoof up again, braced himself, and fitted the shoe to the hoof. The stench of burning hoof made him gag. The stallion smelled it and reared. Laeghaire fell against the anvil. The stallion swung his hindquarters, snorting.

"He doesn't like the smell," Karl said. "That's a pretty boy, whoa now, whoa."

"He doesn't like me. He knows when he's shod, he's going to be ridden, and he doesn't like being ridden. That's why he threw the first shoe."

He found the shoe and washed it in the water. Karl walked the horse around. Laeghaire went for a drink of wine. The smell of the burning hoof had brought the pain closer to his forehead. He looked out at the camp. Two boys carrying water passed him. He could see some of his men talking around their fire.

The shoe cooled and he began to nail it on. The stallion sulked. Karl patted him and talked to him. Laeghaire heard Karl's voice change and looked up.

"Good afternoon, my lord," he said. He had to twist his neck to look at William. William sat on a tall gray horse whose shoulder was no more than a yard from Laeghaire's face. Laeghaire started to put down the hoof, but William said, "Keep on, sir."

Laeghaire spat a nail into the palm of his hand and set it in a nail hole. He lifted the hammer. William made him nervous. He worked slowly.

"The whole camp talks about the newest champion," William said. "I understand you proved your heavy arm."

"I was drunk, my lord."

"I hear different."

Laeghaire put another nail gently through the hoof wall and twisted off the excess.

"I hear you came into an inn and saw fit to kill a man for no reason worth retelling."

"I was drunk, my lord."

"You had just come from me, and you were not drunk when I saw you. Or are you easy with your wine?"

"Very easy, my lord."

"You will plead my pardon."

Laeghaire set down the hoof. He stepped back a little. "Néel was his own man."

"No. He owed his knight's fee to me. Now he can hardly fill it. He died last night. You owe me a knight's fee."

Karl said softly, "My lord." He led the horse away. Laeghaire stepped back farther.

"I owe you nothing, Norman," he said. "I am in the service of my lord of Flanders. Throw your mighty name at someone else."

His head throbbed. William's eyes narrowed with rage. This gave Laeghaire satisfaction. He crossed his arms. "I am a free knight," he said, "and be you the Duke of Normandy or Jesus Christ Himself, you will not try your tricks with me."

The gray horse wheeled. William's fist sledged down. Laeghaire felt it club against the side of his head and he felt his bare back skinned on the stony ground. For a moment he could not see. He sat up. His head cleared slowly. He saw the forelegs of the gray horse in front of him. The hoofs almost touched his right foot.

He got to his feet. He saw the other men gathering around. The Flemings stood in the closest circle. One of them stepped forward and drew his sword. "Sir Laeghaire," he said. He held out the sword.

Laeghaire flung out his arm. "Sheathe it."

"No man can—"

"Sheathe it, or I'll cut your throat with it."

The man pushed back into the crowd.

"You'll be in my anteroom as soon as you're properly dressed," William said. "And you'll plead my pardon."

He lifted the rein. Laeghaire caught the rein. He pushed his hair out of his eyes.

"My lord," he said. "My good, Christian, knightly, sweet lord, before I plead your pardon, you will plead mine. You have my promise on it."

William laughed. "There's blood on your head, Irish." He spurred his horse. The rein tore from Laeghaire's fingers. He jumped aside. The men scattered before the gray horse. They turned to look after him. One man crossed himself.

"Leave me," Laeghaire said.

The crowd lingered.

"Leave me. Where is my sword? Leave me, you oxen."

They wandered off. But Josse came to him.

"You are all pride, Irishman. I wonder you aren't dead."

"Do you know who it was who offered me the sword?"

"Yes."

"Take him my apology."

"He'll forgive you. Any man would."

"Not his high and mighty lordship."

"I meant him."

"Josse, don't be so tender with me, hunh?"

"I'm sorry, sir."

Laeghaire caught his arm. "So am I, Josse."

He went to his tent. Karl was oiling the armbands on his shield. He kept his head bent over it. Laeghaire sat down on the ground. His head was thundering. He stared at the shield, at the dents in the surface.

"I saw," Karl said.

"What did you see, boy?"

"There's water in the bucket, sir. You should wash your head."

Laeghaire put his hand to his head. The touch of his fingers made him wince.

"What did you see, boy?"

He looked at his fingers, slick with blood.

"You were right. You were right. How could he have forgotten his honor?"

"His honor."

"You are a knight, and he had no right to strike you, or to order you around."

"Maybe."

"And if he is overhuman, as they say, he had even less

right than he had, which was none."

"I think he had to do it."

"But you had to do what you did."

"Maybe."

Laeghaire washed his head. The water turned filmy and pink.

"Didn't you?" Karl said.

"I don't know."

"Would you do it again?"

"I don't know. Yes. I would."

"Are we going back to Flanders?"

"No. Get me my surcoat and mail."

"Are you—"

"Do as I say. There are few things I regret. Leave it there. If I regretted having done what I did, I wouldn't go up there."

Karl went silently to the war chest. Laeghaire straightened. The blood flowed freely from the wound. It splattered his mail. When he put on the surcoat the blood spread over the shoulder bright as a badge. He buckled on his sword belt.

"I have your horse, my lord," Karl said.

He went out. Karl held the brown stallion. Laeghaire looked at him. He mounted. Karl said, "Did you want the other, my lord?"

"Don't be so innocent."

Karl handed him up his helmet. He said, "Good luck."

"I'm not going to a battle."

He rode slowly through the camp. He saw them straighten and turn to watch him ride by. He held the reins loosely. His left hand rested on his thigh. The blood clotted again; he couldn't feel it running along his ear.

He thought it had never taken him longer to ride such a distance. Even in the town the people turned to watch him. He wondered if they knew. The brown stallion walked with a long reaching stride. Laeghaire took the rein in his left hand and leaned forward to kill a fly on the horse's neck. A smear of blood spread on the palm of his glove.

The castle gate was open. Fitz-Osbern stood in the courtyard, talking to a page boy. He turned and saw Laeghaire and walked over.

"Who are— Oh. So you came."

Laeghaire dismounted.

"I came, my lord." He threw the rein to Fitz-Osbern, who caught it automatically. Laeghaire went by him and up the outer stair.

The anteroom was empty. He stood, looking at the tapestry on the wall. The door opened, but it was a man in bishop's robes. This man cocked an eyebrow and said, "Do you wait for my lord brother, sir knight?"

"Yes, my lord Bishop."

"He is in his offices."

"Then tell him I came this far."

Odo went into the offices. He shut the door. Laeghaire studied the dried blood on the palm of his glove. He started to draw off the glove.

"By the splendor of God."

William came farther into the room. He turned, went back and shut the door. He frowned.

"What do you intend to gain by this?"

"It occurred to me that it would surprise you if I came," Laeghaire said. He took off his helmet.

"Then I expect a flowery speech." William put his hands on his hips. He cocked his head a little.

"No, my lord." Laeghaire looked around. He saw a bench and sat on it. He crossed his arms. "I keep my word."

"So?"

"I made you a promise."

William's mouth thinned. "And if I do not debase myself before a blood-fouled wanderer, a gypsy knight and a stranger, then you will take my father-in-law's army back to Flanders."

"I said nothing of that."

William thought. His eyes never left Laeghaire's. "You damned man," he said.

Laeghaire said nothing.

The Duke went around the room. He put out his hand to touch a part of the tapestry. He paused by the window. Suddenly he turned.

"I plead your pardon," he said.

"And I yours, my lord."

"For what do I plead your pardon? Hitting you, or saying what I said?"

"Saying that. Nothing more. What you meant to do."

"You are a damned, damned man. Get out."

"As you wish, my lord."

He went to the door. William said, "Sir Laeghaire. The blow. Count it an accolade."

Laeghaire went out. He laughed in the hall. He went down to his horse. Fitz-Osbern was in the shadow of the gate. Laeghaire mounted. He put on his helmet. He waved to Fitz-Osbern. The stallion tugged at the bit. Laeghaire took a strong hold on the rein. The stallion reared and Laeghaire spurred him. They bolted out the gate. The dust of the street billowed up under the driving hoofs. They charged across the half-empty marketplace and out of the town onto the field. In the middle of the camp Laeghaire brought the stallion to a stiff-legged stop. He bent him in a wild, plunging circle. The men cheered suddenly. Laeghaire made the stallion rear and lunge three great jumps on his hind legs. He stopped the stallion and sat panting in the saddle. His men were all around him.

Jehan shoved through them. Jehan looked up.

"A berserker with a horse, too. Did he make you a count?"

"It's between him and me. Where's wine? Shall we get drunk? Wait until I get out of this mail."

Four days later, after Mass, they all set out for Maine. They moved fast, as fast as they could with the foot soldiers. They reached a town called Bellême in three days, marched straight through the town, and met the seigneur at the gate of the fortress. Laeghaire saw William speaking to this lord, up by the gate, and heard nothing. William turned and called up his captains.

"We'll camp here the night," he said.

They dispersed their men to find campgrounds and water. Laeghaire went down with Karl to the common pasturage outside the town. He ordered his men to camp near it.

"What's this all about?" Karl said.

"Who is the lord of Bellême?"

"Robert, I think his name is. He's a great lord."

"Whose man is he?"

"No man's man."

"Then that's what. He doesn't want them tricking him. Now he'll have hostages of him."

"Oh," Karl said. He unbuckled the pack harnesses. "He's a clever man."

"That's the truth."

"What are we going to do when we get to Maine?"

"Ride against a village called Le Barb. The rest—they're going to Mayenne. Or so he says."

"Le Barb?"

"There's a fort there. Get me some wine. I'll make the fire."

They rode on the next day. First William sent twenty knights back to Rouen with two younger sons of the house of Bellême. The land was hilly and they could not move as easily or as fast. William sent out his scouts ahead of him. They rode in a tight mass, with the scouts set out before them like the feelers of a bug.

Once they came on a village, and it surrendered to them as soon as the people saw how many they were. Laeghaire and his Flemings were in the front part of the army. They reined in and waited while Fitz-Osbern rode out to accept the surrender of the town. The Duke sat his horse at the head of the army. He talked with Odo, his half brother.

The sun was bright. Laeghaire turned his shoulder to the village. He hooked his right knee over the pommel of his saddle and stretched.

"Wine, my lord?" Karl said, and unslung the jar from his saddle.

"Good." Laeghaire took it and opened it. He drank.

A horse galloped by him, headed for the Duke. Laeghaire tossed the jar to Karl.

"My lord," the rider said. He wheeled to a halt. "Are we going to plunder?"

Laeghaire turned and looked at the men around him. None of them seemed surprised. He heard their voices, muttering, just as before.

"No," William said.

Laeghaire put his foot back into the stirrup and spat.

They rode through the town, but they neither pillaged nor burned, and out again on the other side. Soon after, Jehan rode up looking for Laeghaire and fell in beside him. "Surprised?"

"Who's he to deny me my rights?"

"Nothing there, anyway. By the way, you have two new members in your force."

"Oh, no. He can comfort and carry his own hostages."

"These are his orders. You take them and you hold them."

"He's mad."

"Well, he's probably right. He's always right. You can leave them in the first village you take."

"Hunh."

They talked about Burgundy for a while. Jehan was happy. Laeghaire could see it in him. Jehan liked being a fighting man and being admired and having nothing to worry about. He wished Jehan was coming with him.

They reached the point where the army was to split up. William sent for Laeghaire. He rode up toward the little council of mounted men. He saw the band of scouts on their fleet ponies, wandering along the creek bank. His men were bunching together, away from the Normans; and his own scouts, Thierry and his men, were near them; he thought he felt them watching him.

Fitz-Osbern was talking to William. The other captains turned and rode off. No one else was around except Fitz-Osbern, the Duke and Laeghaire. Laeghaire dropped the rein over the horse's withers. He put his hands on his hips. Ahead of them there was nothing but the long rolling plain and the trees. He could see the mountains, off to his right, like clouds, only thicker than clouds, sailing on the horizon. The sky was a hard brilliant blue. He knew he had sat in his saddle like this before, waiting for his instructions, on different plains, in hills, by rivers. He remembered them, one after another and all together and jumbled. This was no different. The Duke of Normandy was no different from the Duke of Thuringia, the Earl of Wessex, the Count of Burgundy, all of them, all the others. He pressed his palms against the bones of his hips. It was no different. It was no different.

When Fitz-Osbern turned away, neither he nor the Duke said anything to Laeghaire for a moment. They did not look at him. He thought it was logical. For a moment he thought that they could not see him.

Laeghaire took his Flemings straight down against Le Barb. It was the biggest of the villages he was supposed to take. It had a solid fort in the center of the village. Laeghaire's scouts came back to him the night before he attacked it, and they told him that it was bright with torchlight, shining, and that more men walked the walls than were supposed to be in the whole garrison. Thierry, the chief of the scouts, was worried, and he kept talking about that: that Le Barb should be so strongly fortified. He said he thought there was something important there, some man perhaps.

"They know we're here, then," Laeghaire said.

He sent the scouts in to sleep, and thought about this thing. The spies William had bought from Maine had told him, Laeghaire, that Le Barb's fort could maintain no more than one hundred and fifty men, with all their gear and horses. Certainly they knew that this army was out here, in the darkness. He saw Thierry's face in his mind, clear as if Thierry were there, with the three deep grooves in his forehead.

Just before dawn, Laeghaire led out his men. Le Barb was bright, all torchlit, flaming. He saw the men on the walls.

He sent in his men to fire the huts of the village and burn the fields south of the fort. He rode down with them part of the way. His hornbearer, Lodovic, stayed with him. The fortress shone, and the sentries on the wall gave the alarm. Laeghaire heard the bell ring. He called Karl to him and sent him to bring Thierry. The fort remained closed. Some archers shot at Laeghaire's men from the walls, but the knights inside did not come out to drive them off.

"Thierry. Go with the scouts and burn the rest of the fields. Stay out of bowshot."

Thierry went, still worried. Laeghaire called in his men and made them form regular lines. He sent four of the squires to find a log to use as a ram. They waited there until the fires on the south side had dimmed down and the fires on the north and west had grown up. They attacked in the false dawn, in the haze. The smoke floated over them. The gate crumpled in and they swarmed through the fort and drove all the defenders into the courtyard. There were only one hundred men in the fort garrison.

Laeghaire thought it was a good omen. He sent a scout to William with the news. Thierry and his men went to scout the north. For a while Laeghaire stayed in the fort, with all his men but the scouts. He locked up all the Mainards in the dungeon. After a week or so, most of them consented to join his army. He made them into a special band and told them that they would be the first to attack in any fight and if they showed any reluctance they would be killed. He stayed a while longer, arranging everything, and when he left he left fifty of his men in the fortress to hold it.

He and his men went northwest after that, and attacked two little villages and burned them down. He went around Rougemont, the walled town, and captured three villages around it. All of these villages gave in as soon as they saw him, and he left ten men in each, to keep order and make sure the people did not turn against him. It was planting time and the peasants were interested only in their fields. They stayed quiet.

It was a wet spring. The Flemings did not like riding around in the mud and spring rain. All of them wanted to be town garrisons, and they would come to him and plead with him. He let Josse assign the garrisons, but the men screamed favoritism, and he had to do it himself, by lots. One night, just outside the last northern village he was supposed to take, the whole army suddenly sat down and would not move. It was raining and the rain was warm and sticky. Laeghaire rode into the middle of the camp and dismounted.

"The weather is bad," he said. "I don't like it either. At

least you aren't starving."

"When are we going to take something worth pillaging?" somebody said.

Josse stood up. "This is stupid. You've all sworn an oath of loyalty to the Count, and he sent us all down here. Are you going to sin against God and your lord, merely because you are uncomfortable?"

A man from Ypres leaped up and began to argue furiously with him. Laeghaire turned and saw Karl, sleek-faced from the rain, staring at the two arguing men in surprise.

Other knights quickly joined in the argument, and their voices rose like braying, higher and higher. Laeghaire grinned at Karl. He went forward slowly and shouldered his way into the growing knot of arguing knights. He pushed between Josse and the man from Ypres—Raoul, his name was—and looked at both of them. Raoul fell silent at once. The others quieted down. Josse, aware that he was getting in the last word, shouted, "—be rich and go home and live like—"

Laeghaire bent, scooped up a handful of mud, and threw it into Josse's face. Josse choked, coughed, and sat down. The other men burst out laughing. Laeghaire stood over Josse. Josse clawed at the mud in his eyes and mouth, spitting. He tried to get up and slipped. Laeghaire helped him up. Josse's eyes were bright with anger. He stared at Laeghaire a minute.

Laeghaire began to laugh. Josse fumed, stared, and grinned. He wiped off his cheek.

"The rain will wash me," he said.

Laeghaire went back to his horse and mounted. "Let's ride," he said. They all mounted and rode out after him.

They took that northernmost village a few days later. It surrendered easily. Laeghaire left ten men with it. He and the others rode back to attack Rougemont. On the way he heard that the village to the north had revolted against his garrison and sieged them in the church tower, and was trying to burn them out. He turned around with his army and rode back. They burned the village to the ground and chased the villagers into the forest. Laeghaire had his men trample back and forth in the young grain and throw garbage into the wells and the springs. They rounded up all the animals and drove them off before them. Laeghaire would not let the village priest say a Mass for the dead villagers, but threw them all into a ditch and covered them with ash and dead coals from the burned huts. He took the priest prisoner and brought him back with the army to Rougemont.

Rougemont, cut off from help and raided now and then from captured villages all around, had sent out some of her knights to try to take the captured villages away from the Flemings, but the Flemings, always knowing when they were coming, would ambush them and drive them off. The town's garrison was no more than one hundred and ten. Laeghaire circled her entirely and did not attack. He had only four hundred men, besides the Mainards from Le Barb. These men had fought well against the other villages, but Laeghaire still did not trust them. They made a lot of angry talk in the army, saying that they wanted to get some loot for all the dangers they faced. Laeghaire wished he could get rid of them. He sent them off once to raid, a good four- or five-day raid straight into the middle of Maine, but they came back, and they even had some loot, which incited the rest of the army.

Rougemont was obstinate. The fields went untended and the people inside the wall had little to eat, but the town did not surrender. Laeghaire sent off parts of his army in turns to raid. He decided that he had learned something from the Maine knights' raid. He did not want to attack Rougemont.

The leader of the Maine knights was named Gabriel.

He was big and blond and ugly, and he had a voice like a horn; he could be heard all over the camp. One night Laeghaire heard him talking and went over to see what was going on. Gabriel sat by a fire, with some fifteen Maine knights and four or five Flemings. He was saying that he would take Rougemont if he were leading the army and not— he went off in French about Laeghaire. Laeghaire did not recognize some of the words. He went as close as he could without being seen, sat down on his heels, and listened. Gabriel was not very clever. He kept saying the same things about Laeghaire. The Flemings said nothing, nothing at all. The Mainards laughed in the beginning. They grew silent after a while. Gabriel paused only to drink wine. His voice got louder. Finally Laeghaire stood up. He saw many more men around him, listening. Laeghaire came quietly through the men, past the fire, and faced Gabriel. Gabriel looked up at him.

It was very quiet. The fire crackled. Gabriel's face tightened, all over. Even his eyes looked smaller. He started to stand up. Laeghaire put his hand on Gabriel's shoulder and threw him face down on the ground. Laeghaire put his foot on Gabriel's back. Gabriel tried to break loose. He rolled and flailed with his arms. Laeghaire lifted his eyes and looked slowly all around at the men who watched. They said nothing and their faces turned away from him. He drew his dagger. He took his foot from Gabriel's back. Gabriel stood up, turning. Laeghaire stepped close to him. He put his dagger into Gabriel's belly and tore upward. He stepped back. Gabriel fell slack. He fell almost in sections. He lay touching Laeghaire's right boot. Laeghaire wiped his dagger blade on his surcoat and went off.

Rougemont surrendered less than a week later. Laeghaire stayed in the town waiting for reinforcements. He made his garrisons stronger, and from Rougemont sent out raids. But by this time—by midsummer—they had despoiled much of the land around, and there was little to loot. After Laeghaire killed Gabriel, none of the knights said anything about the campaign and what should be done with it.

Even Josse was careful when he talked to Laeghaire, for a while. Karl acted as if he had never heard about it. He came back now and then from the town to the place where Laeghaire was staying, and told Laeghaire jokes he had heard or some news he had heard, but he never mentioned Gabriel.

The reinforcements came—one hundred and fifty Normans—and they brought news of the southern campaign. William had chased Geoffrey and Walter of the Vexin out of the city of Mayenne and driven them south, fighting almost every day. These Normans come to Rougemont were all older knights, tired of fighting, and Laeghaire decided that William could afford to lose them. He scattered them throughout the chain of villages, packed up all but seventy of the Flemings and Maine knights, and rode out, going south.

Saint-Marc, this village was. Over the earthwork around it Laeghaire could see a single light, probably on the church tower. Thierry had said they had a church here. He turned to look back at his men. In the darkness he could not tell exactly how they were spread out. There was no moon. Except for the single light in the village, everything was blank and dark.

Once, fighting in Thuringia, he had ridden out to check a report from one of his scouts. He rode almost a day away from all his men, alone, and in the dusk came up over a ridge and looked down, and there, on the plain, the whole camp of the Slavs lay, a thousand fires.

Women and children and old men and warriors, spread out over the plain. He remembered standing on that ridge, in the trees, looking down at it, and he remembered something of the feeling, but not the feeling itself. The next day, riding back, he had been afraid.

He arched his back to shift the weight of the mail. His left arm had gone to sleep. He made a fist and opened it. His whole arm tingled. He adjusted the shield over it and tightened the higher strap. It was hot. His fingers slipped from the buckle and he swore. Just as the tongue of the buckle slid into the hole he heard Josse's horn.

"Lodovic," he said, and lifted his hand with the rein.

Lodovic blew two hard blasts on the horn. His cheeks puffed and emptied. Immediately the brown stallion lunged forward, throwing himself up the last few yards of the slope. Laeghaire heard the rising sound of the horses behind him. He drew his lance closer under his arm. The brown stallion swung into a full gallop. Lodovic was galloping to Laeghaire's right and a little behind him.

The village was only a few hundred yards away. Laeghaire spurred the stallion. He swung up his shield to protect his head and the stallion's withers and neck. He bent. The stallion veered to the left, abruptly, and Laeghaire felt and heard an arrow bounce off his shield. The noise was all around him: the whining of the arrows in flight and the slap of their striking the shields. There was a great commotion ahead of them, in the village, and the church bell began to ring. The noise of the bell, the rhythm of it, overrode all the rest of the noise.

They were on the earthwork. Laeghaire remembered the reports—"high as a man, broad on the top, wood spikes"—it hardly mattered; he was going over. He lowered the shield and leaned over the stallion's withers. The stallion jumped, clawing with his hind legs. The spikes rose up, one to either side, like walls. Laeghaire shouted.

He felt the stallion lurch up onto the top. Men were running toward him. He dared not look around. He heard the cursing of his men. He heard a horse scream.

The villagers were swarming around him. He flung the lance, underhand, and saw it break through a man's chest. Two shouting men with axes leaped for him. One caught his bridle. He dropped the reins. The axes chopped for him. He took one on his shield and parried the other on the hilt of his half-drawn sword. The stallion reared, fighting the hand on his bridle, and Laeghaire swung his shield in a flat arc. The edge caught the man to his left on the chin. The stallion leaped forward and was off the earthwork. Laeghaire wrenched his sword out and cleaved open a man's head. The stallion leaped from his hocks and reared. The crowd of defenders mobbed them. Laeghaire bashed at them. His men were coming over the earthwork. The crowd was running back. There were torches flittering in the town.

"Lodovic!" Laeghaire shouted. He charged. The horn blasted all around him. The men of the village had turned; they were fleeing. He led the charge against their backs. The bell was tolling almost over his head. For a moment he was alone, galloping over the screaming stragglers, wrestling the stallion around so that he could use his sword. Suddenly his knights were on either side of him. The horses collided with one another, bouncing shoulder to shoulder, and there was no using a sword.

The torches were dead-ahead. The villagers were massed before them. A dim wall of men stood on the far side. A horse neighed. Laeghaire reined up, lifting his sword arm. His men stopped. They completed the ring around the villagers. Laeghaire breathed heavily in their midst. The torches grew in number. Now even his side of the ring was brightly lit. The faces of the villagers were turned blindly into the torchlight. He panted, staring back at them.

"Josse," he said.

Josse waved his arm silently.

Laeghaire breathed deeply, slackening down into his saddle. He looked around. He waved his arm, and his men moved obediently to close up the ring. Josse's men backed their horses around and left quietly. Laeghaire signaled to Lodovic; Lodovic gave orders to the three men beside him, and they all dismounted and collected the weapons of the villagers.

Laeghaire took off his helmet. A baby was crying. A woman bent over it, trying to quiet it. The baby kept crying. After a moment half a dozen others began to cry too. They wailed in their thin voices. The Flemings sat their horses in a ring. Laeghaire held his helmet in his hands. He listened to the edged dreary wailing.

Josse returned. He nodded to Laeghaire. Laeghaire said, "Two men in each hut. Search it before you do any sleeping. Two men, no more, no less."

They disbanded quietly. Laeghaire sat the motionless horse in the square until every man and every villager was gone. Karl came finally to him, with Josse and Lodovic, and they looked around.

"My lord," Karl said, "you are wounded."

Laeghaire looked down at his body. Blood was dribbling down from a cut on his thigh. It began to hurt while he looked at it. It was a deep scratch. He put his hand on it.

"How many did we lose?" he said to Josse.

"One dead," Josse said. "Nineteen wounded. The wounded are all being bound up. All but four of them can ride."

"Who?"

Josse recited names.

"And the dead man?"

"Martin."

"Is there a priest in this village?"

"In the hut in the churchyard."

"Have you found places to stay?"

"Yes."

"Take Karl with you. Karl, have you brought up the horses?"

"In the pen over there, my lord."

"You must be tired," Josse said. "Is that wound all right?"

"It's nothing," Laeghaire said. He lifted his hand. The blood was clotting.

"You must be tired."

"No."

"You look tired."

"No."

"When will we leave?"

"Tomorrow after the Mass."

They left him, slowly. He watched them go. He rode down to the pen and dismounted. His leg felt all right. He unsaddled the brown stallion and caught the black horse. He saddled him and rode to the churchyard. In the hut a torch was burning. He dismounted and hung his shield on the pommel of the saddle. With the reins over his arm he stepped through the door. The priest was sitting on the edge of a bed that stood against the far wall. In the bed a man lay. The man breathed roughly. The priest was muttering.

Laeghaire waited. The priest lifted the man's hand and felt the beating there. He let the hand fall back. He drew up the blanket to the man's chin. He turned slightly, not rising, and saw Laeghaire in the doorway with the horse behind him. He did not look surprised.

"What do you want?"

"You sing two Masses tomorrow. I want a Requiem."

"You bury your dead quickly, Norman."

Laeghaire said nothing.

"A Requiem then. Dawn."

Laeghaire nodded. "The man will be in the church."

"Come with me."

Laeghaire stood aside to let him pass. He followed, leaving the black horse tethered. The priest said, "That man there, he knew you were coming. He warned us. He said he had seen strange horsemen in the fields. But they wouldn't believe him. They said he had seen couriers of the Count of the Vexin. They said you wouldn't come this far."

"Why tell me that?"

"I don't know. It seemed appropriate. I may be singing a Requiem for him too, soon."

"Man who is born of woman," Laeghaire said, "is of few days and full of trouble."

"He didn't deserve to die so young. He is eighteen years old."

"If he's a good man, he's better off dead."

The corpse was lying on the floor in the front of the church, by the altar. The hands were folded on his breast. The priest looked down at him and shrugged.

"Will you have him buried in that helmet?"

"Yes."

The priest left. Laeghaire looked carelessly at the altar. The priest came back with a shroud. "Lift him for me." Laeghaire hoisted the man—stiffening already, his stomach bloating under the tight belt. The priest wrapped the shroud around him, first over his shoulders, and then around his feet while Laeghaire held them off the ground. They lifted him together and carried him to the bench before the altar. The priest straightened the shroud and sprinkled a little holy water over it.

"Nor good nor bad, nor young nor old," Laeghaire said, looking at the corpse. "Maybe he deserved to die, but nobody gave him any warning."

"You speak a good Latin, Norman."

Laeghaire turned and looked at him. The priest cleared

his throat and looked up at the Crucifix.

"Dawn, then," the priest said.

"Dawn."

They went out together, not speaking, and the priest went into the hut again. Laeghaire mounted. He rode out into the village. He rode back and forth along the streets. The horse's hoofs made soft noises on the packed earth. He passed the huts, dark now. He rode along the earth-work. He kept the black horse to a slow pace. He could feel the long hips and shoulders reaching and the working of the horse's back under him.

The moon rose very late. It gave no light. He rode through the middle of the town. He thought of his child, sleeping up in Ghent, or perhaps Bruges if the Count had moved his seat for the winter. He remembered the crying of the babies. His son. Certainly. By now. Or a daughter.

He dozed, while the horse walked in the long slow walk that drew all his body into a single flowing, his long neck stretched out and his head low, in a perfect even rhythm like the running of the waves of the sea. There was no noise in the long night. Once a man thrust his head suddenly from a window, saw him, and drew back.

All through the summer, while Laeghaire's Flemings were fighting to take the last three villages on the plain, they heard about fighting near Le Mans. Laeghaire's scouts came in once and said that they had seen fresh signs of Mayenne's army no more than half a day's ride away, headed south. A courier from the Duke came some four or five days later and said that the Duke was fighting that day in a forest near Le Mans. The courier was going to the Vexin. He paused only long enough to get water and tell this to Laeghaire.

Laeghaire took the last village a little before Assumption and garrisoned it. He now held ten villages, towns and forts with an army of less than seven hundred men spread through them. He went to Rougemont with two hundred of his men and celebrated Assumption there, with a feast like a great lord's and little presents for his men from the booty they had taken. He wondered if he should send these two hundred out to strengthen the garrisons all around, or if he should keep them near him. He kept them in Rougemont, finally, but he sent his scouts out often to check all along the chain of garrisons. The people of the villages were mostly concerned with working their fields. The harvest would be fine, in spite of the fighting.

One day Thierry came back and said that the camp of the Count of the Vexin was just a half day's ride away. Laeghaire said, "How do you know it's his?"

"I saw the marks on their banner. He fights under the mark of St. Andrew. Everybody knows that."

"Are you tired?"

"No."

"Let's go."

Laeghaire wanted to get out. He was glad of this. He went down and saddled the black horse. They rode off west.

"Do you know where William is?" Laeghaire said.

"Only a rumor. One of my men heard from a Mainard peasant that they're off by the river."

"How far?"

"Two, three days."

"What about Mayenne? Was he with this Walter?"

"I didn't see any sign of it. This was a small camp—maybe six hundred men."

"That's enough to wipe out Rougemont and all the villages around."

It was late afternoon. After they left the plowed land, they rode over the wild hills. Once they saw cattle, with two herders. They saw no villages. Thierry led quickly, certain of the way. At sundown, Laeghaire said, "Do you want to keep going?"

"I can find it, my lord."

It was very dark in the hills. They rode single file. The moon came up. It was only a half moon, and it did nothing for light. It was cold. The wind rose and rustled in the trees and died. Toward midnight Thierry led Laeghaire out onto the edge of a plain. Thierry swore.

"They've moved."

Laeghaire rode out onto the plain. It was trampled all over and dead firebeds lay on it. "We have to find them," he said. "We can track them."

Thierry jogged around. He found their trail and called. Laeghaire rode over to him. He saw the wide track of many horses and nodded. He dismounted. The edges of the tracks were hard. They were all moving away.

"They've got foot soldiers," Thierry said. "They won't move fast."

They set off after the army. Thierry was quiet. The cold grew deeper. Laeghaire set a fast pace. Thierry dozed in the saddle.

Once when he had been in Germany but not in Thuringia, he had been caught in a snowstorm. He had found a windfall and sheltered under it with his horses. He did not remember being cold but he must have been. The snow fell so deep he could not move out for days. Hungry. He did not remember that either. But he had been. Almost hungry enough to eat one of his horses. He had had the brown stallion then, and that bay horse with the speckled face, the one that had been hamstrung his second fight in Thuringia. Snow like that, up to here. Over there a man can ride for days without seeing . . .

That whole winter he had seen only two men. One of them had tried to kill him. The one with the black beard and the . . . the Mainards had maybe a full day's head start on them. If I didn't have anybody with me it would be easier. The plain had turned into hills again. Turning back around toward Rougemont to come down from the north, maybe take one of the . . .

"What is he trying to do?"

"Break the chain. We're keeping him from the Vexin."

The dawn came up and they rode in the pink-tinted air and saw no one. The land was flattening out. Once they jumped a deer from a thicket. The deer bounded off. Her movements were fleet and angular. Laeghaire sat watching her while Thierry looked into the thicket.

"Late fawn," he said. "Come and look at it."

"No. Come along."

But he caught a glimpse of the fawn's back, immobilely arched, under the moving branches of the thicket.

There was no sign of anyone, and this made Thierry anxious; he said, "There ought to be more people around."

"Why? It's not farming country. There's a ridge. We can rest the horses a while and look."

But from the ridge they saw nothing, only an expanse of flat plain, with a creek and trees beside it, and the lift of the next hill.

The horses were tired. Laeghaire did not like this. It was well into the morning. He was hungry. He set the pace faster. Thierry was sleeping again. He swayed to the motion of his horse.

They came to the stream, and Laeghaire dismounted to take a drink. He woke Thierry and told him to look around. He lay flat on his belly and bent his face to the water. He drank in long gulps. The water was cold. He stood back and went to his horse, and Thierry dis-

mounted to drink. Laeghaire led the black horse down-
stream and let him drink. He could see the wide matted
trail of the army. He looked almost into the sun at the
next ridge and the trees there.

"Thierry."

"Aye."

"Where is your bow?"

"On my saddle. What's the matter?"

"Bring your horse over here and water him."

Thierry obeyed. He lifted his head. Laeghaire stood
between the horses. "Keep your head down."

"What's wrong?"

Thierry kept low. Laeghaire took the bow and
crouched, feeling the horse's legs. He strung the bow.
He took an arrow.

"Take my horse. Ride to Rougemont, tell them where
they are, and tell them to get ready to fight. Call everybody to Rougemont. Ride."

Thierry jumped into Laeghaire's saddle, wheeled, and
galloped off. Laeghaire lifted the bow, nocked the arrow,
and shot.

The lump in the fork of the tree there did not move.
Laeghaire mounted Thierry's horse. The stirrups were
too short. He wished suddenly he had told Thierry to
send somebody to William. He rode across the stream
and turned west. He rode quickly.

A horn bellowed almost ahead of him. Another sentry.
He looked back and saw that the man he had shot was
sliding from the fork of the tree. He spurred Thierry's
horse. He topped the rise and swore. He should have
known. The camp was in a crescent-shaped valley. Below him a hundred men stood and pointed at him. He
veered off. The horse stretched out wearily. Its head
bobbed. He looked back and saw fifteen or twenty
knights, sweeping up over the rise after him.

There was a copse of trees over to his right. He veered

toward it. He still held Thierry's bow. He took the quiver from the saddle and climbed a tree. He could see his pursuers through the thin autumn branches. They were almost to the wood. He shot and saw a horse fall. He shot again and missed. The others broke into the copse. He flung down the bow and jumped. He landed on a man riding below and dragged him down out of the saddle. He ducked under the horse's belly and hauled himself up into the saddle. He made the horse rear. The others were all around him. He drew his sword and struck at them. In the closeness of the trees they all piled into one another and struggled against one another. He knocked one man off his horse. The others jammed in against him, pinning his horse. He hauled up on the reins and the horse reared, striking out with its forefeet. He saw nothing but swords and axes around him. He dove from the saddle at a big bearded man. A horse screamed. He wrestled the man down and struggled with him on the ground, under the stamping thrashing legs of the horses. The man shrieked suddenly and started up. Laeghaire looked for his sword. He jumped up and was caught between two horses. A stirrup dug into his back. He caught the sword arm of the man he faced. The horses leaned in against him. He tried to slide from between them. The face of the knight before him seemed detached, disinterested. He tasted blood in his mouth. He caught the horse by the bridle and wrenched.

The horse stumbled away and the pressure was gone. He ducked under the head of the horse. For a moment he thought he was by them. He ran toward the open. His legs ran out from under him and he fell.

The knights and their horses were all around. He could hear them. There was dirt in his teeth. He pushed himself to his hands and knees. A hand caught him and dragged him up and slammed him against a tree. He flung out his hand and tangled his fingers in a beard and let his weight fall. The man landed on top of him. He rolled over. He lifted his hand and drove the heel of it against the man's bearded face.

Somebody dragged him off and held him by the arms. He sagged. He felt his head jerked roughly up. The beard had blood on it now. Somebody hit him, open-handed, across the face.

"That's no Norman. Take him to my lord."

"Who are you?"

He lifted his head. His neck ached and his shoulders and chest were on fire. He grinned and spat blood and dirt and wiped his mouth on his sleeve.

"Do you have a ransom?"

One of his teeth was loose. He pushed it with his tongue. It hurt. He looked at the tall thin man. The man had yellow hair.

"You aren't a Norman. Julien was right. Do you speak French?"

The blood and dirt had made mud in his mouth. He spat again. He decided to think in German. That way he wouldn't know French.

"Guard."

It didn't work.

The guard appeared. Laeghaire turned his eyes toward him. He was very tired. He wanted something to eat and a place to lie down. He wondered what the yellow-haired man would say if he told him that he would barter him all he knew for an offer of hot meat, wine and a piece of dirt long enough to lie on. The yellow-haired man wore a surcoat with patterns on it in red and gold woven in like lions, and a baldric . . . black with silver studs . . . all the long ride . . . gray wine from . . .

He woke up to the Count's insistent voice.

"You're tired. You're wounded. You're hungry."

Laeghaire yawned.

"Who are you?"

He was aching. He took the loose tooth between his thumb and forefinger and pulled. His head scorched. The tooth lay in his hand, bloody.

"Give me something to eat," he said.

"Who are you?"

"Jehan Stromrand. I serve the Duke of Normandy. I'm hungry."

"How do I know you're telling me the truth?"

"You guess." Laeghaire smiled at him. "You guess, my lord."

"Where are you from?"

"Burgundy."

"Too far to ransom. Guard. Come tie him up. Tie him to a tree somewhere."

"And give me something to eat?"

"Feed him."

The guard took him, watched while he ate, and tied his wrists together. He tied the other end of the rope to a tree by the horse lines and tied Laeghaire's feet. Laeghaire lay down under the tree and slept. . . .

He had never seen a wolf that big. The wolf snarled from the underbrush. It was a black night. He stopped his horse and dismounted so that he could see the wolf better. The horse ran off and he knew he should have stayed on it. The wolf's eyes blazed and glittered. The wolf sprang. He ran it through with his sword and the wolf fell and lay bleeding. He bent over it. The wolf sprang up and buried his fangs in Laeghaire's hand. Laeghaire saw the tips of the bottom teeth come out through the top of his hand. He clubbed at the wolf with his fist. The wolf lay still, with the sword through his body, and his eyes fixed on Laeghaire glittered. His teeth ground in Laeghaire's hand.

* * *

He woke up. He was cold to his bones. The fog had come in around him. He heard the horses moving near him. They had stayed here all day. Maybe they had scouts out.

He sat up and looked around. He was thirsty. He could hear the horses moving around. He studied the knot on the rope around his wrists. They had bound him with his hands in front of him. They had left his boots on and tied the rope over his ankles. They were fools. He bent over. This was bad. He had no purchase. He wiggled around until he sat with his back to the tree. He bent and caught the boot with both hands and pulled. The boot stuck on his heel. He twisted it and it came off. The rope went with the boot. He pulled off the rope and put his boot back on.

Somebody was coming. He tucked his legs under him. Two knights went by, looked incuriously at him, and went into the mass of horses. He heard them cursing the fog and the horses. He stood up and went around the tree to where that knot was. It was tight. He pried at it with his fingers. His fingertips were numb.

I have to get away from here.

He worried the rope back and forth. It slid suddenly. He threw his whole weight against it. It slid free with a slick whipping. He fell on his back. He turned and ran. In the fog he could not see. He stumbled over something and got up and ran again. A thin line caught him across the stomach and flung him back. The horse line. He ducked under it and sank into the restless surging line of horses.

His hands were still bound. He had forgotten about that. He coiled up the long trailing rope. He stood still. The horses crowded against him. He leaned against one of them. The horse nickered. He slid along it to its head

and felt from the halter to the end of the rope. The rope
was tied in a slipknot. He pulled it loose. He led the horse
straight out. He was afraid he might be headed into the
middle of the camp. His ears strained until they hurt.
The horse followed him willingly. He could not hear the
other horses any more. He walked on. He stepped out
and into nothing and fell. The horse splashed by him and
dragged him a little. He came up onto his feet, to his
knees in silent water. He went to the horse's head. The
horse lipped at his hand. He led the horse out of the water. He took a handful of mane. He swung himself up
onto the horse's back. He turned it. They walked. The
horse moved willingly. He felt the sharpness of its back-
bone and hitched himself up onto its withers. The horse
went on, quietly. He listened for men chasing him. He
heard nothing. He was cut off from sound and sight. The
fog wrapped around him. He let the horse move. Suddenly they were in the middle of trees. He slid off. He
tied the horse to a tree and lay down and shivering went
to sleep.

When he woke up it was bright starry night. He got
to his feet. The horse was dozing. His hands were numb.
He gnawed at the rope. It was tight and it had been
stretched; the knot was immovable. The slack trailed
away from his hands. He coiled it up and held it between
his wrists. He went to the horse and woke it and
mounted. He rode west. He was not really awake. He
kept seeing things. He saw men chasing him. He held
onto the horse's mane. He made sure he was riding west.
He saw a deer jump up from the trees and leap by him.
He would hold onto the antlers. Deer were faster than
horses. He saw the wolf again. Its great glittering eyes
shone down on him, steady and blind.

He fell off. The ground heaved under him. He lay

there and wished he would sleep. The sky swung majestically over him, back and forth. The stars made arcs. He saw the moon. He had not noticed it before. The old man and his bundle of sticks. He stood up. The horse stood watching him. He tied himself onto the horse with the slack of the rope on his hands. The horse walked on. He saw nothing more. The wolf had gone, afraid of the moon. The deer had gone too. In the afternoon all the deer in Ireland go up to the slopes of Knockmeal down and graze on the banshee's graze. The moon was the sun now and the horse was grazing. He lay along the horse's back. The horse grazed. Fierce is the wind tonight. His mother was dead. And the white hair of the sea lay way off on the coast of Ireland. Where Brian Borumha walked with his shield arm toward the sea.

He was dead-cold. He was hungry. He saw the stars out and wondered where he was. He had drifted. He remembered a little. He looked to see what way he was going. He was headed west. He put the horse into a canter across a deep meadow. The grass was almost to the horse's belly.

Lord, he thought. A pack horse. If I'd got a war-horse I'd be dead by now. The horse ran easily.

They had tied him that way for some reason. So that he could feed himself and drink and make water without anybody's having to come and help him. They didn't care much whether I got away or not. No ransom. Landless knight from—I think it was Burgundy. I took Jehan's name, that was it.

"Halt, in the name of the Duke of Normandy."

"I'm friendly."

"Stop, then. By the Virgin, it's Jehan's Irishman."

The sentry was in the tree near him. He looked up at the man's face.

"Is the Duke here?"

"Yes. Ride straight on. The camp is dead-ahead. Give

good warning or you might be killed."

He rode on. He paused every once in a while and listened. The horse was tugging toward the other horses. He rode a few feet and saw the camp. The fires were carefully banked. He would have taken the dim light for moonlight.

"I'm friendly," he said loudly. He rode into the camp. Sleepy men looked up at him from their blankets and someone said, "Who is it?"

"Hunh. It's the berserker." A knight stood up. "You want Jehan, Irish?"

"The Duke."

"He's sleeping."

"It's important."

"Hunh. It's your neck."

The knight pointed to a tent. Laeghaire rode to it. He dismounted and his legs caved in under him. The guards looked down at him. He stood up.

"Cut me loose."

"Sweet Jesus." The sentry took a dagger and cut the rope. He unwound it. It had made grooves on Laeghaire's wrists. The blood swam back tingling into his hands.

"I'm going in there," Laeghaire said, and pointed.

"He's asleep."

Laeghaire brushed by them. He stamped into the tent. There was a rustle of blankets and William said, "Stand where you are. Who is it?"

"Laeghaire from Tralee, my lord."

A silence.

"There's a torch on the floor there. Light it."

"I have no fire."

"Go out for it."

He took the torch and went outside to a banked fire and lit the torch. He went back. The Duke was sitting in his smallclothes on a war chest, a cloak wrapped around him. Laeghaire laughed.

"Do I amuse you? Where have you been?"

"I was a stranger in a strange land, and they took me in."

"Leave off that. Answer my question."

"Walter's army is a day's or two day's ride."

"I know."

"Shall I tell you about them?"

"I have scouts too. I know everything."

"Commendable."

"I am foul-tempered of waking." William pointed at Laeghaire's chest. "If I were not aware of your sometime virtues, I would be foul-tempered now, and you would spend the next few days under arrest. Are they coming after you?"

"I doubt it. They don't know who I am."

"Oho. Oho. A little arrogance here. A little sinful pride. No matter. I won't judge you, Irish." William grinned suddenly. "I have him now. He's in a certain amount of trouble. I sent you two hundred men at Rougemont. Fitz-Osbern is half a day's ride from here and north of him with five hundred. He's in a funnel if he comes any farther north, and if he doesn't I'll follow him until he's cornered and fight him there. Were they breaking camp?"

"I don't know. I didn't wait."

"I've got him now."

Laeghaire applauded him.

"You're filthy. Go clean yourself up. You look like a slave."

"Yes, my lord."

"Laeghaire."

"Yes, my lord?"

"The Count of Flanders has told me he wants you back in Flanders by Epiphany. Don't go. I want you here."

"I am his captain, my lord."

"Quit him. Send them back by themselves."

"He pays me."

"Go, then. If it suits you. Leave me."

Laeghaire slept in William's camp. He was awakened and put on a horse and moved once, and slept again. Jehan came and saw him and said that Laeghaire must have been sick, to sleep so long. When at last he woke up of his own accord, he went back to Rougemont. He rode fast. One day before he reached Rougemont, he cut the track of the enemy army, headed suddenly northwest. Laeghaire rested his horse and studied the track. Walter must have seen Fitz-Osbern. Laeghaire rode on wondering about it. Walter had more men than Fitz-Osbern.

When he got to Rougemont it was almost dark and he was tired. Thierry and Josse had called in all but five men from each of the villages, and Rougemont was full of knights. Thierry came to the room where Laeghaire slept and told him everything. Laeghaire heard him and sent him away and went to bed. He was hardly asleep when Thierry woke him up again, all excited. Laeghaire sat up. He knew what it was. He started to dress.

The room was full of people; Josse, two other knights, and three of Thierry's scouts. Laeghaire put on his mail shirt. Thierry was shouting. Josse told him to shut up and he did. Karl came silently over and gave Laeghaire his surcoat.

"Where is he?" Laeghaire said.

"Four, six leagues south," one of Thierry's scouts said. "And riding fast."

"South? Josse. Get everybody out and armed and ready. Does anybody know where Fitz-Osbern is?"

"He was half a day's ride north yesterday," Josse said quietly. "One of Thierry's men saw him. Headed due

:south, slowly."

"Send somebody to find him. Bring him back here."

Thierry signed to one of his men.

One of the other knights came forward. "My lord, I am Mishel of Sées. The lord Duke sent me here with—"

"I know. I saw him yesterday. How many besides these?"

"Five hundred."

"Get them armed. We'll ride out as soon as everybody is ready. Karl, go get the stallion ready. Bale," he said to the sentry, "when Fitz-Osbern gets here come out and meet me. I'll be southwest."

He buckled on his sword belt, picked up his shield, and went out. Down in the town square all the knights had gathered. They streamed in from their quarters into the square. The bell was ringing. He had not noticed it. The bell in the church tower. He mounted the brown stallion. Karl held his stirrup.

"My lord?"

"Stay here."

"Be . . . Good luck."

Laeghaire called for Lodovic. Lodovic blew his horn. They rode out the main gate and swung southwest.

Mishel rode up to him. "My lord, he shouldn't be there."

"Why not?"

"Fitz-Osbern's supposed to be keeping him in contact. I was there. When the Duke told him, 'Keep him in contact.'"

"Fitz-Osbern's been lost for a long time, then. He didn't have him in contact when I— He was headed northwest a couple of days ago; I crossed his track."

It was dark. The stars were hidden. They rode through trees.

"He's been moving fast."

"He rode north to see if Fitz-Osbern had any kind of

touch with him, found out he didn't, and swung down to catch us off guard. He doesn't know about you. He thinks I'm undermanned. He's trying to get to the Vexin. Bypass Rougemont to the north or south, as he can."

"Why didn't he just go through farther south?"

"Country's against him. He'd never get there before William did. William would catch him out in the middle of nowhere, too far from Mayenne and too far from his own country. Cut him to shreds."

"He's scared of my lord," Mishel said.

"Maybe."

"My lord hates his name."

Epiphany. He thought suddenly of his child. Born now. Certainly born. He wished it were nearer Epiphany. A son. Maybe. His son.

They reached the edge of the plain. Laeghaire called a halt. He sent Mishel up to the ridge just ahead. Mishel's horse cantered off. The hoofs beat on the ground. The sound died slowly. Mishel topped the ridge. He wheeled and waved his arms wildly. He rode back.

"Within bowshot," he said.

Laeghaire lifted his arm and drove it down. He spurred the stallion. The horse was rank from too long resting. He bolted. The others swept after him. They galloped up the ridge and over it. The army below them was all stretched out in files. Laeghaire pulled out his horn and blew a long and a short blast. He glanced over his shoulder. His men were packing in, close together. The army ahead was bunching, turning. They were spread out too far. Laeghaire and his men struck that army in the side. For a moment they had to slow, fighting. The swords rang together. The horses surged and bumped each other and reared. Laeghaire broke through the line of men. He galloped off. His men followed him. The stallion bucked and kicked. Laeghaire reined him down. His men raced after him, by him. The army of the Vexin turned and was following.

More than there was supposed to be. Only part he had seen, then. Other part going north or maybe left back here. That's how he lost Fitz-Osbern. A thousand, easily.

He wheeled and rode after his men. Thierry and Mishel saw him coming and turned back. The two bands of men, one chasing, one flying, raced over the plain. Josse swung in toward Laeghaire.

"He's lost his foot soldiers."

Laeghaire turned. The men chasing them were all horsemen. Way behind them the Vexin foot soldiers were grouped. Abruptly the horsemen chasing them turned and rode back.

"Hold up."

Lodovic blew his horn. The Flemings stopped and waited, all spread out. They weren't all Flemings now; there were two hundred Normans and those sixty Mainards.

"What a mess," Laeghaire said.

"What do we do?" Thierry said.

"Where's Josse?"

Josse rode up. He had a cut on his arm. He wrapped a scarf around it.

The Vexin army was headed off, straight toward Rougemont. Laeghaire turned to Josse.

"Take the Flemings and go back. The Mainards too. Get ready for a siege. Barricade the gates. Find out where Fitz-Osbern is. Mishel, you and your men come with me."

Josse sent ten of his band down to pick up the dead and wounded on the plain. Thierry clung by Laeghaire.

"Shall I go with you?"

"Stay with Josse."

Thierry rode over toward Josse. Josse and his men started off, riding fast.

"We don't stop," Laeghaire said to Mishel. "We hit

them. We don't stop."

Mishel nodded. Laeghaire turned and rode after the Vexin army. The Normans grouped up and followed him. They galloped past the men searching for wounded in the uneven litter of bodies there on the plain.

He chased and harried the Vexin army all the way back to Rougemont, leading off the mounted knights now and then. Whenever he took the knights after him the Vexinois foot would gather in a circle. It was light when they reached Rougemont. The Vexin army drew in among the few huts outside the wall and would not leave. Laeghaire saw his archers shooting at them from the walls of the town. He and the Normans pulled back.

"They'll hold them off for a while," he said.

He set up a round of men to watch the Vexin army and let the others sleep. He slept himself. He did not dream. He woke up at a shout from one of his guards, and the first thing he thought was that he was thankful for not dreaming.

The Vexin army had drawn up against the west wall of the town. On the wall men ran back and forth, waving things. Laeghaire mounted up.

"Mishel."

Mishel came.

"Ride around and come in from the north. Take—" He turned. He pointed to a tree standing in the middle of the mass of Normans. "Every man right of that tree come with me. The rest of you go with Mishel. Don't stop."

They rode down, split into two bands, and circled the walls. When they reached the west gate, the Vexin army had almost rammed down the gate. Laeghaire charged his men into the middle of the fighting. They used the wall to protect one flank. The defenders on the wall cheered wildly. They shot arrows and threw stones and wood down on the Vexin knights. Many of the townspeople were on the walls too, defending. The Vexin knights stayed, fighting steadily, holding their shields against the arrows and stones. The gate gave way with a great splintering of wood. The men inside the town had heaped carts and wood against it, so that the knights could not easily get through. At that moment Mishel attacked from the other side. The Vexin army turned and raced off. One part of the infantry was caught against the gate. Laeghaire and his men cut them down. When Laeghaire turned from the fighting he saw that Mishel had followed the rest of the Vexin army.

He reached for his horn. But Mishel turned just then and rode off. The Vexin knights chased the Normans. The Normans scattered. The foot soldiers stood motionless in their circle, watching Laeghaire. Finally the Vexin knights came back to them and the whole bunch of them moved steadily off, back to their huts.

Laeghaire and Mishel stayed by that gate until the people inside had barricaded it. It was dusk by then. The people inside the town handed down food to Laeghaire and the Normans, in bread baskets hung from ropes. They ate in their saddles.

That night the Vexin army left, going south. Laeghaire followed them and harried them. It was difficult in the darkness and he was tired and his men were tired. The Vexin army could pick their own way. Laeghaire got an arrow in the shoulder. He lost them just before dawn and rode back. When he got back he was sick again. He went to his room and slept for two days.

When he woke up, Karl told him that Fitz-Osbern was there and wanted to see him. Laeghaire sent him down for Fitz-Osbern and got out of bed.

Fitz-Osbern came in, put his helmet on the table, and sat down. "I hear that you were wounded."

"Not serious." Laeghaire scraped his hand over his jaw. His beard felt like a boar's pelt. He stropped his dagger. Karl came in with water in a dish.

"Why didn't you hold them until I got here?" Fitz-Osbern said.

Laeghaire turned on his heel. "Hold them? With six hundred men? He outnumbered me by a full set of infantry. Nearly two to one. Why didn't you keep contact with him? You lost him, Fitz-Osbern. Not I."

"My orders were to keep him from coming north."

"Your orders. He came north. You lost him. He knew where you were all the time and you didn't know where he was. He almost bypassed us and went on and got away."

"So much the better. Then we would have had only Mayenne to fight. We could have cut them down at our leisure."

"Hunh." Laeghaire turned and shaved half his face.

"It probably would have been better so."

"You tell that to the Duke."

"I had my orders directly from him."

"Did they include leaving one thousand men free to turn and attack us when we move?"

"I will grant you, sir, that I lost contact. I should have known his position exactly. That was my error. I still believe you could have held him here until I arrived. Together we would have outnumbered him sufficiently."

"How?"

"Fought him, instead of running and chasing him as if you were one to his ten. As Sir Mishel has told me you did."

"I would have liked to see you try it, outnumbered."

"You overjudged them."

Laeghaire finished shaving. He wiped his face on his

sleeve. He turned and looked at Fitz-Osbern, sprawled easily in the chair.

"I meant no offense," Fitz-Osbern said. "I was merely pointing out that we have both made errors."

"My lord." Laeghaire put his hands on the table and leaned on them. He stared at Fitz-Osbern. "The next time you err, err against me, and not what we're fighting. The next time you make an offense, make it against what we're fighting, and not me."

Fitz-Osbern stood up. He looked at Karl. "Boy, you are witness. I'll have you to accounts for that remark, mercenary." He turned and went out the door. Laeghaire jumped around the table and opened the door and stuck his head out.

"I'll say it again in front of twenty witnesses," he shouted after Fitz-Osbern. "I'll write it down and sign it."

Karl laughed.

"How did you mean that?" Laeghaire said.

"Don't be angry, my lord. You looked so funny."

"You keep your mouth shut. Get me something to eat."

Karl left.

Laeghaire sat down. He rested his chin on his fists. He thought about the fighting. He thought that maybe Fitz-Osbern had been right. Not right. He was not right. Maybe he was less wrong than Laeghaire had thought at first.

He wanted to go. He wished he could ride back to Flanders. He felt the walls pushing against him. He wondered what his men were saying.

Just after the first snowfall, the news came north that William and the Normans were sieging Le Mans. They had caught Walter of the Vexin there, but the lord of

Mayenne had apparently slipped out. William sent word that Laeghaire and his men were to stay, holding the line between Maine and the way to the Vexin, but he called Fitz-Osbern up to Le Mans. Laeghaire and his men fretted. It seemed that Le Mans, all gold and women and good one-sided fighting, was to go to the Normans.

Laeghaire went up one night to the bell tower in the church. Josse was there, standing early watch, with a young Norman from near Caen. They were playing the fingers game when Laeghaire came in. They saw him and stood up quickly. The Norman locked his hands behind his back.

"Good evening, my lord," he said.

"It's hard to keep watch against nothing."

"Aye," the Norman said.

"My lord," Josse said, "is there anything new from Le Mans?"

"Nothing new." Laeghaire leaned on the windowsill. "This quiet is enough to make me go crazy."

"That's sure. Rolf, go fetch me some water, can you?"

Rolf slid off through the door.

Laeghaire turned. He slacked his weight against the windowsill. "You are always kind, Josse."

"My lord?"

"I used to know every man I rode with, everything they thought and wanted. And now I don't know half the faces. Much less the names."

"No one expects it of you, my lord. You have captains for that."

"I am growing old and feeble-minded and . . . quite possibly crazy."

"My lord, you're joking with me."

Laeghaire turned his eyes toward the moon.

"My lord," Josse said, "if anyone is fit to . . . say anything about you—"

"You were about to say 'judge.' "

"Well, then, judge you, it is the men you lead. And not since that fool Gabriel has any man in this whole army said one word except in your greatest praise. I—my lord, we could not follow anyone but you."

"You'll have me weeping, Josse."

Josse put his hand on Laeghaire's shoulder. "When we fight again, you'll feel better."

Laeghaire shrugged.

"Who is somebody named Hadrad?"

"Who?"

"The King of one of those Norse places."

"Harald Hardraada."

"Yes."

"Why?"

Josse's face was sly. "Oh, someone mentioned him last night, and the men had an argument, who was better, you or he."

"Hardraada is a sea pirate. He gives orders. I am a land pirate. I take orders."

"Some of the men maintained you were better."

"Maybe I am."

"I've never seen anyone fight the way you do. You fight as if you had no mind."

Laeghaire threw back his head and laughed. "What a compliment, Josse. Tell me, had you ever heard of me before you met me?"

"No, my lord. But I had never heard of Hardraada before this afternoon."

Rolf came in with a jug of wine. "I got it from Franzes. He was just going by. My lord, there's a messenger come from Le Mans, I think."

"Good." Laeghaire went by him. He saw Rolf's eyes follow him. He went down the ladder and came out of the bell tower into the churchyard. He could hear the noises of the men gathered by the messenger. He started toward them. They were gathered by the gate of the

house he lived in. Suddenly there rose a ragged cheer.
Laeghaire broke into a run. He shoved into the crowd
and caught the bridle of the messenger's horse.

"What's this?" The noise was all around him. He
wheeled and raked them with his stare and they stilled.
He turned back to the messenger.

"Laeghaire of the Long Road?" the man said.

"Yes."

"My lord, I came to tell you that Walter of the Vexin
was taken prisoner. Le Mans has fallen. Also, that the
lord of Mayenne with some seven hundred men is coming north. I passed him at noon. He's headed for the île."

"Are you sure?"

"My lord, I'm headed there myself." The messenger
smiled. Laeghaire waved to the nearest man to take the
horse. The messenger dismounted. He said, "My name is
Robert of Montgomery. The Duke's sent me to Paris."

"I'll give you fresh horses."

Laeghaire started into the house. Robert of Montgomery followed him.

"My lord, I won't need them. I sent my escort on to
take the messages. And if they need someone of great
name, one of the d'Avranches is with them."

"Did the Duke send me any orders?"

"He said that I was to tell you that Mayenne was coming."

"Nothing more?"

"No."

"And he gave you to think nothing?"

"No. Will you fight him?"

"My lord, I'll fight him all the way to hell. Thierry."

Karl, sleepy, suddenly appeared. He turned and ran
off, shouting for Thierry. Laeghaire opened the door
into his room. Montgomery went in and sat down.

"You've ridden all day, my lord," Laeghaire said.
"Sleep a little."

"When will you ride out?"

Laeghaire put on his mail. "I'll ride now. To look. I'll send my orders. Why were you going to Paris?"

"To reach the King before Mayenne does."

"The King?"

"The Count of Flanders is in Paris now."

"The—"

"He's your master, isn't he?"

"He pays my wages. If he intends to . . . pull Mayenne out of his—"

"The word was that he had recalled you for Epiphany."

"He knows I'm caught here and not likely to do anything but sit. And now . . . sleep, my lord. I'll send a messenger."

Laeghaire took his gloves from the table. He thrust them into his belt and went out. In the hall he met Karl and told him to saddle both horses. He went out into the street and called up as many of his men as he could find in a moment, and told them all that Mayenne was somewhere near and that he was going to find him. Thierry arrived all at once, lacing up his shirt, his reins looped over his arm and the horse protesting every step. Laeghaire sent all the men to wake up the others and tell them to be ready to ride at any moment. Karl trotted out with the horses.

"Can you ride the black?" Laeghaire said. "Here." He tossed Karl into the saddle. The black horse leaped once and stood shivering. Thierry mounted. Laeghaire put a hand on the black's neck. "He's never carried anyone but me," he said. "I broke him." He turned and mounted the brown stallion. They rode down the street and out the gate. The whole town roiled and shouted behind them.

"If he's headed for Paris and the messenger passed him from Le Mans," Thierry said, "there's only one way he could have come. You know how the land slopes down from the edge of that forest down there?"

Laeghaire nodded. "And if he's seen the messenger and knows how strong we are, he'll have turned off."

"East," Thierry said.

Laeghaire grinned. "West. I'll lay odds on it. While we're watching all the possible approaches on the east he'll ride west, turn north, and cut past us north of Rougemont. Avoid the Vexin and reach Paris from the south."

"Where will he be?"

"Right on the track Vexin took when he was up here that time."

They trotted under the full moon. Like wild deer or outlaws they dodged into the trees that ran unevenly over the plain. Laeghaire wished he had brought his bow. He asked Thierry for his.

"I had my scouts out all to the south," Thierry said. "I wonder why they haven't reported him."

"They've grown careless from no dangers."

The wind rose and fell. Karl had some difficulty with the black horse. The horse tried to bolt and came up close to Laeghaire. Laeghaire caught the rein and snatched him. The horse stopped dead. Laeghaire patted him quickly on the neck and jogged off again. The horse followed, sulking.

They passed through a meadow, up a slight slope, and into a fringe of trees. In the trees, like deer or outlaws, they froze. Far, far down the plain the army of Mayenne lay under the pale moon. Everything was silver-blue from the moon, and the fires looked bright and smaller than usual.

"Karl. Go back. Wake up the lord of Montgomery. Bring him with every man out here. Tell him to move fast. Thierry, come with me."

Karl wheeled and rode off. The air swallowed the noise. Laeghaire and Thierry rode into the thickest part of the trees. The snow lay light and dimly tracked all around them.

"They must have sentries. They must have seen us."

"Perhaps."

Laeghaire tethered the stallion and climbed a tree. He saw Thierry, on the ground, watching him with wide eyes. Laeghaire settled himself comfortably into a fork in the tree. He looked once down at the camp. The horses beyond it moved slowly, grazing, drowsing. Thierry had sat down at the foot of the tree.

They had not seen them. There was no movement down there, but for the horses. He counted them roughly, thinking that perhaps they had figured this all out and left this camp and those horses as a trap, and he counted at least five hundred. He leaned his head against the tree trunk and smiled and dozed. . . .

He woke suddenly, flinging out his arms, and his hands struck against the rough bark. He twisted his fingers around the branch. The bark came loose and bits of it clung to his palms. The wolf.

"They are coming, my lord."

He slid down from the tree. He mounted the brown stallion and waited. All through the trees they came, and he could see the others, strung out behind them. He shook his head to forget the wolf. His hair fell over his eyes. He tossed it back and rode past the first men. He rode along the line, slowly, telling them to be still and wait, and telling them where the army of Mayenne was. From these trees they could not see them, for the little rise.

At the end of the long string of men he found Montgomery, on a borrowed horse. Laeghaire rode up a little, over the rise, and saw the camp below from the other side, differently. He saw a sentry, too, and the sentry saw him.

The sentry wheeled. His tiny arms jerked. Laeghaire

took his horn and blew a charge.

They burst out of the trees. Some of the horses staggered in the brush. Laeghaire saw Karl, a full stride ahead, shouting. Below them the camp jumped awake. They crawled out of blankets and darted around to get swords and horses. The horses began to mill.

Laeghaire's men struck the camp with all those men still dashing around and looking for things. They crashed through the empty blankets and scattered them underhoof and galloped on. The enemy, on foot, rallied to stop them, to hold them. Some of them were swept up and carried along on the ends of swords and lances. Some of them stopped the charging knights and fought to a standstill with them, fought reaching up and died falling down. The rest turned and ran.

"Give quarter," Laeghaire shouted against a noise like twenty thousand men all shouting. "Give quarter—I want prisoners."

He had no idea if they heard him or not. They were chasing men all over the camp and through the neighing colliding mass of free horses. He battered through them, shoving them off. He beat his way straight into the last clump of fighting Mainards. They leaped at him like wolves and he pounded them down. The horse reared and lashed out with his hind legs.

The Normans were pressing in against the fighting Mainards. Laeghaire flogged them with his sword.

"Quarter!" one man cried.

"No quarter!" another shouted.

"Catch me that man." Laeghaire pointed to the man who had cried "No quarter." His own men were all around him. The man started, thinking of fleeing, and stood, with his head up. The others around him ceased fighting and threw down their weapons. Laeghaire's Normans surrounded the man. Laeghaire turned in his saddle. All around the fighting was over. Josse trotted up, hitching his shield around.

Karl was right beside Laeghaire. Laeghaire dismounted and gave him the rein. His men parted to let him through to the surrounded man. Everybody grew quiet. Laeghaire said, "My lord of Mayenne?"

The man smiled only.

"Is there anyone here who knows Mayenne?"

Montgomery, with a slash on his cheek, rode his horse into the swarming knights. Laeghaire said to the man, "Take off your helmet."

"I am Geoffrey de Mayenne." He looked up at Montgomery. "Who is commander here?"

Laeghaire turned and told Josse to herd all the captives together and start them back to Rougemont. He heard Montgomery say, "He is." Laeghaire turned back toward Mayenne.

Mayenne took off his helmet. His heavy-lidded eyes turned on Laeghaire. "Laeghaire of the Long Road. I'll surrender to you, Montgomery. There's no merit in giving one's sword to a noted butcher."

Laeghaire grinned. "Truss him up. I think you'll find it makes no difference one way or another. Karl?"

Montgomery and Laeghaire took Mayenne to Le Mans. They went with a little escort. By the time they reached the city, William was holding court within its walls. They came into Le Mans late at night, and slept before they saw William.

That next day William took the homage of Geoffrey of Mayene, and with his hands between William's hands, Mayenne swore himself into vassalage. He commended all his men with him and the sour expression on his face made William smile. He sent him and Walter of the Vexin off to their quarters and had them guarded. He called for wine and beer, and when the captive steward said there was no beer, he told him to have some brought from Germany, or at least from Flanders.

"The finest beer is German beer," he said. "Sir Laeghaire, isn't that so?"

"German beer is better than any wine, my lord."

William laughed. He was in a good humor. Laeghaire had never seen him so loose with his laughing. William's head swung toward him. In his eyes was a peculiar glitter. Laeghaire stared into his eyes. They were like the eyes of the wolf in the dream. He cursed the dream. The eyes of drunken men glittered like that. Let this wolf bite him.

He sat on a low stool, with one leg stretched forward and one drawn up, so that he could rest his arm on the knee. He took the cup of wine and drank it off and caught the page before he could leave and poured another.

The other knights talked boldly. William talked with some of them. He called Laeghaire once and Laeghaire went over to him.

"I don't think that your lord meant you to do me that service," William said.

"He sent me no order."

"He outtricked himself."

"My lord." Laeghaire could not think of anything to say. He looked straight into William's eyes. William grinned, and Laeghaire felt himself grinning.

"You shaggy-headed Irish."

"I'll crop clean as a monk to please you, my lord."

"My lord." Fitz-Osbern stood up. The other men turned to watch him. Fitz-Osbern was a man of stature in Normandy. "I want no interruption in your triumph, my good lord, but this is an affair of my honor."

Laeghaire stood up and went off a little to the side. He stood with one leg relaxed. He crossed his arms.

"Then tell it," William said.

"It concerns the Irish knight," Fitz-Osbern said.

"My lord," Laeghaire said. "The Steward and I had some words. It seems he thought I should carve even more of his meat for him."

There was laughter. William leaned forward. "When was this?"

"When we turned Walter back."

Fitz-Osbern said, "This Irish knight, this wanderer, this sometime brigand to be sure, this landless fighting man for hire, this—bought man of the Count of Flanders, dared to tell me that I had mislaid my orders. Like a quick-tempered baseborn slave he took offense at the slightest comment I made, when I only meant to show him his error, and he turned it against me like an insult, and then offered comments of his own, none of which were complimentary or recognized my rank—"

"I am a free man and a knight, and whatever high-flown title you may have smiled and fawned your way into, my good lord meat-carver, gives you no right to plaster me with—"

Fitz-Osbern drew off his glove and threw it down between them. Laeghaire started for it.

William said, "Irish, leave it where it lies."

"My lord," Fitz-Osbern said.

"Lord Steward," Laeghaire said, "if you would care to come outside—"

Fitz-Osbern wheeled toward William. "Am I to take these insults and baiting from a mad, unnerved, bastard of a bastard—"

"You put me in good company," Laeghaire said, "you lawfully begotten son of a fishwife and an errant demon out of hell that lost his way in a dark night."

William came down between them. He stopped by Fitz-Osbern and said, "He's got your measure for quick-tongued talking, sir. Leave him alone."

"As you wish, my lord," Fitz-Osbern said. He turned

and marched out of the hall.

William turned toward Laeghaire. "Your pride itches. By God's Splendor, if you weren't a berserker knight, I'd let you fight him."

"But I'll kill him, and if I were no berserker knight, I'd have no pride."

William laughed. He started back to his chair. "Then leave off attacking sure targets. If he killed you, you'd have no pride, but I doubt if I'd want that, and you'll talk prettily to him. Not quite so prettily as you have today, and remember, he is older than you and he is after all the Lord Steward of Normandy."

William went back and sat down. Laeghaire took more wine. He drank it all down in one gulp. He was getting drunk. He felt good for it. He would have shown Fitz-Osbern that they bred killers in Ireland.

From then until Epiphany, William sent Laeghaire on several missions, even using him before Fitz-Osbern as a messenger. Once he sent him to take the homage of a certain town and gave him an escort like a lord's. The town was called Remy, and lay in the south. Laeghaire rode there in a day and was back again the next. It was simple. He took the homage of the elders of the town in the common pasturage and afterward rode through the town with his escort to show that William of Normandy had taken the town for his son. On the way through the town, the people were gathered to watch. A woman stood by a trough for watering cattle, near the far gate. She had a child by her. The child started out toward the lines of knights, and the woman caught it and pulled it back. She saw that Laeghaire was watching her and the child, and she put her hand across the child's eyes.

"Devil," she said. "You Irish Devil."

When he was back at Le Mans he thought of it. The woman had known who he was. He had never been to Remy before. She had known who he was.

"I have given an order," William said, "to send the Flemings back. I wish you to remain here. Until Easter."

"My lord, my son will be full-grown before I see him."

"You are dead-certain it was a boy she bore, aren't you?"

Laeghaire grinned. "Or if it was a girl, my lord, I'll want a chance to try again."

William frowned. "You have the boldest tongue. Go back, if you wish. And do me one favor. I want Walter of the Vexin and his wife transported to Falaise, in Normandy. You will command the guard that takes them there. That way I can keep Montgomery here."

"As you wish, my lord."

"When you get back to Flanders, Irish, the Count will have no more use for you."

That Laeghaire had not thought of.

"He sent me a letter and said that he will offer you a place in his court. It suits him to have a gentleman of reputation with him. Would you accept that?"

"Yes, my lord."

"And not go . . . wandering?"

"It's no life for a child and a woman, my lord."

"How right you are. And if I were to tell you that I might have need of you at some later occasion, and that I wished you to swear to me to come when I want you, what would you say?"

"You do me honor."

"The question, Irish."

"I dislike being bound, my lord."

"God's Splendor, man, you're bound. You have a wife and a child. What further binding does any man need? You're tied into life because you must keep them alive, and tied in one place to protect them, and— Answer the question."

"Yes, my lord."

"Good. You have my leave to go."

Laeghaire stood.

"You and your men shall prepare to leave before the end of this week. Walter and his wife will go with you. Give them only into the hands of the chatelain, Hubert. He is an old man, but he is absolutely trustworthy." William picked up a warrant and folded it. He put a tray of wax over the candle flame. "He served my mother's husband. Who was, as you so gently pointed out a while ago, not my father."

"I have never noticed you lamenting it, my lord."

"No." William spilled a bit of wax on the warrant and sealed it with his signet ring. He put the ring back onto his little finger. "Do you fight very much in Ireland, Laeghaire?"

"Like dogs, my lord. There's nothing we like better."

"Take this, give it to Hubert. And to none but him."

"By your leave, my lord."

He went to the door. William said, "Irish."

Laeghaire turned back toward him.

"You have the gift of second sight," William said. "My father-in-law said in the letter that your wife bore the child safely. And it is a boy."

The old chatelain at Falaise took the prisoners and the warrant, without a comment. He sent for his warders. He made out a letter saying that he had the persons of Walter of the Vexin and his lady Biota of the knight Laeghaire of the Long Road, and he gave it to Laeghaire.

The escort which William had given Laeghaire was made up of Normans, and they dispersed when the mission was finished. Laeghaire spent the night in the castle of Falaise. He meant to go on to Ghent the next morning. It seemed impossible to him that he was almost there, and yet he was sure of it. He felt fresh and clean. He thought of his son.

In the morning, however, there was a messenger, a page, from the court of the Duchess at Falaise, saying that the Duchess wished the knight Laeghaire to attend her at her house. The page waited to take him there. Laeghaire could not decline to go. He went with the page. The Duchess had a house in the center of the town. They rode through the outlying part of the town. The smell of tanners' vats clung to everything. It was still early but the people were out curing hides on the frames by their huts.

"The lord Duke was born in Falaise," the page said.

"Why did you say that?"

"You looked surprised, my lord."

His mother had been a peasant. He remembered now. A tanner's daughter. Some people said her father had been a sexton's assistant. The smell of the tanners' curing waters filled his nose. A Duke now and a great lord, the greatest lord in . . .

The page took him in to the Duchess's chamber. The Duchess was with her ladies, doing whatever it was that ladies did alone. When the page announced Laeghaire, she stood and came a step forward. He walked toward her. The ladies of her chamber were still. Their eyes and their arched Norman noses turned toward him. He saw the fine cloth of their gowns, all draped and shadowed. He knelt before the Duchess. She was so small that even when he was kneeling he hardly had to look up to see her eyes.

"Sir Laeghaire," she said, "it was good of you to come."

"At your command, my lady."

"Please rise. I am not your lady, sir. You had no need to come." She sat down. "It was good of you to come. I wished to hear some news of my lord."

"My lady."

"Is he well?"

"Very well."

"And happy?"

She held off his answer with her tiny hand. "Yves, fetch a stool for Sir Laeghaire."

The page brought a stool. It was a lady's stool, very small. Laeghaire looked down at it.

"I would rather stand, my lady."

"My dear sir, I would rather you be uncomfortable than I." She laughed. "You hurt my neck, standing. Please, sit."

Laeghaire sat.

"You are very paltry with your answers, sir. Is it a

habit among your people? And I know that you speak Flemish. You were in my guard once, at Bruges; I remember seeing you. Please, sir; be free with me."

"As you wish, my lady."

"And my lord. He is happy?"

"As happy as he could be, my lady."

She wrinkled her nose and laughed. "Explain yourself, sir."

"He is never happy."

"How well you know my lord. Is he an easy man to follow?"

"For some, my lady."

"For you, not?"

"I would take Hell for him, if he wanted it."

"By 'some,' then, you mean, all good men."

"No. No. Only fools and madmen, my lady."

"Why, that's a pretty passage from your tongue. I hear that you killed poor Sir Néel in Rouen when you were there."

"Yes."

"Why?"

"I did not like him, my lady."

"Oh. That's awful."

The other ladies murmured like wild bees. Laeghaire glanced at them. One of them put her hand quickly over her eyes, but her mouth smiled at him.

"You've beguiled my ladies, sir." The Duchess frowned at them. "They are always fascinated by bloody, devilish men. I trust my lord reproved you for killing poor Sir Néel."

"Not overmuch. He had some need of me, and no need of Sir Néel, who was beyond need."

"What a pretty tongue you have, for a murderous man. Will you stay to have some dinner with me?"

"I am going to Ghent, my lady."

"Only stay a while. I weary of these chickens."

"I have—" He looked at the ladies. "Soon after I left to go to Maine, I had a son born, and I have not yet even seen him once, my lady."

The smiling mouths pouted.

"By all means, Sir Laeghaire. It was good of you to come. I had no idea I was keeping you from anything quite so urgent." She rose; he rose; the ladies swept up to their feet, all their skirts and sleeves rustling. "Although it seems so odd that such a bloody man as you should have a home and family. You have my leave."

"My lady."

He went toward the door. He heard the women whispering behind him. When he came out into the courtyard and mounted the black horse, he saw a glimpse of a white face and a full sleeve at the window, and he heard them giggle, shrinking back.

It was a bad ride north. It rained a lot. He rode during the day and slept at night, at first, but the closer he came to Ghent the more he wanted to be there, and he rode almost all the time. He let the horses graze and sleep from dawn until the sun was past noon, every day, but he slept very little himself. He thought, I miss Hilde. He had not thought of her all the time he had been away. Now he missed her. I'll tell her that. She'll be happy.

He rode in the dripping afternoon, with the rain beating on his shoulders and head and running over the black horse's neck and mane, and the brown stallion crowding after him under the pack. He was going back to where his son was and his woman. In the deep dry heat of the kitchens full of the smells of food and cooking and Lisabet fat from tasting, and the ovens singing with the heat and the kegs of beer and wine standing double and triple height against the far wall, and the flour and salt in sacks, where Hilde was with the child she had borne, all alone when he was far off and maybe only a dream to her, Hilde dragged out of her home and sold to him. The rain made all things neither far nor near, just wet. He rode on, very happy, and sang an Irish song to himself, a song he would teach his son.

He would call him Murrough, after his brother, and after the prince the pin-blessed warrior had loved enough to throw away his life and Aoife for. He would teach him Gaelic and listen to Hilde sing him German songs and watch her suckle him. And watch the milk he had put into her breasts by his loving her make his son grow.

Ghent was quiet in the rain. He rode at a gallop through the town to the gates of the castle. The gate was shut.

"Who goes?"

"Laeghaire of the Long Road."

The guard shouted his name back into the castle. The gate inched up. He rode through it into the courtyard. He drew the men there toward him from all directions, all running toward him. They cheered him. He dismounted and someone snatched his reins and he crowded by them, and their cheers became laughing.

He went into the corridor and it became familiar to him, and a warm shock came over him, to be back here again. He walked down to the kitchens. He heard Lisabet's heavy voice even before he opened the door. She was screaming about something. He opened the door and saw her beating a scullion over the head with her spoon, down by the great ovens. For a moment he could not find Hilde.

She was chopping vegetables. Her hands moved deftly with the big knife. Her feet were bare and wide-spread on the floor. Around her waist she had a bright red scarf.

He went into the kitchen, ducking the eave over the steps, and passed Lisabet. "Shut up," he said to her. She stopped and turned to gape at him. He went on down to Hilde. The kitchen people grew quiet and stared. He put his arm around Hilde's waist and kissed her ear. She turned, gasping, with the knife in her hand, and he caught her waist.

"You'll have my head yet," he said, laughing.

"Laeghaire. Laeghaire."

The tears welled from her eyes. Her eyes were blacker than he remembered. She threw her arms around him and kissed him. Her mouth moved from his mouth to his cheek and eyes and nose. He laughed. She backed off just far enough to get a running start and flung herself into his arms again.

"I was afraid you'd died and they didn't want to tell me. I thought you wouldn't come back ever. Oh, dear God, oh dear sweet God, my own dear Laeghaire—"

He kissed her mouth. He wanted her.

"No. No. Wait. You have to see the baby."

She backed out of his arms, teasing him. "Wait 'til you see him. He's perfect. Where is he? Lisabet—"

"He's here, lady." One of the scullions came forward. He held the baby. Hilde went to take it, but Laeghaire was there before she was, and he took the baby and held it in his arms. The baby wailed and fought to get away.

The kitchen people began to laugh. Laeghaire felt himself blush. He looked around at them. The baby screamed and beat at him with its fists. Its face twisted with anger and got bright red. Laeghaire took it to a stool. He sat down and held it on his knee. He held its face to look at him. Its eyes were blue, and its hair was black. It looked like him.

"Don't yell like that," he said. He said it in Gaelic. "You make them laugh at me. I'm your father. Do you want to make your father a laughingstock?"

The child stopped yelling. It took hold of Laeghaire's

hand, leaned out, and caught for his surcoat. Laeghaire drew him close. The child stared up at him. He talked to it in Gaelic. He had not spoken Gaelic for nearly six years. He had saved it to be spoken to his son. He watched the baby's eyes and saw its mouth try to say words.

"You're happy," Hilde said.

"Yes." He looked at her. "Yes."

"What shall we call him?"

"Murrough. For my brother."

"I thought maybe we could call him Klaus."

"Let's go someplace else."

She stood up. She took the child from him. "All right." She smiled at him.

Laeghaire started off. Hilde turned suddenly. "May I go, Lisabet?"

Her voice rang clear in the kitchens. Lisabet took a step forward.

"Yes." And she bowed, awkwardly. "My lord."

"I missed you while you were gone."

"Ummmmmmm?"

"Did you have any other women?"

"Every woman between here and the city of Le Mans."

She bent her head and bit him where his throat joined his shoulder. He jerked her away.

"You're not bleeding. I meant to make you bleed." She put her hand where she had bitten him. "I bled."

"You're meant for it."

"Were you hurt?"

"Once or twice. Once a horse almost crushed me."

He had to tell her about it. He made love to her again after that.

"Let's call him Klaus."

He was half asleep. "Go feed him. He must be hungry."

She climbed over him and went and got the baby. She brought him back and fed him. Laeghaire yawned.

"Why Klaus?"

"I've always liked that name."

"I want to call him Murrough."

"If you wish, my lord."

"I wish."

They were building a ceiling over the old underground stable, a roof to the vault that would be a floor for the stable on top. The old stable would be a storage room. The Count said that the old vault had been too small. Hilde said that a giant and a giantess were buried in the earth of the vault floor, and that they had cursed the place. She said that Lisabet had said that the horses' hoofs were falling off because of it. Laeghaire went down to the stable and watched the men building.

All that spring he thought he would go crazy from boredom. There was nothing for him to do. The Count called him in once, to pay him for the work done in Maine, but at the same meeting the Count told him that he ought not to have gone and captured Mayenne. Laeghaire said that he could hardly have known that. The Count insisted that he did know it, and that he had done it because he loved William of Normandy, that everybody loved William of Normandy, and an ordinary Christian could not find men to do his work for him any more without their falling into the hands of William of Normandy. He sent Laeghaire once to Paris, just after Easter, with a special message all sealed up and wrapped in a wax-coated cloth.

Laeghaire spent much time with Murrough. The child

had learned that Laeghaire was his father. He was just beginning to talk. He would say things in German and in Flemish and in Gaelic, all at once. He liked to be with Laeghaire. Laeghaire taught him games, like the games he had played when he was little. When he was gone, he made Karl watch the baby.

Hilde had gone out of the kitchens. The Countess thought that a woman with a young child should not work so hard. Besides, she found Hilde interesting. She gave her presents and taught her to speak the language of the court. Hilde talked about the other ladies of the Countess's court with some pity because they had no men. She was pregnant again by the beginning of the summer. She had changed. He knew it and he learned it every time he saw her, every time he was with her. She spoke differently. She wore her clothes differently. Often he found her making new clothes for herself. She made him things, surcoats and tunics. Karl would sit and play with the child while Laeghaire was off on some minor errand of the Count's, and when Laeghaire came back, Karl would tell him something of the child and something more of Hilde, and when Karl spoke of Hilde it was with a strange tone in his voice.

"Everybody in the guard thinks of her," Karl said once. He leaned against the shield he was cleaning. Murrough played on the floor a few feet away. "As if she were a saint. But she hardly even knows they exist. Isn't that strange?"

"I think you're a puppy baying at the moon for love."

"Oh, my lord, I can't love your wife."

"Karl."

"My lord?"

"She is not my wife."

It was a small distinction. Maybe it was no distinction at all. He stayed in Ghent because of her and Murrough. She had given him Murrough and she would give him another child in the winter. He remembered what William had said, that he was bound. But that had been different when William had told him. He had been a fighting man, a knight, and an honored and respected captain, and here he was a hanger-on. Néel's words. Dead men's ghosts behind him.

In the early summer Lanfranc, the Prior of Bec, came to Ghent. He came to parley with the Count before he, Lanfranc, left for Rome. Guillaume told Laeghaire that William wanted to return to the Count's good graces. Laeghaire could hardly see that William had left them.

He met Lanfranc in the little side chapel when he went to confess before the Countess's holy day. Lanfranc was sitting before the altar, with his hands clasped, but he was not praying. Laeghaire could see him, when he went down to the altar to pray, and he saw from the corner of his eyes that Lanfranc had stood and was coming toward him. He shut his eyes. The wood of the altar floor creaked, and Lanfranc, kneeling by him, said, "My lord said that I was to give you his deepest regards."

"Give your lord my answering deepest regards, priest."

Lanfranc's long narrow face turned. Lanfranc smiled.

"The finest swords rust from disuse," Lanfranc said. "I was only to tell you that he does not forget your service."

"And for this we behave like spies, meeting in a chapel and praying?"

Laeghaire got up and went off. He heard the priest laughing behind him.

Later, the Count told him that Lanfranc had come to find out how much the Count would give to have the marriage of his daughter to the Duke of Normandy, long under the ban of the Pope, made lawful and blessed. The Count told Laeghaire that he had told Lanfranc that he would give nothing, because it seemed that William was giving everything. William was sending Norman warriors to Italy, to help this Hildebrand against the Emperor and against the other monks and priests trying to gain the Chair. "He wants to make a pope, be King of England, and teach God. He's a wild man."

"He is, that."

"You do love him."

"My lord." Laeghaire grinned. "As you do, my lord, only as much as you do."

"What is he? What damned beast is he? You hated him, before. Remember? In my offices you told him things I have never heard any man say to him. They think he's half God. He's muscle and bone and meat, like the rest of us—the poor fool."

Laeghaire lifted his head.

"Could you beat him in a fight?" the Count said.

"I've never seen him fight."

"He's a very devil. He does everything better than any other man. I've never seen you fight. But Sir Josse tells me that the men you led swear you sprout horns when you see enemies and that you cured a wound by passing your hand over it. They say—"

The Count shut his eyes and opened them.

"They say you walked into the middle of a group of men and killed one who had maligned you, without speaking a word, smiling. Is that why you love him? What kind of man are you?"

"My lord, you're unsettled."

"Have we lived this long to pass the world on to such as you and he?"

Laeghaire blinked.

"I'm sorry. You must excuse me. I have pressing . . . things on my mind. I am . . . old. You must excuse me. I meant no offense."

"My lord, I took none."

"I honor you and respect you. You must excuse me.

Please. You have my leave to go. I— For your comfort, they say that Harold Godwinson—the Earl of Wessex and the closest man to holy Edward—is in Normandy now, to swear England into William's hands a second time. In Edward's place, or as his chief man. Is he his chief man?"

"There are other great men."

"Good. Then. Please."

"Yes, my lord."

Later he sat in his room and watched the child sleeping. Murrough lay still. His damp hair clung to his head. Laeghaire wished he could take the child and put Hilde on the brown stallion among the packs and ride back to Ireland, ride the wet sea and ride the hills, and come at last into the house where his father sat under the eaves, talking to his sons' sons of the great old folk of Ireland.

All summer long he did nothing. He rode out often. Once he thought of buying another horse, and spent nearly a full month dickering with a man in the town of Ypres, going there for days on end, but at the end of the month he did not buy the horse. He spent the rest of his time with Murrough. They played the fingers game and Laeghaire told Murrough stories out of Irish history, of Cuchulain and the others, and how the Irish came to Ireland before the Flood. Murrough would pull himself up and try to walk, swaying like a drunken man, and he would almost always fall, and Laeghaire would laugh at him and tell him he was a colt to be trained, and when he laughed he would see the boy's eyes like a colt's and his strong round cheeks and his shouting mouth laugh back.

By the time the summer was over Murrough walked all the time. He would follow Laeghaire, if Laeghaire went slowly enough, but if he didn't, Murrough would stand and cry to be picked up and carried. He knew he could not keep up with Laeghaire if Laeghaire walked fast. Sometimes he tried, and always fell and skinned his knees.

Sometimes Laeghaire went to the armory, to oversee the smith with the new weapons. He took Murrough with him there. The boy crawled and climbed around the great empty room. One day he knocked over a shield and sat, amazed, while the shield thundered and rolled on the floor. Murrough began to laugh. He laughed uproariously at the shield that rolled and thundered on the floor.

"Hunh," Laeghaire said. "It might have hit you, little one, you sprouting colt."

"Father, do you fight giants ever?"

"Not very often, little one."

Murrough climbed up and sat on Laeghaire's shoulders. He pulled Laeghaire's ears and drummed his heels on Laeghaire's chest. "Tell me a story."

"What story?"

"Mac Datho."

Laeghaire told him. Mac Datho had a hound that the King of Ulster, Conor, and the Queen of Connaught both wanted, and to keep them from getting it, Mac Datho had a banquet. At the banquet he served up a pig that he had been fattening for seven years, and there was a quarrel between the Ulster men and the Connaught men over who should carve the pig. They all told stories, one after another, about their deeds and how many men they had killed—

"How many men have you killed, Father?"

"Of Ulster men, none, but of Connaught men, quite a few, and of Germans and French and various others, even more."

"Are we Ulster or Connaught, Father?"

"We're Kerry men, and no better fight in Ireland."

This satisfied Murrough, as it always did. "And in the end," he said. "Go on, Father."

He told the rest of the story, of Cet Mac Magach and Conall the Winner of Battles, and he thought telling it that the Irish heroes could have their fancy epithets. When Cet told Conall that it was true that Conall was the better man, Murrough began to rock back and forth, excitedly. " 'But if my brother Anluan had come, you would be the second only,' said Cet Mac Magach, 'for Anluan is the greatest warrior of Connaught, and Connaught breeds the best warriors in the world.' And Conall said, 'Your brother came here tonight, and I brought him.' So saying, he took from his belt the head of Anluan Mac Magach, and threw it down, and all the Connaught men had to give way to Conall the Winner of Battles."

"I like that story," Murrough said.

"That's obvious."

Hilde came in soon after that, with bread and meat and wine, and they ate there in the armory. Murrough chattered about what had occurred to him during the story. He spoke part German, part Flemish and part Gaelic. Laeghaire understood it all, but Hilde did not, and Laeghaire told her what was in Gaelic.

"It's not right that he should speak a Babel like that," Hilde said.

"Let him. When he grows older he'll know the difference. I do."

"You are . . . much older."

"Naturally."

Murrough went off to play with the fallen shield. Hilde came into Laeghaire's arms. Laeghaire kissed her mouth. "Are you unhappy?" he said.

"I'm not unhappy. I love you, and I think that you love me, and I'm not unhappy."

Murrough was christened in the autumn, when he could say his prayers correctly in Latin and Flemish. The Bishop of Ghent christened him, and the Count of Flanders stood as his godfather. There was a great ceremony and a feast afterwards. Laeghaire got drunk from toasting his son too much, because he began toasting Murrough at the beginning and ended toasting him long after Murrough had gone away to bed. In the middle of the feast, Karl came and sat near him and told him, with much excitement, of a campaign the Duke of Normandy had fought in Brittany. Laeghaire was unhappy because the Duke of Normandy had seen fit to carry on a campaign without the greatest knight in all Christendom, and he told Karl so.

"But my son will do greater things than I. His godfather is the Count of Flanders. My son will be a great man."

"He is your son, my lord."

Laeghaire put his hands to his face. He massaged his eye sockets with the heels of his hands.

"I'd have him a lord," he said. "I want him honored. He's the bastard of a runaway monk and a girl who deserted her betrothed to be sold to a killer."

"You're drunk, my lord."

"Yes. Am I talking loudly?"

"No. No one's heard you but me."

"You know everything about me anyway. I had the finest hand in the monastery, Karl."

"My lord, you do all things well."

"No. No. No. No. I've wrecked my life."

A long time later or maybe just a little bit later he heard Karl say to Hilde that he had never seen him this drunk before, and Laeghaire wondered because nobody was really that drunk, and he went up to his room with only a little help from Hilde and lay down on his bed and slept.

In the deep cold of that winter, Hilde's baby was born dead. She was sick for a long time afterward. Laeghaire was afraid that she would die. He sent Murrough down to stay with a woman in the town. Hilde lay in the bed with her face turned to the wall. She breathed lightly. When she was fed her eyes barely opened.

He wondered if she knew about the baby. He told Murrough about it, one time when he rode down to visit him. "You had a baby brother, but he died." Murrough turned his head a little, tilting his face. "Died? Who killed him?" Murrough asked him once, another time, about Hilde, and Laeghaire said that she was resting. The child's round face looked at him, thoughtfully, serious. Deep blue eyes, the thick straight black hair. Laeghaire put out his hands and touched Murrough's cheeks with his fingertips. Murrough climbed up onto Laeghaire's knee and sat. He drew Laeghaire's arms around him.

"He doesn't understand," Karl said. "He isn't old enough."

Laeghaire watched Murrough playing with the children of the Flemish woman. Hilde lying under the heavy coverlet dry and empty never moving or talking or even looking. Murrough's high loud laughter made him recoil. He went to his horse and mounted. Never moving or talking or looking, tight, surrounded, packed in. Get out of here.

"He was frightened because he saw your face. You were frightened and he knew it. That's all."

Karl solemn patient crossing himself against death, now riding earnest beside him, trying to cheer him. Riding back to the castle and the room tight and cramped in with the woman trying to put something back into that corpse there, the life standing right at the lips ready to leap out and go, the room thick with the smell of the corpse and the nurse woman and the dead child. Two children born in that room now one dead the woman dying.

Murrough had not been conceived in that room. Murrough had been born in the late spring. Murrough she had conceived under the trees in Germany. Born in that room but not. . . Murrough was different. Murrough turned and waved to him now. Laughing he waved, bristling with energy.

They went back to the castle.

In the beginning of Lent, Hilde grew stronger, suddenly, and she got out of bed just before Palm Sunday. She laughed about being dead. She did not mention the baby.

* * *

It was a wet spring. The Count went once to Paris and left Laeghaire in charge of the castle of Ghent. He had to hear the complaints of the castle people and judge between them, and be sure that they all did what they were supposed to, make out schedules for sentries and hear reports from the chatelains of other castles in the Count's domains. The Countess helped him. She knew much of the affairs of the county. She never overruled him, and she would not advise him unless he asked her for advice, and even then she was quiet and gentle. She told him nothing, but asked him questions that made him see what she thought ought to be done.

Once when he went to see her, she asked him if the Count had told him anything about christening the son of the Count's heir.

"No," he said. "Nothing of it."

"Perhaps he means to put it off until he returns. I received a messenger this morning from my son. He is in Bruges and keeps his court there. He prefers much younger company to ours. I doubt if he has been here at all since you came, sir."

"He was here for the Christmas feast the year that the Duke was here, my lady."

"Oh yes, he hunted with us. I remember now. He was here when you were in Maine, too."

She turned her head slightly. Her brows drew together. The skin of her cheek was very fine, very soft.

"Please, sir," she said, "forgive me if I intrude on you. My daughter's husband—my lord William—my husband says that you love him much. Do you believe—I fear for my daughter. She loves him too much, I think. He may destroy himself."

Laeghaire glanced at her maids, tatting in the far corner. The room was small. It was dark. The tapestries moved with the drafts and the rain beat against the shutters. In Falaise the sun had poured in over the skirts of the women. That one . . .

"I beg your pardon, sir. I have intruded."

The Countess stood up. She looked up at him. The wide bones of her face made her eyes seem deeper. Her eyes were like claws, reaching for him.

"No, my lady. I was wondering what you were asking me."

"Is he a good man?"

"Good? How do you mean, good? He won't be beaten."

Her eyes tried to draw the thoughts out of his eyes. "He frightens me. He wants so much. I don't understand him. Or you. How do I mean, good? Is he a monster, or is he God's chosen?"

Laeghaire made a small gesture with his hands. His throat was dry and he swallowed. Her eyes ran needles through him. "I don't know," he said.

"I'm sorry. I have confused you. Here. Sit down again, and someone will bring you wine. Jan, come here, please."

They talked of the affairs of the castle. Laeghaire went down to the kitchens to eat. He could not understand her question. He did not know how she could think that he would be able to answer it.

The Count came home after a while. Hilde was pregnant again. She served the Countess very well, because Laeghaire got many presents of the Countess. She said once that she thought the Countess was half in love with Laeghaire. Laeghaire didn't believe that at all.

The christening feast for the Count's younger grandson began on the Assumption. The great lords of Flanders started arriving long days before that. The young King of France came, too, and a great train of servants and attendants. Finally, on Assumption Eve, the Duke of Normandy rode into the castle of Ghent.

The castle was jammed with people. Most of the horses were stabled in the town, and some of the lesser lords stayed in the houses outside the wall of the castle. Pages charged around fetching wine for their masters, carrying messages, demanding help. Lords met in the courtyards and stood talking, while the wagons bringing supplies shoved and crushed through to be unloaded. The steward of the King of France started a fight with the Count about the position of the banner that proclaimed the presence of the King. Someone had apparently hung it on the left of Baldwin's standard, and the Duke of Normandy's on the right. Fitz-Osbern heard about it and showed up in the Count's cabinet before the royal steward had got the argument completely out of his mouth.

Laeghaire was with the Count. He stood against the wall behind the Count and listened to the royal steward's latherings. When Fitz-Osbern came in with three retainers, Laeghaire moved to make room, but there was no room. He finally opened the shutters and sat on the windowsill. The Count rose to greet Fitz-Osbern, and the royal steward wheeled, and the shouting started up all over again. The Count sat down. He was smiling. He looked over at his son, the heir Baldwin.

Baldwin came forward, speaking softly, and separated Fitz-Osbern and the royal steward. He could not separate them by much; there were eighteen men in the little room. The two stewards stopped shouting and stood, their faces bright red.

"My lords, my lords. This is most unsettling. My lord father wants me to advise you that you are arguing with the wrong man. Present your cases to the lord Herald of Flanders."

"My good lord," Fitz-Osbern said. "I was unaware

that Flanders had this honorable post. In previous years, your lord steward has adjudicated these disputes."

"My lords." Baldwin turned. "My lord father."

The Count rose. "The lord Herald of Flanders, my good lords. Sir Laeghaire of the Long Road."

Fitz-Osbern stiffened.

The Count looked at Laeghaire. "Settle this dispute, if it please you, my lord." He bowed, and Laeghaire bowed. He could not get off the windowsill; the Count's chair was against his knees.

"My lords," he said. "The banners are on the gate, are they not?"

"Indeed," the royal steward said. "The Count of Flanders' standard flies from the crossbar center, and my lord's standard, the royal standard of France, has been placed on the left upright. The left, my good lord."

"Approaching the gate how, my lord?"

"Why—from the town, of course."

"But coming from the castle, it's on the right, is it not?"

"But—"

"And coming from the town, the Duke of Normandy's standard is on the right, is it not?"

"This is—"

"So. You are both in the right, my lords, and I fail to see the difficulty."

The royal steward turned and crowded his way out of the room. His attendants followed him.

"Now we have room to breathe in," the Count said. "My dear Sir William. Most pleasant to have you here again."

"My lord Count." Fitz-Osbern bowed. "And may I congratulate your lord Herald on his solution of the problem."

"Thank you, my lord."

"Hebert will attend to any difficulty you might encounter," the Count said. "My compliments to your lord and lady."

"My lords." Fitz-Osbern bowed and went out. His retainers followed him.

"Very good," the Count said. "Laeghaire, you amaze me."

"No more than you me, my lord."

"It seemed to have its advantages at the time. You may take your place among my court officers, if you like, or resign."

"My lord, I'll resign."

Baldwin, the Count's son, turned abruptly. "Do you dislike honor, sir?"

"He is my man only in name," the Count said. "His real allegiance is to your good and dutiful brother-in-law."

"I should think it might have been dangerous to ask him to judge that decision, then."

"Not at all. I have it on good authority that our friendly Irishman is not listed among the admirers of William Fitz-Osbern. Isn't that so, Laeghaire?"

"We almost fought once."

"Or twice, or three times. Enough of that. You have my leave, sir."

Laeghaire slid off the windowsill. He passed by young Baldwin and went out.

With Murrough he sat on the rampart and watched the swarming mass of people in the courtyard. Murrough pointed excitedly to various things going on and asked what they were. Laeghaire held him by the belt, in case he decided to fall off the rampart.

"Have you nothing to do, my lord Herald of Flanders?"

William sat down beside Laeghaire. Two knights and

a page loitered dutifully at the foot of the ladder.

"A herald's life is an easy one in a peace-loving place, my lord. Besides, I resigned."

Murrough looked up at William. He stood, got a good grip on Laeghaire's coat, and leaned out to grab for William. Laeghaire pulled him down. "Sit still," he said.

"He looks much older than he must be," William said.

"He's a good lad."

"He looks like you."

"He does. Sit still." Laeghaire switched to Gaelic. "Sit still or I'll skin your tail end."

"Fitz-Osbern was very upset."

Laeghaire grinned. "He looked upset. I heard you fought in Brittany."

William nodded. He was still watching Murrough. "With Harold the Saxon. Did you know him?"

"A little."

"He is a good man."

"For whose purposes, my lord?"

William looked at him. They both laughed at once.

"You knew him well enough, then."

"My lord, he's not a secret kind of man."

"Unlike some. His brother is one."

"Which?"

"Tosti."

"Oh. Tosti."

"You knew him?"

"Yes. Did you get what you wanted of Harold, my lord?"

"Oh, a small oath. Just a little oath." William threw back his head and laughed. Murrough began to laugh too. Suddenly Murrough hiccuped.

"On all the bones and relics and cow's skulls I could find," William said. "It was an oath to bind the Pope himself."

"Will you have to fight for England?"

"I don't think so."

"I think so."

William frowned. Murrough hiccuped again, and Laeghaire tilted up the boy's head. Murrough suddenly frowned too, and looked back at William.

"If I do, I'll send an honor guard for you," William said. "You have my word on it."

"I'll take it, my lord."

The feasting and hunting and drinking lasted seven days. Laeghaire talked with William often. One night he spent drinking with William and William's retainers, in a little hall; the Normans made no sign that he was not one of them. They all knew him, they laughed at his mistakes with French, and everyone told stories. They told many stories about Maine. Another time they hunted together. Murrough liked William and imitated him when Laeghaire and William sat talking.

After the feasting everybody went home. The rest of the summer Laeghaire spent training squires and running errands for the Count. Hilde was round with the next baby. She sat often combing her long pale hair, thinking. He knew from the curve of her mouth that she was happy. He lay in bed one morning, playing with Murrough, and watched her comb her hair. Her hair fell over her shoulders. It shone in the sunlight from the window. He remembered the weight of her hair on his fingertips.

"What are you thinking about?" she said.

"Your hair."

She smiled. Her eyes were half closed. She sat like that often. He could not reach her. She was full with a life completely dependent on her, surrounded by her, and he could never understand it. Murrough, impatient, tugged at his hand, and he got up. She did not need him now.

She had someone who needed her absolutely. She could let him look at her, without speaking; she liked to be looked at.

He shaved himself and dressed and took Murrough with him down to the field where the squires practiced. He knew that she sat there, alone, and combed her hair, and thought about the child growing curled up in her belly.

In that early autumn he could taste the peace of this place. The harvests were good, and the merchants had many things to sell. The people wove cloth and the cloth given to the Count lay in heaps in the storerooms, all colors, changing color where the shadows and light fell on it. He remembered the year before, when he had been nearly mad with boredom. Only a year before.

"Laeghaire," the Count said. "I have a favor to ask you."

"Ask."

"In return I will give you your freedom to follow the Duke when he calls you. You have always had it, but I'll give you my blessing."

"Thank you."

"You know that Tosti Godwinson is married to my half sister."

"Yes. I forgot. I remember now."

"He has been exiled from England."

"Exiled. Why?"

"I don't know. Some misadventure."

He overstepped himself, Laeghaire thought. Wanting to make absolutely sure. Secret Tosti.

"He is coming here, to Ghent," the Count said. "I want you to watch him. He will bring with him only a few retainers. None of them speaks any Flemish. My sister does, of course, but I think she will stay with my

Countess. He will need a companion who speaks the language and knows his way around. And I want to know
everything in his mind."

"Yes, my lord."

"I don't want him to go to Normandy. That is an order. If you suspect that he might want to go to Normandy, dissuade him. If you cannot, tell me. And by no
means give him aid or go with him."

"Yes, my lord."

"He will be here shortly before Allhallows."

Tosti came in the first snow of the season, almost
alone. He came from the coast, with five retainers and his
wife, the lady Judith, and two packhorses. The Count
received him in his antechamber, with the Countess and
the steward Hebert and Laeghaire. The woman was
tired. Her eyes sank into hollows and her mouth was thin
and blue with cold. The Countess took her up to the
women's quarters right away. The Count sat in his chair
and studied the others, the six men. Laeghaire saw the
skin tight over the Count's jawbone. He crossed his arms
and waited.

"You cannot expect me to do you much benefit," the
Count said. "You may sit."

The retainers sat down, still holding their cloaks tight
around them. But Tosti remained on his feet. He looked
guilty and proud. His face was sharp. His eyes were
dark. They smoldered. Laeghaire remembered him
younger. Seeing him now brought back all the memories
of him and his brothers. Laeghaire might have left England only the day before; he remembered it in every de-
tail.

"There was a time," Tosti said, "when you rejoiced to
give me benefit, my lord Count."

"That was before you lost an earldom and had yourself declared an outlaw. You should never play big games with men who know more of the rules than you do."

So the Count knew, too.

The Count lifted his head. "You are in disgrace. I can offer you a place to spend your exile until such time as you may return peacefully to England. If your father were still alive, there might be better hope for it."

"My father."

"While you stay here, I will place my most honored knight at your disposal." The Count laid his hand on the top of the desk. He stared at it. "You will find that he is an adequate spy. I do not wish you to leave Flanders without notifying me first of your intentions and destination. Is that clear?"

The Count did not look up. Tosti's face changed slightly. It seemed to Laeghaire that the bones moved, fitting together in a different form. The sleek new eyes like a cat's were full of lies.

"As you wish, my lord," Tosti said. His eyes moved slowly and thoughtfully to Laeghaire. "Well, Irishman?"

"Your memory is as long as I hope your discretion to be," the Count said. "You have my leave to go."

Tosti turned and went out into the hall. Laeghaire followed him.

"I always wondered where you went after you left us," Tosti said. He spoke Saxon now.

"I have been other places."

"You must have. Your reputation penetrated even Edward's rather dull court. At least some of the tales told about you must be true. The old man's sick, you know."

"How could I know?"

"Ears, ears, ears, ears. I heard your name once in connection with a man I should pretend to hate and loathe, since his connivances lost me my title. Where are we going?"

"To your chambers."

"I have nothing to hide from a spy. I will tell you everything, if you care to listen. I'm a great talker, you know. My brother says it's my worst fault. My brother. You recall my brother."

"Which one?"

"Harold. Since Sweyn died, he has been the head of our family. Harold the Lucky, they call him. You should see him now. Are these my chambers?"

"Yes."

"Sumptuous. Aldric, go find us something to eat. Tell him how to get to the kitchens, Irishman."

"He can find a page just down the hall, in the alcove."

"Call him then, Aldric. The rest of you leave me. Aldric will feed you."

Aldric returned with the page. "He doesn't understand me," Aldric said.

Laeghaire wheeled. "Boy, go to the kitchens and have them send us food for six and a cask of wine. The good wine."

The page glanced at Tosti from the corner of his eyes. "On your orders, my lord."

"My orders. Hurry."

Tosti snapped his fingers and pointed to the door to the next room. Aldric went to it, opened it, and looked in. He came back, yawning.

"They've all fallen asleep, my lord."

"Good. Aldric was my reeve, Irishman. He stayed loyal to me by his own will. The rest of these dogs had to. They would have been torn to pieces otherwise. I was their only means out of England." He looked around, saw a chair, and dragged it over to the fire. He flung off his sodden cloak and sat down. He propped his feet up on the logs by the fire. "Ah. Warmth. It's damned cold. What did you tell the page, Irishman?"

"To bring you food. I don't hold deep speech with

pages." Laeghaire drifted around the room. The King of France had occupied these chambers. He ran his fingers over the surface of the tapestry. It showed Charlemagne at the hunt, his beard divided neatly over each shoulder as he charged, crossbow aimed, after a pard.

"The second Charlemagne. He caused me much trouble." Tosti stretched. "Still, it had to come. And it weakened my brother considerably."

"What happened?"

"Oh, I was to swear myself into the hands of the honored master of God's will in England. Serve as his vicarius, I think the phrase is, in his hot campaign for the crown of England. Unfortunately, I wanted too much. He offered my brother a daughter to marry, but he would not marry his son to my daughter—who is, incidentally, now a hostage to my brother in York. Pleasant city, York. Also, I wanted some estates in the south. He is a man of meager thanks. He decided that I wanted too much and gave too little, and—zip." Tosti snapped his fingers. "Of course, the house of Mercia has had certain designs on my head for a long time, and this played into their hands. I might add that he gained a powerful enemy in the north, if by any ill luck or trick of the Devil he should take England. What do you think of him?"

"He will take England."

"Oh. Oh. I see how the land lies. The proverbial sword in the right hand. Yea verily. Irishman, he'll use you until he has no more use for you, and he'll fling you into the sea."

"No, he won't."

"He can be as sweet-tongued as the very Devil, to whom, I am sure, he is a close blood relative. Among his other connections. Here's the food."

Tosti and Aldric ate in silence, bolting down the meat and bread, swallowing it half chewed. Laeghaire felt sick at the sight of them. He went to the door. "If you want me, I'll be in my room or at the stable. Send the page for me."

"He'll come for you when I leave, anyway," Tosti said. He swallowed. He smiled viciously. "How pleasant to have seen you again, Irishman."

Tosti rested for a while. Every day he would send the page for Laeghaire, and they would walk together around the castle and into the town. Aldric was always around, but the others of Tosti's retainers soon disappeared. The Count told Laeghaire that they had all left Ghent by the fourth day of Tosti's visit, sick of their master and longing for better chances. The lady Judith rarely left the Countess's chambers.

Tosti took his meals in his own chambers. Laeghaire wondered why, since everybody knew who he was and he never stayed inside during any other time of the day. One night, however, several days after the last of the retainers had gone, Tosti suddenly appeared in the dining hall when the meat was being put on the table. He excused himself to the Count, turned, and scanned the table. He headed straight for Laeghaire. Laeghaire told Hilde to move over on the bench.

Tosti sat down. "Well. I thought to join the quick." His eyes flew over the men nearest him. A servant put a cup and a trencher in front of him, and he carved himself meat.

"Your wife is at the table with the Count," Laeghaire said. "Go eat with her."

"So eager to be rid of me, Irishman? My beloved spouse and I are not speaking. I have disgraced her." Tosti broke off a chunk of bread. He began to eat with great energy. Laeghaire thought he did nothing more hatefully than eat. He glanced up at the head of the table. The lady Judith was staring at Tosti. Suddenly she rose and left the hall.

Now everybody was watching Tosti. He lifted his head and looked after his wife. "I thought so. My very presence in a room as wide and airy as this has sickened her. Put her off her feed, like a nursing cow."

The Count stood up. "Your voice penetrates even this wide and airy room, Saxon."

"May I call to your attention, my lord, that I may have lost my earldom but I did not lose my birth, a fact you and your bootlicking Irish hound seem to feel free to ignore."

Laeghaire got up and backed away from the table. He looked at the Count. Tosti kept his back to him.

"Cut the leash," Tosti said to the Count. "You can be rid of me within the hour. I assure you I am no match for the far-famed Laeghaire of the Long Road."

"Sir Laeghaire," the Count said, "you will accept the lord Tosti's apologies. And he will, I hope, accept mine."

Laeghaire turned on his heel and walked out of the room. He walked the length of the table to the back door. He slammed the door after him.

He stood in his room looking at Murrough, asleep in the cradle by the fire. Hilde came in. She skirted the table and came to him. "Don't be angry," she said. She stood behind him and put her arms around him. His muscles tensed.

"You haven't been angry for so long, it's been so wonderful. Please don't be angry."

He put his hands over her hands. He could feel the bones under his fingers.

"He gave you an insult, but he's a fool, and nobody will think any less of you if you do not repay him for it."

She rested her cheek against his back. He turned around and kissed her. She sighed. He patted her belly.

"Go to bed."

"You aren't angry any more?"

"No. Go to bed."

She smiled and began to undress. There was a knock on the door. Laeghaire said, "Who is it?"

"Tosti Godwinson."

Hilde put her hand on his arm.

"Just a moment," Laeghaire said. He sat on the table. Hilde took her clothes and went into the alcove and drew the curtain. Laeghaire told Tosti to come in.

Tosti opened the door. "I wanted to express my most abject apologies. I seem to have let my rancor get the upper hand."

"Be quieter. You'll wake the baby up."

"Baby?" Tosti crossed to the cradle and looked down. The torch was behind him. It cast a glow all around his head. He rested his hands on the side of the cradle.

"Is it yours?"

"Yes."

"It's a boy, isn't it."

"Yes."

Tosti was silent. He stood looking down at Murrough.

"When did you marry?"

"I didn't."

"Oh. My mistake. I seem to be extra clumsy tonight. I couldn't get a son. I have three daughters."

He looked down at Murrough again. "Deal wisely with him, Irishman." He turned and left.

Hilde came from behind the curtain in her shift. "What did he mean?"

"Who knows? Go to bed. You must be sleepy."

Tosti and the Count suddenly became friends, and Tosti sat at supper by the head of the table with the Count. The lady Judith at first dined and supped in her chambers. But she could not avoid Tosti, especially during Advent, when everybody went to services three times a day. Laeghaire always stood by Tosti in the chapel. He watched them, day by day, draw closer together. Finally, after the Vespers of the fourth day before Christmas Eve, they left the chapel together. Laeghaire went out after them and crossed the courtyard to the outer stair. He saw them walking slowly together, apart from the others. Tosti's head was bent toward Judith's. He was talking. His left hand moved in an easy gesture. Suddenly Judith turned to face him and smiled. Her eyes shone confidently.

It was beginning to snow. Laeghaire went into the castle.

Christmas was quiet. The Count invited no guests. He gave presents to all the children. Murrough got a wooden horse set on wheels, with a cord to draw it around by. The grown-ups held a feast. The Count knighted Karl the next morning, in a single ceremony, and Karl had presents from all the people in the castle. His knighting had been a gift from the Count.

"When it stops snowing," the Count said, "we will have a mock fight, Sir Karl. Between you and Sir Laeghaire."

Karl laughed. His laughter and the expression on his face remained with Laeghaire a long time. He did not remember the last time he had himself laughed. He was not unhappy.

He took his spell of guard duty on Twelfth Night. The lights of the hall and the Feast of Fools and the Court of Misrule were nothing for him. He thought of Karl laughing and Tosti and Judith, their heads bent together, smiling. He thought of Murrough, pulling the wooden horse after him, running in the hall, the wooden wheels clattering on the stone. He was not unhappy. The thing that lives in a cocoon, he thought, is not unhappy either. I see with my eyes and my ears hear and I touch with my hands.

Somebody scrambled up the ladder and came swiftly toward him. It was Hilde, wrapped in his old cloak. He knew her by the giggle that came from the depths of the hood.

"False monk," she said, "I brought you your piece of the cake."

A hand crept from the cloak's folds and deposited a crumbling bit of cake in the snow. The great mass of the cloak turned and staggered off.

"Come back here. You'll hurt yourself. Or the baby." He drew her down by him. She sat between his knees and leaned back against his chest. He put his arms around her and pulled the edge of his own cloak over her. She shook off her hood. In the dark heavy lump of the cloaks her hair shone. She smiled. She put her head against his shoulder.

From the hall came a burst of noise. The lights flickered over the empty courtyard. Laeghaire closed his eyes. He smelled the scent of her skin and her hair. He dozed.

Tosti came hunting him one day, when he sat playing with Murrough in the stables. Tosti drifted in and stood watching until Laeghaire looked up.

Murrough stood. Laeghaire said, "Go play. Go find your friends."

The boy stared at Tosti. He backed off a few steps, suddenly shy. He turned and trotted off. Tosti watched him.

"You've been lax in your duties, Irish," Tosti said. "You are supposed to accompany me."

"Even courting?"

Tosti grinned. "No. Not at my courting, my dear man. Not at my courting." He wandered on light feet around the back part of the stable. "Aha! What's this? The earth has opened and will swallow Ghent whole?"

"What?"

"A fissure, one might say a veritable cleft. In the floor of the stable." Tosti banged his heel on the stable floor. "Hollow. A shame. I thought to see marvels. Hallo. Yes. It even echoes."

"That's the old vault. It's underground and it gave the horses thrush or something. The Count closed it up."

"Leaving a gap? Bad judgment on the part of your estimable carpenters. A man could fall and break his neck."

"It's a little narrow for that."

"In truth. Your boy is very handsome."

"Yes."

"My dear man, you are supposed to thank me and immediately raise your opinion of my taste some two or three notches. Not admit it."

"Have you convinced the lady Judith that she is unshamed?"

"Indeed. You have a knack for acquiring the verbal idiosyncrasies of the people you converse with. Do not mock me."

"I'm sorry."

"I came hither the bringer of substantial news. A messenger appeared this morning from the coast, was ushered into the Count's presence, and there gave him news that the King of England is dead. God rest his immortal and most holy soul." Tosti crossed himself, and Laeghaire did, too. "And, further, that my dear brother has crowned himself King. On Epiphany, before the corpse was hardly chilled. And thus, Irishman, I need your aid."

"To go where?"

"To Normandy."

"No."

"I feared as much. 'To go where?' You revealed yourself, dropped your shield. Then I shall go myself."

"I'll have to tell the Count."

"Tell the Count, my dear. I shall go alone. Aldric is too old to play these games, and Judith must remain here. Until I can return her to her place as Countess of Northumbria. Under a King who owes me at least one part of his crown. William of Normandy, perhaps; a Northman, perhaps; even an Atheling—but not my brother."

"You talk too much."

"So I do. So I do. Let me talk a moment more. My brother is going to die."

"All men die."

"Ah, but I am going to kill him. The first, most terrible crime."

"Why hate him?"

"I don't know. I've always hated him. He always means well, but he has gotten us into more trouble than anyone else. King of England. Is he a fool? Doesn't he know what he's doing? Do you remember my father?"

"Yes."

"My father was as near to God as any man I have ever known. As near as holy Edward."

Tosti spat. He went out. His boots rang on the floor.

The next day he was gone. The Count raged a while and at last admitted that no man could have stopped him. Laeghaire hardly cared. William was going to have to fight for England. William would need knights. Laeghaire remembered Maine like a fire. He waited for William to call him. For two or three days he waited for each moment because each moment might bring him his summons.

Hilde had the baby, very quickly. One moment she was coming to Laeghaire, telling him that she was going to have it, and the next she was lying on the bed, asleep, and the new baby wrapped in swaddling in the nurse's arms. It was a girl. Hilde called her Traude, and Laeghaire called her Dierdre. Hilde was well right away and very happy. Six days after the baby was born, she died, and they buried her in the castle graveyard outside the wall.

"Don't worry. We'll get another," Laeghaire said.

"But I wanted this one. I wanted my little girl. You have Murrough, and I wanted a girl."

Murrough sat on the bed, looking from one face to the other. Laeghaire put his arms around Hilde. "We'll get another. She'll be happier where she is."

"She wasn't christened." Hilde pulled away from him. "And we will never have another. It's a punishment on us, for our sin. I'll keep having them, and they'll keep dying, they'll just keep dying. I hate it. I hate it."

"Murrough, go outside."

"You go too. Go away."

He went out after Murrough. Murrough turned and looked up.

"What was my mother mad about?"

"Your little baby sister."

"Where is she?"

"She's dead, Murrough."

Murrough caught Laeghaire's hand. "She's dead? I can't see her any more?"

"No."

"Did she go to Heaven?"

"Yes."

"Why did she die?"

"I don't know."

"When I die, will I go to Heaven?"

"Stop talking about it."

Murrough's fingers tightened around Laeghaire's. His face turned up toward Laeghaire's. Suddenly he began to cry. Laeghaire picked him up. Murrough wept.

"Hush. Be quiet. Don't worry. Hush."

"Why are you mad at me?"

"I'm not. I'm not."

Murrough was a heavy weight in his arms. He stood in the hall with the child in his arms. Murrough cried against his shoulder. He should marry her. It would not take away the sin. They had lived together for a long time, slept in the same bed, without a marriage. He did not think it would take away the sin.

He fought the mock fight with Karl, with a wrapped sword and a padded shield. The whole castle came to watch, in the field where the squires trained. The snow was melting and the horses moved in mud to their fetlocks. Murrough sat by the Count. Hilde was with him. The two horses were well matched, although Laeghaire's stallion was much older and wiser than Karl's horse. Karl fought well. Laeghaire rapped him several times across the ribs. Once Karl beat down Laeghaire's shield and almost tapped him on the shoulder. They fought for nearly the whole afternoon. Twice Karl fell off his horse. The people cheered wildly and threw snowballs at them when they made bad moves.

Finally Karl thrust up his hands. "Quarter," he said. He took off his helmet, laughing. "By the Cross," he said, "you killed me a dozen times."

"You'll be a good knight," Laeghaire said. "Hold your shield higher. Cover your neck with it."

"Yes, my lord."

Murrough ran up. He danced around them, laughing. He caught the brown stallion's stirrup. Laeghaire bent and swung him up. Karl said, "That's dangerous."

"He plays in horses' stalls. He's an Irishman. We're half horse."

"When I grow up," Murrough said, "I'll be like my father."

"He'll be a very devil of a knight," Karl said.

"No, he won't. He'll be a landed lord, a count, like his godfather."

The others were all around them now. Murrough jumped up and down, hanging onto Laeghaire.

"Where?"

"It doesn't matter."

No word from William. Rumors. William had sent to Rome for a special blessing on his claim against the oath-breaker. Tosti was in Normandy, helping William. The Pope would call a holy war against the usurper Harold. Harold had been crowned by the Archbishop Stigand, who was not invested from Rome, and the Pope hated him. The Emperor was sending aid to William, the rumors said. They said that the Spanish Moors were seeking an alliance with Harold Godwinson, and with Harold's help would crush Christendom.

There was no word from William. Laeghaire thought of going to Normandy uncalled. He did not want to. He wanted William to send for him.

Hilde was better. She was merry most of the time but sometimes she would be quiet and sit alone and think. He could not reach her any more. He made love to her once but she was dull and empty in his arms. After he was finished he lay in the darkness, trembling, and listened to her fall asleep.

He took his horses for long gallops to condition them. He worked often with Karl and one or two of the squires. All the long spring he fretted. The Count knew it, and called him in one day to tell him that it would be a while before William would send for him. England was a bigger enterprise than Maine. Wait. Be calm. Wait. He rode hard, leaping the horses over the swollen streams and the windfalls of the gone winter. The brown stallion ran at the end of the whipping rope, his great body flecked with lather. Both horses began to trim down. Laeghaire sat in his saddle one day in the late spring and watched the brown stallion stamp and wheel at the end of the rope. The stallion was fresh and wild. He had not been ridden since the fight with Karl. His legs bent and drove down, smashing at the ground, tearing clods of turf out of the ground. He played like a colt, arching his neck. Spring wildness. He wanted a mare. His eyes rolled. The muscles of his haunches arched and flattened and his tail, cocked high, flew back and forth. Laeghaire could not stop watching him. He had had the stallion since he was a colt. Now the stallion was in his prime, sleek and strong and proud in the mean glitter of his eyes. He wished he were the stallion and could leap and dance and strut, fling out his hoofs and claw open the ground.

When Laeghaire went back to the castle that day, Lanfranc the Prior of Bec was there. Lanfranc said that he had only come to visit and bring some minor news, but when he said it he looked at Laeghaire, and Laeghaire thought, It's a fine honor guard, my lord. He laughed. The Count turned, surprised, and Laeghaire made his face straight.

That evening, Lanfranc sought him out and said, "I must go back to Normandy in four days. The Duke said that if I saw you I was to tell you that he is calling knights to take England."

"For the fun of it?"

"England is rich. Booty, land, women . . ."

That night he dreamed that he rode in English fields, and saw a witchwoman there. He dreamed they stood and stared at one another for a long time, and suddenly he jumped for her and caught her, and in the middle of the sunny fields he raped her. In the dream he was happy about it, but when he woke up he saw Hilde and was a little ashamed and put it out of his mind.

"We're going to Normandy, aren't we?" Hilde said.

"Yes."

"When?"

"In three days."

"I'll get ready."

"Good." Laeghaire called to Murrough.

"Here, leave him here, he's sleepy. He woke up again last night. Where are you going?"

"I'm going to run my horses."

"Normandy?" Murrough said. "Normandy? Are we really going to Normandy?"

"Yes." Laeghaire picked him up. "You sleep. You're sleepy." He grinned. He grinned at Hilde also. He put Murrough into the bed and went out. He went up to the armory and got his shield and sword. He took them down to the smith's forge, at the back of the stable, and pounded the dents out of the sword. The smith came to watch. He asked about the ball on the pommel and how it was set in. They talked about swords for a while. Laeghaire took the horses and rode out, down south to the open flat land.

When he came back in, he was hungry, and he put the horses up and went to the kitchens to get something to eat. He was sitting there with a bowl of stew when Hilde came to him.

"Laeghaire. I can't find Murrough."

"When did he wake up?"

"I don't know. I left right after you did—I had to sew some things."

"And he's not in the room?"

"He isn't anywhere. Nobody has seen him."

"Did you look in the armory? He goes there sometimes."

"He isn't there. I looked there, in the stable, every-where."

Laeghaire got up so quickly that the bench fell over. He ran out of the kitchens and down the corridor. The courtyard was empty. He ran across it. His boots rang on the stones. He threw open the stable door.

"Murrough."

The stableman came from behind a stall partition. "What?"

"Have you seen my son?"

"No. When was he here?"

"How long have you been here?"

"I just came back."

"Murrough!"

He looked in all the stalls but Murrough wasn't in any of them. He looked by the haymow and under the saddles. In all the long stable there was no sign of Murrough. Maybe he had gone to the kitchens. Maybe he was in the armory. Laeghaire went slowly to the cleft in the floor. The boards seemed to bend under him. He kicked his heel and the echo came up to him, softly. It was dark down there. There would be spiders. The vault gave horses thrush. He went slowly out to the courtyard and got a dead torch and went back to the stable. The cleft grew wider under his eyes. The stableman stood silent in the middle of the stable. He crossed himself suddenly. Laeghaire knelt and swung himself into the cleft. He rammed the torch through his belt and lowered himself down. He hung at the length of his arms. The darkness swallowed up his legs and hips. He dropped. His boots struck the stone floor and he went to his knees. It was a long drop. The noise echoed softly, slowly. He took the torch and lit it. He saw cobwebs dripping from the ceiling of the vault, and the great shadows racing away from the torchlight and the dark floor, damp and solid stone. He saw Murrough. He went slowly down and laid the torch on the floor and picked him up. He was cold already, damp and cold as the stone.

"Did you find him?"

Laeghaire shut his eyes tight. The darkness slithered in around him. It was a slimy darkness. He tasted it lapping at his mouth. He rocked a little.

"Sir Laeghaire."

He crushed Murrough against his chest and pressed his face against Murrough's neck. The skin was unyielding and smelled of the dank vault and the cobwebs. The creeping darkness giggled in his ears. The torch guttered and died.

"I've found him."

His breathing filled the vault and came back to him, almost covering the gibbering of the darkness and the clammy dribbling of its fingers down his spine. He heard many feet on the ceiling over his head and bodies sliding down over the edge of the cleft. They could not reach him. He felt himself walled in by the thick stinking body of the darkness, pressing in on him, damp and horribly smooth. Their torchlight rebounded away from him and never touched him, and their hands only moved the darkness around him. He opened his mouth and swallowed up the darkness, and in the light but with the darkness inside him he let them help him up.

"He'll be happier where he is," Hilde said.

He wheeled on her.

"That's what you said to me. We'll get another, you said. That's what you said to me when my baby died."

"Get out."

"Laeghaire, oh Laeghaire, I'm sorry, please, let me be sorry too? Don't shut me out. I was his mother, Laeghaire."

He stared at her. She floated above the ground. She

floated in the light from the window. It was still after-noon, afternoon of a million days.

"Laeghaire," she said, and caught his arm.

He threw her off. She fell against the wall. He stood watching her. If she got up he would kill her. She looked at him. She shook her head.

"Please, Laeghaire—"

"I'll kill you if you don't go."

"Laeghaire." She stood up. She put her hands out. "Please, please . . ."

He stared at her. He took a step toward her. She turned and ran. He heard her sobbing. She tore open the door and ran. He could hear her crying.

He looked at the open door and the shadows. He raised his fist and took a step and hit the door and it slammed shut. His fist split open. The blood spat out and lay on his hand. He clenched his fist again. He turned wildly. He took a step and hit the chair and fell over it. He rolled over on the floor and got to his knees and stood up and sat in the chair.

Church bells. Nothing. The bed and the wall and the way the wall ran up to the other wall. Three of them all gone. Murrough. The eyes looked at him. The face laughed at him. The flesh peeled back in strips and the bony skull lay beneath it and jaws laughed at him and maggots crept from the eyes. His throat was blocked. In Ireland the women keened but the men never keened. If he screamed they would all hear him. Hear him scream. His eyes blurred over. He put his hands to his face and drove his nails against his cheekbones.

The door opened. He whirled up and jumped into a corner. It was Lanfranc. He stood in the door.

"Your woman sent me."

"No."

"You cannot deny me that way. Sit down."

"Spiritual comfort for the bereaved? The aid of Holy

Mother Church for the distraught father? Tell me, priest. Comfort me. Aid me. Tell me how he is gone up to Heaven and sitteth at the right hand of God."

"You don't believe it."

"Believe it. Believe it. He was my son. He was my only son. He was three years old, priest. Why should he have to die? Why didn't I die? Why strike me through my son?"

"You fool."

"Don't judge me, priest."

"I will judge you. Your pride cannot negate God's law and God's will. God has judged you."

"Damn God."

Lanfranc circled the table once and sat down. "Judge yourself, then. God is all-just. He measures all men. You cannot damn God."

"Leave me alone."

"You are already alone. You are a man living in a box, blind and deaf and dumb. But just because you can't see doesn't mean that everybody else is blind."

"They taught you all the words, didn't they? All the pretty little answers strung like— I wish to Christ I were blind."

"Do you realize that she loves you?"

"Stop asking me questions."

"You bought and paid for her. But she loves you. She is a human being, like you, and she is a creature of God, and she needs love. You need love. But you will not bend to that, you will not admit it, you will neither love nor live with her, you come to her when you are hungry."

"Shut up. Shut up, will you?"

"I don't think it's my words that bother you. You need them. Do you know what kind of suffering you have put her through? Three children, all dead, a man who leaves when he wishes and never thinks of her, never talks to her, never shares anything with her—"

"Leave me alone."

"If I stop talking, you'll have nothing but silence, and you would be even more frightened of the silence. Come here, sit down. I know that you're frightened."

"You know all the answers. If something happens—there"—he jabbed his hand toward the ceiling—"if you want something, you know where to get it."

"The same is true for you."

"No."

"Laeghaire. Listen to me. Think about this. God is all-merciful. Perhaps He meant to teach you something. To instruct you. Learn from it. An animal is something that cannot learn. A man learns. The learning will be hard for you because you are a man perhaps valuable to God. Be worthy of being severely tried. There is comfort for everybody. There is a place and a time for everybody. You have a right to grief. You have no right to destroy yourself by it."

Laeghaire went slowly to the bed and sat down on it.

"Grieve," Lanfranc said. "But let her share it. And let God share it."

Lanfranc rose. He smiled. "And remember that he has an immortal soul."

He left. Laeghaire lay down on the bed. He shut his eyes.

I want at least five thousand men," William said. "But them—them I can get. I need you to run errands for me. I need men I can trust to handle some details of this."

Laeghaire said nothing.

"Are you alone? Do you have a squire? I can quarter you with my retainers, if you wish."

"I have a woman with me."

"Oh? Ah. The yellow-headed wench."

"Yes."

"Camp-followers. Then make a camp somewhere, within the city wall. I—what's the matter?"

"What do you mean?"

"What's wrong with you?"

"My son died."

"Your little boy? What happened?"

"He fell into the lower vault of the stable."

"He was very—"

"I suppose he's better off."

"Do you still want to fight?"

"Yes." Laeghaire raised his eyes. He looked up at William's face. "Yes."

"A stupid question, perhaps."

"Yes."

"You have my condolences."

"Thank you."

William circled the broad table and sat down. He leaned back. He looked out the window.

"It doesn't ever really work," he said. "A man knows that he has everything he wished for, but there is always something missing, or something gone. Even when you are happy you're impatient for something."

"I was happy."

"Maybe. For how long? I say I will be happy when I

have England. I don't know."

"Maybe it's not in us."

"You and me? Or the rest of the world as well?"

Laeghaire reached over onto the table and took an arrow that was there. It was a crossbow bolt, new, with clean feathers. "You answer that."

"Why should we have to be different?"

"God's . . . will."

"God's will. If I had waited on the will of God— Irish, I'll give you land in England. I'll give you land in the south and in the north and the east. You can build castles and hold forests and every day you can ride out and watch your serfs working the land."

"You have that now. Are you happy?"

"No. I want England."

"Why?"

"I have blood right to it."

"Blood. A wolf has blood. And you won't be happy."

"No. We'll never be happy. But we can be great and unhappy."

"I dreamed about England. About riding in an English field. I met a witchwoman and took her."

"God's Splendor. That's a prophecy of a dream."

"Is it?"

There was a knock on the door. William stood up. "I'll summon you when I want you. I have much to do. Go pitch your camp."

"Yes, my lord."

He went back and made his camp, under the shadow of the wall around Caen. Hilde went about building a fire. She went for water. When she came back, he said, "William will pay me for this in land."

She bent over the fire. "And you will be a lord."

"Yes."

"And take a lord's daughter for your wife."

"No. If I live to take the land, I will have you for my

lady. I promise it. I owe it to you."

She turned. "Oh, Laeghaire. Laeghaire, thank you."

She put her arms around him. He held her. After a while she left him and made their supper.

William sent him to the Dives's mouth with Fitz-Osbern, to bring him information of the boats being drawn up there. Fitz-Osbern told Laeghaire a lot while they rode. He acted as if they had always been great friends. He told Laeghaire of how the old King of England had died of a long sickness, and how Harold had been named King by the Council of Ancients, but that many of the Saxon lords would not call Harold their master. This William's spies had brought him.

"It might have been better if he had attacked when the old man was King," Laeghaire said.

"No. The old man was holy. God would have struck us down. Why else was it that no raids, no wars, nothing, troubled his reign, and he a gentle king?"

"There was a war. Godwin threw out the Normans."

"That wasn't important."

Laeghaire grinned.

"He holds much of the coast," Fitz-Osbern said. "And all the men who come will have boats, too. Thousands of them."

At the Dives they inspected the boats that had been built and even went out in them, a little way from the shore, to see if they were sound. Laeghaire said that was stupid, because if the boats had holes in them he and Fitz-Osbern would drown. Fitz-Osbern only shrugged. They poled the boats out a little, into the mouth of the river, and they did not sink.

There were seventeen boats there, but some of them belonged to the fishermen. The fishermen made camps on the shore at night, hung their nets, and cleaned fish.

The shore stank of fish. Laeghaire and Fitz-Osbern made a camp with the fishermen and ate fish. They talked little. The fires were big and made the darkness of the shore seem immense. The water boomed evenly on the shore. The foam glittered in the firelight and glowed white of its own light all along the beach.

They slept wrapped in their cloaks. Laeghaire woke up in the night and went off to make water. He looked up at the sky. He cried out. Fitz-Osbern and the others woke and rolled out of their cloaks. They laughed at him, standing with his leggings down. He swore at them and pointed at the sky and they looked where he pointed.

"What is it?"

"Can't you see it?"

The fishermen knelt down and prayed.

"It's a star," Laeghaire said. "It's a star with a tail."

"I can see it."

He pulled up his leggings and tied the thong. "They can see it, can't they? Back in Caen?"

"It's an omen." Fitz-Osbern crossed himself.

The fishermen were praying very loudly. He stared up at the monster star, with its huge tail all spread out like a cloak after it. He thought he could see it move. It was huge. It was brighter than anything else, brighter than the moon.

"What is it an omen of?" Fitz-Osbern whispered.

"I don't know."

"The Duke will know. Perhaps—"

"It's about us. About the expedition."

"Us? How could God make something that great just for us?"

"The Duke. God's chosen. God is marking him. It's for him."

"Do you believe that?"

Laeghaire went off. He went down by the sea. He

stood looking at the star. All out of nothing it had come.
So huge out there. Maybe the wind just blew it together
and it caught fire from the sun on the other side. Maybe
it would be there forever. It was so vast, that sky, like the
edge of another ocean.

"There was a star like that when our Lord Jesus was
born," Fitz-Osbern said. He was beside Laeghaire again.
"A special star, like that one."

"Yes."

"Maybe this is the same one."

"That one went away."

"It could have come back. There are all sorts of stories
in the old chronicles. Of stars like this one."

"Not like this one." He went away from Fitz-Osbern
again, watching the star.

They prayed all night back by the banked fire. He
watched the star. He lay down to watch it. He dozed off
and woke starting up again. But by dawn he was so tired
that he went to sleep on the sand. He dreamed of many
things all pushed together, and over them all rode the
star.

"Did you see it?" Hilde said. "Did you see it?"

"Yes." He pulled the reins over the black horse's head,
looked up at the sky, and back to her. "Did you all see it
clearly?"

"Yes. It was terrible. I wanted you to be here."

She reached out her hand and touched his arm. "What
did it mean, Laeghaire?"

"A sign from God, perhaps. About this."

"Good or bad?"

"Good."

"A boy came. From the Duke. I think he's a Norman.
I can't talk to him."

"Where is he?"

She turned and called, "Rolf."

A young boy, about as tall as Hilde, came from behind the tent. He stood awkwardly. "My lord Laeghaire?" he said.

"Yes."

The boy began to speak rapidly. Laeghaire said, "Slow down. My French is not very good."

"I'm sorry, my lord. My lord the Duke said I was to attend you."

"Do you have a horse?"

"No. But I have a dagger. He says I am to stay by your lady."

Hilde was watching him, waiting for him to explain. Laeghaire told her in German. She smiled. "Your lady."

"Good," Laeghaire said to the boy. "Take this horse and put him to pasture." He threw the boy the reins and went into the tent.

"We'll be going down to the coast soon," he said to Hilde. "And half the knights in Christendom will be there. The Duke wants you protected when I'm off on his business."

"Is it dangerous?"

"It could be."

"For me?"

"Yes."

Rolf came in. "My lord, there is a man here from the Duke."

Laeghaire went out. Jehan, the big Burgundian, sat in his high saddle, in half mail. Jehan grinned. "So you did come. I thought it was you."

"Of course I came. Am I a man to let something like this go by? Come down and have wine."

"I can't; I am supposed to hie you straight up to his lordship the Duke of everywhere."

"Rolf, go fetch me a horse."

Jehan leaned back and let his reins go. He turned to

watch the boy skitter away. "By the Virgin, you made some great name for yourself in Maine. They still talk about you in the halls."

" 'That devil Irish.' "

"Well, something of that. According to some of them, arrows passed right through you without hurting you and you killed men with the looks of your eyes."

"The perils of the profession."

"How is your offspring?"

"Dead."

"Ah. I'm always stepping into traps."

"It doesn't matter any more. What does he want of me?"

"Oh, your mighty arm, your quibbling tongue, your deep thoughts. Here comes your horse."

Rolf trotted up with the brown stallion on a leading string. Laeghaire frowned. He said, "Next time you bring me a horse to ride to a council, bring me the black."

"He's tired, my lord."

Rolf saddled the brown stallion in the open space by the wall.

"Nonetheless, bring him. It's not far and I don't like to ride that one except in a fight. No, don't worry about it now."

"I'm sorry."

"You didn't know."

Jehan wrinkled his forehead. "You're uncommon careful with your war-horse."

"It spoils them to be ridden around like palfreys."

He sent Rolf for his cloak.

"You rode the brown horse when you went to give the Duke your apology, after he hit you."

"That was different."

"Did you really make him apologize to you?"

"I swore I would, didn't I?"

"My mistake. I overlooked the value of your oaths."

Laeghaire put on the cloak and gathered up the reins. He vaulted into the saddle. They rode off.

"This is no council," Jehan said. "I think it's something to do with his spies."

"He still has his spies out, then."

"Of course."

There were many knights in the town, and archers, all sitting in the marketplace, drinking and talking. Jehan waved to some of them. They called to him. One of them called Laeghaire's name. At once the marketplace was queerly silent. It broke into a little mutter.

"You are a famous man," Jehan said.

"Famous men die," Laeghaire said.

"You're in a sweet mood."

"So I am."

"I'll wager he puts you to command one of the flanks. His great men know you and respect you. He could use you instead of one of them. They would not object to it."

"They wouldn't dare."

Jehan grinned. They rode into the courtyard. They went up to the little hall and found William there with Lanfranc and Odo, the Bishop of Bayeux, and two men in palmer's clothes. William nodded to them when they came in.

"Are you all acquainted, my lords? Odo, that big bear is Jehan of the River's Edge, and the tall thin one is Laeghaire of the Long Road. Sit down, knights."

The two palmers looked disinterestedly around. Laeghaire found a stool and sat on it, but Jehan stood.

"One moment," William said to them, and turned to the palmers. He spoke to them. Laeghaire understood it and suddenly realized that it was bad Saxon the Duke spoke. He had not heard Saxon since Tosti's disappearance. His ears stretched to hear. The palmer who answered talked of a fyrd, and for a moment Laeghaire struggled to remember.

"Hunh," he said.

William raised his hand. "Sir Laeghaire?"

"Nothing, my lord."

He said it in Saxon, and William laughed. The palmer who had been talking turned toward him.

"Saxon?" he said.

"Irish."

The man grinned. He said, "What a polyglot band he has."

"This Irishman," William said, "has the gift of tongues. I'll put a white dove on his banner if he lives long enough. Here, let's get back to this."

The door opened and a Norman peasant trotted in. He brushed by Odo and Jehan without a pause or a look and came up by the palmers. He was a small, thin man with a face like a wild dog's.

"What?" William said.

"The Norwegians have been sighted off the coast of Ireland."

"The Norwegians?" Odo said.

"When?" William said.

"A good two weeks ago," the serf said. "Fishermen from Ponthieu saw them. They sailed in today."

"What were they doing fishing in the Irish Sea?"

The serf shrugged. "It's a poor season for fish. Why not?"

"How many of them?"

"Some fifty ships, they counted."

"Fifty. How many men to a Viking ship?"

"Eighty to a hundred and twenty," the serf said. "Or so I've heard." He looked around him. Nobody said anything.

"Harold will have his hands full. Irish, can he beat the Norwegians?"

"If he's not outnumbered and he can pick his ground," Laeghaire said. "Godwin's house has always been good warriors and he has the housekarls. The Norwegians aren't knights, either."

"So?"

"It's knights will beat the Saxons. Knights and horses."

"How do they fight?"

The serf looked at Laeghaire. Laeghaire shrugged. The serf said, "If you've been there, you can tell him better than I."

"On even ground, he'll put his housekarls in the center and the fyrd on the flanks and charge. The line will hold, and when they close ranks they'll make a wall with their shields. Against men on foot he has the advantage. No one can break that wall."

The serf nodded. He drew designs on the floor with his toe.

"And if he is attacked?"

"He'll choose his ground and stand behind that wall."

The palmer said, "That's so; I've seen it so."

"Good. Odo, I will see you this evening." He dismissed the palmers in Saxon. He waited until the prelate had left and the palmers, and turned to Jehan.

"Sir Jehan. You will be in charge of the camp by the coast. No violence and no drunkenness."

"My lord, they must have drink."

"They can drink without being drunk. Make some arrangements about women."

Jehan grinned at Laeghaire. "All women?"

"Leave his alone. You may leave."

The serf had sat down and was staring at the floor. William looked down at him. "Guy," he said.

The serf looked up.

"This knight is Laeghaire of the Long Road. I will put him in charge of the spies."

The serf looked at Laeghaire. "He's all right."

"Your judgment flatters me," Laeghaire said. He thrust out his legs in front of him. "I would not want to impose myself on you."

The serf's face darkened. Laeghaire glanced at William. William was watching the serf. His face was almost gentle.

"Your serfling has no sense of humor," Laeghaire said to William.

"He has no need of one."

"Then he's a lucky man."

"Your French is better than it used to be."

"You are a bright flame to learn by, my lord."

"Nor brighter than a star."

"Why, my lord, if stars will burn for you, you have no need of any other light."

"He has a quick tongue," Guy said.

"As merry with my tongue as any apostle," Laeghaire said.

"And easy with your sword as any devil," William said. "I'll start a church for you, Irish; God's Splendor, you need a Mass now and then."

The gentleness was gone out of his face, and his eyes glittered like the wolf's in the dream. Laeghaire grinned at him.

"Tomorrow," William said, "you'll go down by the Dives. I will have all the spies from England sent to you. Report what you think I might need to know."

He left by the rear door, and the serf Guy by the side. Laeghaire went after Guy. In the corridor he called after him. The serf turned and waited. Laeghaire went up to him. He stood a full head and shoulders taller than the serf.

"Will you be down by the Dives?" the serf said.

"Yes."

They went down to the courtyard. Laeghaire said, "If you hear more of Norway, tell me as well as the Duke."

"Why?"

"So I can understand what happens. Don't be an arrogant serf; I have no quarrel with you."

"I'll tell you. I hear from the fishermen. You ought not to talk to him like that."

"If you talk to me like that, I'll have a quarrel with you soon enough, and it's only a guilder for serfs. I mean nothing against him by it. It's my game, and I'll play it. He knows it."

He mounted his horse. "Are you going somewhere?"

"Yes," Guy said. "I'm going off to my lowly hut and sleep."

"My tent's by the wall, down from the east gate. See me tonight, or I'll come looking for you tomorrow."

"Yes, my lord."

Laeghaire laughed at him and rode out.

He talked that night with Guy and learned who came from England and why and when, and Guy also told him all that was important that had come before with the spies. They sat on the ground inside the tent and Hilde gave them wine and sat looking at them. Laeghaire saw her watching Guy. He told her afterward what they had said.

The next day they went down to the Dives and camped there, up on the rise behind the beach, very near the river. The fishermen had gone. Many knights, already come, were setting up their tents and pasturing out their horses. Jehan told four of them to hunt for better pasturage. Jehan sat in his saddle like a thick-shouldered Joab, giving orders, pleased with himself.

The knights began to come into the camp, alone, in pairs, in bands, from Normandy itself and from outside the duchy, from the Norman counties in Italy and up from the Spanish frontiers, from the Empire and from

Rome. They pitched their tents and put their horses to pasture by the sea and sat by their fires talking. They fought often, sometimes in mock jousts, and sometimes meaning it. Jehan was hard put to keep them from killing each other. They did get drunk, and they had their women. The only thing they dared not do was raid the villages near the river's mouth. The camp was a shambles, full of horses running loose and men shouting. The shouting never ceased. All night long they drank and fought and boasted, and all day long they boasted and fought and drank. The only difference was that at night they could not see where they were going and tripped over people and things and the fights were more dangerous.

One day Laeghaire rode back to Caen and spent much time with William, telling him what the spies had told him, and on the way back fell in with a band of knights from Italy. It was twilight by the time they reached the camp, and in the twilight the shouting and laughing were louder. Laeghaire separated from the Italian knights and went off toward his tent. Rolf came out to hold the horse. On his face was a great bruise.

"What happened?" Laeghaire said.

"A knight came by and tried to ride off with your lady."

"Is she all right?"

"Yes."

"Is the knight all right?"

"Yes. I shouted and he hit me and we wrestled, and then he ran off."

"Do you know who he was?"

"That big dark man at the fire by the rock that looks like a horse's back."

Laeghaire reined around and rode off. He passed by Jehan's fire and waved. Jehan waved back. Laeghaire came up to the rock that looked like a horse's back and rode around it. The fire was built against it. Three knights were there. One of them, a big dark man, had a smear of dust on the back of his surcoat.

One of the knights heard Laeghaire coming and started to turn. The black horse veered a little, shying from the fire, and Laeghaire wrenched him back. The rising knights jumped to either side. Laeghaire knocked one of them down with a swipe of his free arm. The black horse jumped the fire. His hind hoofs struck coals and scattered them in high arcs. Laeghaire saw the dark man running off and charged after him. He caught him in three of the black horse's long strides. He bent down, clinging to the reins and mane, and grabbed the knight's shoulder. He heaved him up, clawing and screaming, and the surcoat tore, and Laeghaire snatched at him with both hands. He flung the man across his saddlebows and spurred the horse straight for the sea. The horse, wild from the fire, bolted down into the water. They smashed through the breaking waves and were soaked through. Laeghaire was blinded by the salt. He spurred through water and the sea lapped up to his thighs and the horse began to swim and Laeghaire threw off the fighting screaming knight. Immediately he turned the horse back to land, and when he felt the horse's hoofs touch the ground he stopped and wheeled to look.

The knight could not swim. He thrashed and gurgled in the toppling waves, went under, and came up again, his mouth wide and running salt water. His flailing arms took him under again. Laeghaire turned to look over his shoulder. The shore was massed with men, all shouting and pointing. The knight came to the surface, a little closer; he was pushing himself up on the sea bottom. He staggered in that way until he was standing, in water to his armpits.

He screamed curses and waved his fist at Laeghaire, and Laeghaire began to laugh. The man floundered on.

Laeghaire turned the horse casually to block his way. The man tried to get around him but Laeghaire moved the horse each time. Finally the man jumped against him, trying to catch him and pull him down, and Laeghaire lifted his foot, put it on the man's chest, and pushed. The man fell and went under. When he came up, panting, Laeghaire said, "Don't bother my woman again."

He said it loud enough so that the men on the shore could hear.

"Let me by," the knight said.

"Pledge me your honor you will not bother my woman again."

"I pledge it. Let me by. I'm cold."

Laeghaire reached down and took him by the hair and shoulder. The man clung to Laeghaire's arms. The horse jumped back to the shore. Laeghaire dropped the man in the sand and rode off at a fast lope.

Jehan came to him later, when Laeghaire was in the tent and Hilde was hanging up his wet leggings. Jehan said, "You should not have done that."

"I did him no violence. He did me violence."

"You are no different. The rules are the rules."

"I have my reputation to consider. If I told you, and you had him punished, what would it do to my reputation? And now no man will bother Hilde."

"I still think it was wrong."

"Then it was wrong."

Jehan blew out through his nose. "You're going to get in trouble someday."

"I am always in trouble."

The next day, Laeghaire showed Rolf how to clean his mail and left him to do it while he went up to check his horses. At noon Hilde came to where he was combing out the stallion's tail. She had dinner for him. They sat down and ate.

"Are you really going to marry me, Laeghaire?"

"Yes."

"I don't think it's right."

"Why?"

"Rolf treats me as your lady. But that man tried to—to take me like a common camp-follower. I'm not fit for you."

"Sometimes I think it's the other way."

"Why? It's not true."

"Because I am not worth what you will give me."

"That's not so. That's what that man said, that priest, that Lanfranc. That's wrong. You're fine and noble and wonderful."

"That's what you wish I were, maybe. I'm not."

She shook her head. "No. Don't even talk about it."

"All right."

"It's pretty here, by the sea. Will you have land by the sea?"

"He'll give me land in the south and the north and the east."

"Let's have a place to live in by the sea."

"All right."

They talked of this for a while. He got up and untangled the burrs and snarls from the stallion's tail. She was happy. She got flowers and made a chain for her hair.

Laeghaire went off to Caen again the next day, to take to William a spy who had some special news of the Saxon coast guard. He came back that same night, very late. He rode up to the pasturage and unsaddled the black horse and started down toward the camp. He saw the three men in the little fringe of underbrush just before they jumped. He flung the saddle into one man's face. The two others pulled him down. He snatched out his dagger and stabbed and that man flinched away, gasping. In the dark he could not see their faces but he knew who they were. He caught the last of them around the waist and wrestled with him in the dirt and brush. The thorns scratched his hands and face. He felt the man's arms tighten around him. The others were urging him on in low voices. The man he fought wrenched him suddenly and fell on top of him. Laeghaire thrashed around. He felt the man's thumb grope for his eyes. He forced his hands down under the high collar and around the man's throat. The thumb jammed into his eye. Fire colors leaped inside his head. He brought his knee up hard into the man's groin. A hand tore at his arm. The man on top of him winced and his hands drew away. Laeghaire flung him off. The others closed in on him. One stank of blood. He fought to his knees. One of them kicked him in the chest. He caught that foot and yanked. The four bodies all crashed together. Suddenly one of them stood and ran off, bent over under the few trees. Laeghaire reached out blindly and caught a sleeve and staggered to his feet. He hit that man in the face with his fist. He felt bone break under his knuckles. He hit him again. The other man hit him in the small of the back. Laeghaire wheeled. He grappled with the other man and they went down. He heard running footsteps, going away. Only the one, now. His fingers curled around the man's windpipe. He rolled him over and lay on top of him and pressed his fingers down. The hands clubbed at him and the knees jabbed vainly. The man caught him by the hair and tried to tear him off. Laeghaire let go with his right hand and brought his elbow smashing into the man's face, once, twice, again. The hand in his hair loosened and fell, limp.

Laeghaire stood up. He took the man by the heels and dragged him out into the moonlight. It was the big dark man. He was still breathing. Laeghaire thought of killing him. He remembered Jehan and decided against it. He went back to where the brush was trampled down and found his dagger, covered with blood. He put it in the

boulders on the slopes.

"Your woman," Guy said. "She's Flemish."

"German." He wondered how much of her Guy had seen in the dim tent.

"And speaks no French."

"No."

"She must be lonely."

"I suppose she is."

They sat down. It was very dark outside the torch-light. The surf whispered, down on the beach.

"You fool, to bring her here."

"She wanted to come. Anyway, she's with me. I speak French."

"You're a fool anyway."

Laeghaire shrugged. "Any news of the Norwegians?"

"No. You?"

"Sighted off Skye a while ago."

"What's Skye?"

"One of those islands up there. Up at the north end of the Irish Sea. You know."

"Did you know Tosti?"

"Yes."

"He was here a while. The lord gave him money. The lord thinks he went to Norway."

"He hates his brother."

"Yes."

"What did he do with the money?"

Guy scratched his head. His long hair hung over his eyes. "He attacked that island, the big one, just off the south coast in the—"

"Wight."

"Yes." Guy grinned. His dog teeth were crooked. "He didn't take it."

"He's a strange man."

"Doesn't it make you feel important, to be working so close to things that move the whole world? We are changing things, you and I."

"Important? No."

Guy scowled. "But why not?"

"Because whatever changes we make aren't changes. And we aren't the men who would make changes. Only great ones make changes. And nothing important ever really changes, anyway."

"I'm a change. I was a serf and now I'm a servant of the Duke of Normandy, who is going to be the King of England."

"And you're still a serf. To them, you're a serf. To me, a serf."

"I am no man's man."

"You are William's man."

Guy frowned. He turned his head from side to side. "I'm going." He got to his feet. "I'll be in tomorrow, with him."

"Don't get angry, Guy."

"Why not?" Guy said. He turned and was gone. Laeghaire watched him go. He flung the torch into the sand and covered it up. He listened to the men and the sea. His face hurt. Why not? He looked up. The great star was long gone. It had stayed only eight days. He felt his ribs burning. He turned away from the swarm of the camp. He thought, Big star, take me with you. He put his hand against his side. His heart was throbbing too hard. He hated those knights. He hated the fires and the sea. His heart pounded and he heard the sea break in conflicting rhythms on the shore. His heart leaped under his fingers. He heard the sea break and saw in his mind the waves curling in their foaming glowing break, a long progression down the shore into the dark.

"Laeghaire?"

She was beside him; she put her hand on his arm. "Laeghaire, what are you staring at?"

"Nothing. Come on."

* * *

The knights knew when William had come and they calmed down for a while, but one night there was a great fight over some of the women, and William rode down on his gray gelding and flogged them with his voice until they quailed and drew off. The camp was too big to control, and the men fought despite William; but when William came they stopped and stood, watching him. He prowled around them like a wolf, waiting for one of them to do something wrong, and as soon as he was gone the turmoil and the fighting and drinking broke out again. There was never any silence, even at night. The summer was hot and the days full of sun. Hilde grew brown as a farmer and her hair hung dead-white down her back. No man touched her.

The boats lined the shore, hundreds of them, and the horses they led on and off to accustom them to riding on the sea. The men joked about it, but it was hard work. The horses were frightened of the boats and would rear and try to leap off when they saw the land going away from them. One of Fitz-Osbern's horses climbed over the rail of one boat and swam all the way back, dragging his boy through the waves.

Guy taught Hilde a little French, more by his persistence than her learning, and she talked haltingly with him and with Laeghaire and listened when they talked. Laeghaire went to the councils, where the Duke gave out orders to stop the fighting and drunkenness and the women, orders that never had effect, and every day knights paid their fines to him. They said his treasury had doubled since the knights came.

The archers swaggered in bands and practiced on the hillside. Laeghaire went to watch them and heard them joking and saw them shooting their bolts over long distances straight to the mark, easily as if they shot quail.

He heard them talking, and he answered questions that they asked him. They knew him; they all knew him. He shot a little, with his long German bow, but the range of his bow was less than that of the crossbows.

By midsummer they knew they should have sailed. The winds blew contrary. The winds were north or west, never right. The wind blew steadily out of the north and there was a week of rain, and that only made them fight harder, while William rode along the shore in his fur cloak and cursed the wind and the rain and the boats that could not sail into the wind. The blue banner that flew by his tent hung sodden in the rain, or stood on the wind that blew from the north or the west. Every day the Duke came out of his tent and looked at that banner, blessed by the Pope, and swore up and down against it and the wind.

They said—the Saxon spies, fewer now, with the Saxon coast guard and Harold Godwinson the usurper and the breaker of oaths watching every day for the Normans to come—they said that the Norwegians had been seen off the coast of the Scots. The wind blew contrary, and William swore and said he would fight Harold, either Harold, the Saxon or the Norwegian, whichever held England. There was rebellion in the north of England, which did William little good, and William fretted that the Norwegians would use that to win England.

The King of Norway was Harald Hardraada, the great warrior, the fabled victor of the Bosporus. They told stories about him by the fires. Laeghaire heard them and half wished that Hardraada would win England, so that he, Laeghaire, could fight him. He wondered if Hardraada knew his name.

The summer ended in a fit of west winds. After the equinox, Laeghaire met a little wizened man from Wessex, and sat for a few moments with him in the tent. He went out of the tent, stopped only to call Guy, and rode to William's tent. He spat at the base of the banner staff and went into the tent without a word. The guards said nothing to him.

"What now?" William said.

"Harold has summoned out the fyrd again. The Norwegians have landed in Northumbria."

William flung back his head. "By the glorious, the almighty, the magnificent splendor of the one true God. How is the wind?"

"Due west."

"I am sinned against."

Guy came in. Laeghaire told him of the landing. Guy looked at William. His eyes were hot and sharp.

"We sail," William said.

"The wind," Guy said.

"Nonetheless, we are sailing. We can go with a west wind up to the mouth of the Somme. To Saint-Valéry. It's closer."

"Do we hold the Somme?"

The Duke went by him. Guy looked at Laeghaire again.

"It's the great ones who change things," Laeghaire said. He could hear the horns blasting. He went out and rode back to get Hilde.

So they sailed to Saint-Valéry, on the mouth of the Somme. Hilde was sick all the way, and Laeghaire held her in his lap so that she would not slip under the hoofs of the horses. They went ashore at Saint-Valéry and camped, and during the night the wind came up in a full gale and veered around the circle. By dawn it was blowing steadily from the southeast. By the time the sun was fully up, the orders were out to board the boats again.

Laeghaire and Rolf led the horses onto their boat. The

black horse kicked and reared. He broke from Rolf's grip and charged across the boat and came up on the edge and snorted, pawing at the rail of the boat. He backed up in a wild rush and knocked over several barrels.

"Catch that horse—"

Laeghaire threw the stallion's lead rope to Rolf. He shoved away two men that stood bewildered before him. He shouted, "Clear this boat." The black horse was bucking on the deck. His hoofs rang on the boards. Barrels and a bale of hay skidded under his hoofs. Laeghaire dodged them and caught the rope. The horse reared. He bolted. Laeghaire braced himself. The horse dragged him a few feet. He reached out and wrapped his arm around the mast. The horse came up hard on the end of the rope and fell. Laeghaire ran to him and sat on his head. He shouted for more rope. Immediately there were men around him, dodging the horse's striking hoofs. He took a rope and hobbled the horse and stood up. The horse got to his feet and stood, shaking his head.

"What happened to him?" Rolf said.

"Nervous." Laeghaire took the horse to the back of the boat and tethered him.

"He was all right yesterday."

"He gets a little wild sometimes. Besides, I led him on yesterday. Get the stallion up here."

The stallion came on quietly, steadily. Laeghaire turned to look back. The whole shore was dark and swarming with men and horses. They floundered in the shallow breaking waves and howled for help. A horse broke loose and dashed back up the beach, and twenty men chased it, shouting and waving their arms, and the horse neighed, wild-eyed, and bolted on. The boats that were filled were moving away to make room, and the swarm spread out, pushing into the water, bobbing on the waves.

Laeghaire went back for Hilde and brought her on the boat. He stayed there with her for a while and they watched the crowd. She was flushed and happy. "It's wonderful. It's wonderful."

The boat next to theirs shoved off. The sails opened. The canvas snapped taut. The horses quivered and arched their necks. Three men sat on the rail, their legs trailing over, and shouted to the people on the next boat.

"I have to go with William," Laeghaire said. "Rolf will take care of you."

"Why do I have to stay here?"

"Because I said so."

"Cast off," somebody shouted.

Laeghaire shouldered through the mob. He could smell the sweat of excitement on them. He pushed away from them, vaulted the rail, and waded ashore. The beach was almost empty now. He stood a moment, looking at the empty beach. Horse tracks and man tracks and scattered dung littered it, as far as he could see. A forgotten piece of equipment lay on the sand up by the high-tide line.

"I'm going to England," he said.

He smiled at the empty beach and spat into the sand. He turned and walked down the beach toward William's boat. It was the last to cast off. The blue banner stretched out on the wind. He waded out and hoisted himself over the rail.

Guy was immediately beside him. Guy's eyes were bright and his mouth worked. He pulled Laeghaire's sleeve. "Isn't it exciting?"

"Hunh."

Guy turned on him. "It is. We are all going on a great adventure."

"You sound like a child."

"I've never gone far from my own place before. I've never left Normandy."

"You'll leave once too often, if you take up fighting for pay."

Guy was angry. He turned and bulled his way through the massed knights. They stepped aside and called angrily after him, but he never turned; he went straight on and out of sight. Laeghaire stood at the rail and watched the waves and the fading shore.

He was violently sick as soon as they reached the rough water. The sight of the chopping waves and the gulls that followed them made black dots jump before his eyes. Half the others were sick too. They lay on the deck with their heads over the edge and vomited into the crisp blue sea. Or they lay in the middle of the deck and now and then stumbled to the edge, trampling on the men prone beneath them, because William did not wish his boat fouled.

Laeghaire recovered quicker than most of them and sat with his back to the mast, weak-legged, listening to the sailors tell stories to the knights. One of them had seen a sea serpent. He swore it was five hundred yards long and that it had three heads. The knights made appropriate noises. They moved carefully, watchful of their light stomachs.

Nobody ate anything all that day. By nightfall, Laeghaire was ready to try something. He got up and walked around, feeling much steadier and stronger. He found Guy playing the fingers game with an archer and said, "Do you have anything to eat?"

"There's meat up on the foredeck." Guy held up his clenched fist. He counted. Laeghaire stepped by him. On the foredeck he found a small fire and meat on skewers. The Duke sat cross-legged on the deck with his hands greasy from eating. William was talking to a man in a jongleur's clothes. The jongleur said something and

William laughed.

"Tell your jest to the Irish," William said. "He's the great wit of my captains. Irish, come here."

"My lord."

The jongleur reached for his lute. He sat back and began to play. William glanced at him.

"I saw you were sick," William said to Laeghaire.

"Yes."

"No fit place for a knight. What do you know of Wessex? What is Pevensey?"

"Old fort. Very old. Roman, maybe. Nothing but a bunch of stone walls."

"Has it got a harbor, or a bay, or anything?"

Laeghaire shut his eyes. Wessex. "No. Not Pevensey. There is a harbor a little way up the coast from it."

William's head turned. "Guy."

Guy came up to the foredeck.

"Is there a town near Pevensey? Northeast of it? Go on, Laeghaire."

"It's a fishing village," Laeghaire said. Parts came back to him. He tried to fit them together. "Two rivers, and a low sandspit between them—that's the town. Very well protected. There are hills just inland of it, good rolling hills."

"Yes," Guy said.

"Hastings," Laeghaire said.

"Yes," Guy said.

"Good," William said. "We will occupy that town, if we can." He paused. His eyes burned steadily on Laeghaire. "You have a good memory, Irish."

Laeghaire nodded.

"From this town, if we can take it, we will attack all the country around. My lord d'Avranches."

D'Avranches swung his head toward them. He was a broad-faced Norman and William's greatest lord. William told him what they would do. D'Avranches listened calmly. He asked a few questions and turned away. He got up and went slowly down the deck, crowding men out of his way. He met the lord of Warenne, a way down the deck, and stood talking. William's eyes stayed angrily on him.

"Someday," he said, "I will make him a little less dangerous."

"When it suits you, my lord," Laeghaire said.

William laughed. "I hope your sons' sons are as good as you, when my son's son is on the throne."

"Your Grace."

"When you raid, Irish, burn and loot. Whatever loot you take is yours. You'll need it, to furnish your earldom."

"You are kind, Your Grace."

"I'm not King yet."

"Who doubts?"

William smiled. "Tailleford," he said. He turned to the jongleur. "Tailleford, play us a war song."

In the twilight they bound torches to each corner of the boat and to the top of the mast. The other boats also did so. Slowly, the torches multiplied, spreading out, glimmering on the water between the boats. The bits of fire, blown by the wind, stretched on and on and on, deep into the haze, past sight, and still went on. The sun was down, and the blackness closed in around them, but on the deck of William's boat the light filled all the corners.

Laeghaire went to sleep on the foredeck, with his cloak wrapped into a bundle under his head. He woke up in the false dawn. The deck was littered with sleeping men. He went to the side of the ship and made water. On the way back to his place, stepping over the bodies of the sleepers, he paused by the mast and drank from the wineskin there. It was still chilly from the night air. He stood a moment, rolling the water on his tongue. The ship rolled slightly under his feet. He went back to his place. William sat in the bow, asleep, leaning against the angle of the rail. Laeghaire rested his weight against the rail and studied William. He smiled in his sleep. His hair was redder and his skin glowed in the first light of the sun. There was gray in his hair. The ridge of his cheekbone showed through the skin there.

He's only a little older than I, Laeghaire thought. We are neither of us young men any more. I am nearly forty. He was born to it, what he is, and I was born to what I am. And our sons . . .

He watched William come awake. He woke easily, stretching, saw Laeghaire and grinned. His eyes were half closed. Laeghaire saw them glitter. William got up and went down the deck. He yawned and moved his shoulders, loosening his muscles. His shadow ran over the men lying dull asleep on the deck of the ship; his shadow was long as the boat, from the sun that had just risen.

The English coast was long and low and gray. They moved swiftly on into it, the hundreds of little boats, nosing through the faint mist. Laeghaire watched the coast move in toward him. The features of this shore defined themselves and grew slowly familiar, as if he were coming home. He thought it might be that. He would have an earldom here, and a castle, and lands and serfs. He would have his own band of retainers. He would have his own knights and his own tenants. He would sit in the King's council, and when they spoke of him, he would be Laeghaire, Earl of Such-and-Such, not Laeghaire of the Long Road. When he died he would have six sons to carry his coffin to the churchyard of the church he would build, and his daughters with silvery hair would weep for him. He would never leave his land.

"All in my hands," he said, and Guy turned to look up at him.

"Will you build real castles, knight?"

"Yes. Of solid stone. Get along, serf."

They nosed in against the beach, and the shock of their landing toppled two men into the water. The others cheered. They leaped off in droves, laughing. They drew their swords and hacked at the soil. Laeghaire climbed over the rail and felt the strong land under his feet and shouted. He almost fell over; the land seemed to move under him like the deck of a ship. He turned to help Guy down.

"Any more noise," he shouted, "and we'll have the Saxons down on us."

Guy, laughing, ran a few steps backward. He turned and flung up his arms. "The Promised Land."

William climbed over the rail before they put out the plank. He jumped. He took a step and stumbled and fell on his face, in full sight of all his men.

Guy gasped and put his hand to his mouth. Fitz-Osbern leaped to help. The Duke shook him off. He stood. He raised his hands; he had sand on his sleeves. He cried, "I have seized England with both hands."

His voice rang in a stony quiet. The men cheered suddenly. They turned, relaxing, reassured. The horses were coming off the boats, clattering down the gangplanks. Laeghaire saw William turn, say something to Fitz-Osbern, and walk up the beach, apart from the others. Laeghaire jogged through the crowd, wheeling by horses and laughing men. He found Hilde and Rolf, standing by the boat, watching the freed horses fly off the plank to the solid ground. Laeghaire put his arm around Hilde.

The brown stallion came easily down the gangplank and stopped, and Rolf went to bring him. The black horse galloped down with a neigh and kicked up his heels. The other horses began to neigh.

"Listen. They are cheering for us." Jehan rode up, grinning. "The Duke wants you, as usual."

Rolf was saddling the black horse. Laeghaire drew Hilde in between the horses and trotted off to William.

"That Roman fort is about a hundred paces down from here," William said. "Get some men together and make an earthwork in it."

Laeghaire went back, mounted the black horse, and rode around collecting men. He took the largest groups he could find, the archers and the foot soldiers, who had nothing to do. They got spades from the supply boat and followed him up to the fort. The fort was almost overgrown. Laeghaire took his lance and drew a circle around it, riding with the lance dragging in the soft earth. The men bent and began to dig. They talked incessantly. Laeghaire rode back and ordered up some knights to guard them. The sun rose higher; it would be hot. He took his feet out of the stirrups and relaxed, watching the men dig.

Below, on the beach, the rest of the army was getting organized. The boats drew off and were anchored offshore. Laeghaire could see the men gathering around the banner staff blessed by the Pope. He saw a band of knights gallop off to the east, along the coast, going to find Hastings.

The sun climbed up to the zenith, and Hilde brought him dinner. A new group of men came up to relieve the diggers. On the beach, the last of the boats was unloaded. The knights came back and met William. Laeghaire wanted to go down there and find out what was happening. He rode once around the fort; the earthwork was almost completed.

That night they slept inside the earthwork. Hilde, wrapped in blankets, shivered beside Laeghaire. It was not cold. She dreamed, and woke him once, muttering and sighing in her sleep.

At dawn they gathered again on the beach. William's voice rose over them. He ordered some four hundred men to stay in the fort of Pevensey. They growled and moaned and went up to the lonely little fort. The rest of the army prepared to march. Within moments the beach was a swarm of men and horses. Laeghaire put Hilde and Rolf both on the brown stallion. The stallion stood in the jumble of bodies, calm, taking the shock of colliding horses, never moving. Laeghaire put his hand on the horse's neck. The stallion lowered his head. His forelock dipped into his eyes. Once in Thuringia they had gathered up, and heard the Duke there talk of the great and glorious work they were doing for God against the pagans.

The tangle of horses and knights and archers was sweeping quickly into order. Laeghaire watched the men fall into groups, and the groups into lines. The banner blessed by the Pope traveled swiftly along the beach. Behind it William rode at full gallop. His fur cloak swirled around him. The men sent up a great shout for him. It grew, as he passed, into a roar that made the waves silent. Laeghaire sat without a word, beside the stallion that never moved. He watched the Duke ride after his banner. William was the finest horseman and the greatest warrior in his army. Laeghaire felt as if the cheering were for him.

The shouting died slowly. Under it grew the steady noises of the march. They rode at an easy pace. The men on foot marched a little apart from the others. Laeghaire heard them laughing and telling stories. The men around him were silent. They were all knights, horsemen. Laeghaire felt the black horse moving under him.

"Where are we going?" Hilde said. She looked down at him from the brown stallion's back. She held the rope of the pack with one hand, and her body moved easily with the movements of the horse.

"Just a little way. I'll have to go raiding. I'll leave you with Rolf."

"You'll be all right, won't you?"

"Yes."

"It would be so horrible if anything happened to you now, when we have everything almost in our hands."

"I won't die."

Her face was troubled. She looked at him strangely. When she turned her face away, she was still frowning.

"What's the matter?"

"I don't know. I had a feeling . . ."

"Sh."

He saw William, riding under the shadow of the blue banner. He thought he could almost see William's muscles and bones through his surcoat and mail. Muscles and bones like me. I'm not a young man any more.

In a few days, in a few months, it would not matter if he were young or not. He watched William riding, his head dark against the sky.

They rode along the shore. The scouts rode on ahead of them. Laeghaire saw some of them riding in the thin cover of trees on the top of the cliff by the sea. Guy was riding a chunky dun horse, up ahead, crouched awkwardly in the saddle. He was not a horseman: Little spymaster, you're useless now. The army stretched out around him. The boats followed them, close in to the shore. The army ran easily over land and water.

Hardraada. What had happened? The Norwegians and Tosti must have invaded. Perhaps they had not. The legend was very big. Breaking the golden chain across the straits by Constantinople with the prow of his longship. Sooner or later we will have to fight him. Unless Godwin's son had beaten him. The housekarls are . . .

Nonetheless. Hardraada was a king, Harold was a king. I hope we fight him. I fight him. There was Hastings.

He called to Rolf to saddle the brown stallion, but the old men of the city were already out on the sand, waiting, and they surrendered Hastings almost before the army had stopped its marching.

Odo said a Mass the next morning, under the dawn sky. His voice was strong and wild. He blessed them all, the men crowded into the market and the boats in the harbor. Laeghaire swung his weight from one foot to the other. "Go out and raid," William had said. "Be back here by sundown tonight. I want your report on what you see, what you take, whatever there is that you know that you did not know when you left. Everything." And, turning, slower, "The old men here say that the Norwegians landed in the north. They took York but the—but Godwinson rode north and fought them. Hardraada is dead. And Tosti Godwinson too. He was with Hardraada."

"Tosti."

"And now in all Christendom there is no greater warrior than you, Irish. Your rival's dead."

"My lord."

"One of my lords told me. Tosny. He's traveled in Italy. He remarked that I had you in my army, and said that as fighting men go, you ranked only below Hardraada."

"I've never been to Italy."

Odo's voice slid through his ears and he shut it out.

"Not in the flesh, perhaps. But you've been to Italy. . . . What does your trade say of the d'Hautvilles?"

"Dirty fighters. Low pay, long wars, bad risks, good booty, good women."

"Who told you that?"

Laeghaire shrugged. "My informers."

"Informers."

"Merchants, gypsies, innkeepers on the roads, other fighters."

"What do they say about me?"

Laeghaire grinned. "Bad pay, no women, hard fighting. The fighting's good, they say."

"Hunh," William said through Odo's voice.

Odo finished and they prayed. Laeghaire prayed deeply. He wanted to come back. Hardraada was dead. He prayed for Hardraada. He turned away and waved his arm. The horns were blasting all through the marketplace.

"Mount up," he shouted, and went to his horse. His men gathered and mounted, all separate from the others. It seemed to Laeghaire that the whole army stood and watched them mount. These men, his men, two hundred men, so few compared to the others. But when they had mounted they seemed greater. He lifted his hand and they were ready, like unhooded hawks. He thought he saw something in the faces of the vast crowd that watched him; he could not understand it.

He rode up to William and saluted him. William said, "Come back, remember."

"My lord, would I leave you?"

"Fare well."

Laeghaire put on his helmet and rode back. He signaled to his men. They rode off at a jog. They rode north.

They burned several fields that day and were back in time to eat supper with the rest of the army. The Saxons made no resistance. He saw nothing of them but the peasants' backs, running for shelter in the walled houses. The land was open and rolling, with many trees and little forests. They rode easily through it. It was rich, dark land.

The next day they rode again, and the day after that. The Saxons tried to defend against them that day, when they attacked a village. The Saxons fought them in the streets. It was easy fighting. The horses ran the Saxons down and they fled. Laeghaire had his men torch all the buildings. That night they did not return to Hastings until the moon had set. They slept all the next day and did not ride the day after that.

Hilde was very happy. She had a little hut all to herself, except for Laeghaire and Rolf, and she pretended it was a castle. She swept it every morning and cooked in it and sang all day long. Laeghaire enjoyed this. He had made her happy. At night when she slept next to him he listened to her breathing and thought that she smiled in her sleep. Her songs were happy songs. She needed him to make her happy.

William ordered him out after the few days' resting and told him to capture a Saxon and ask him what Harold Godwinson was doing. William told him to stay somewhere near Hastings but that he had no need to come back every night, if his Saxon gave him any reason to stay out. Laeghaire rode out with fifty men. They rode due north, well past the farthest limit of their previous raidings, and Laeghaire spread his men out in a long line through the fields and little stands of oak. In the midafternoon they brought a Saxon to him. He ordered them all to make a night camp, and took the Saxon into the shade of an oak tree.

The Saxon was bound hand and foot. Laeghaire got some dried meat and ate it. He looked at the Saxon. "Take off the rope," he said.

"My lord—" the Norman said.

"Cut him loose. I want to talk to him, and a man who's bound can't talk right."

He drank water from a bucket while they untied the Saxon. The man's eyes followed his hands.

"Are you thirsty?" Laeghaire asked in Saxon.

"Yes."

Laeghaire put the bucket in front of him.

"It's Norman water," the man said.

"It's English water."

"It's a Norman bucket."

"If you're thirsty, drink."

The man plunged his hands into the water and scooped it up and drank. He drank feverishly.

"What is your name?" Laeghaire asked.

"Byrth."

"Where are you from?"

"I have land of the lord of Dunmer."

"Much land?"

"No."

"Do you hunt? In these woods?"

"Yes. That's why they caught me."

"Then you know the land."

"Yes."

"Good," Laeghaire said. "You'll guide us."

"No."

"You want your land, don't you?"

"You'll never beat Harold. Not King Harold."

"He's a foul oath-breaking usurper prince."

"He'll kill me if he finds out."

"He'll never know. Besides, he doesn't seem to be in any great hurry to come and catch us."

"He's coming. He's in London already."

"He'll never come out. He's frightened of us."

"No, he isn't."

"Then why doesn't he come fight us?"

"He will. You wait around."

"We will." Laeghaire grinned.

* * *

He sent all this by a messenger back to Hastings. He collected his men and set off to scout the countryside. So far they had not taken any booty. After moonrise, they turned a little west, and found a walled house, near a river. They withdrew and pretended they were going away, and in the middle of the night attacked it and burned part of the wall and one of the inside buildings. The Saxons surrendered, and they spent the rest of the night sacking the place. Laeghaire found a little chest of silver pieces hidden in the floor under the lord's chair, where a lot of Saxons kept their hoards, and carted it back to Hastings. He woke up Hilde and told her about the raid. She was happy. She smiled at him.

A few days later William gave him permission to go off again. Laeghaire took the same fifty men and rode toward London. He still had Byrth and he made Byrth guide them. Byrth tried to take them onto the wrong road but Laeghaire knew enough of the way to keep them straight. In the night they slept until the moon rose and rode out to a little village Byrth knew of.

The Normans kept to the woods as far as they could, and charged across the half-harvested fields to the village. They waved their torches and made a lot of noise. The people fled out of the huts, running for the fort. The Normans, whooping and whirling their torches, set fire to the huts. The flames caught quickly and leaped up with a merry crackling.

Laeghaire rode up and down the square, shouting and making his horse buck. His men galloped around the burning huts, and some of them set the field on fire. Laeghaire collected several of his men and sent them to herd out the cattle and swine that were in the common pasturage, before the fire caught in the dry grass. He turned and rode back up the square. His men were racing off, bored with this sport.

He passed close to a building. Something struck the side of his helmet. He reeled in the saddle. He straightened and wheeled the horse. A slight man burst out of the shelter of the burning building and ran off through the high grass behind the village, headed for the narrow band of the woods nearby. Laeghaire spurred the horse between the fires. The slight man was far ahead of him, running fleetly. Laeghaire kicked the horse. The horse bolted after the man. He shied suddenly and Laeghaire almost went off. He looked down. A wide ditch lay before him. He laughed and galloped along it. The slight man had almost reached the woods. Laeghaire found the shallow part of the ditch, put the horse across it, and chased.

That small figure vanished in the trees. Laeghaire charged across the last of the field and into the forest. He saw nothing. He rode around and put the trees between him and the fire. He began to laugh. The man was huddled in a fork of a tree, clear against the leaping fire.

Laeghaire rode straight to the tree. The man knew he had been seen; he leaped down. He ran two steps. Laeghaire swore. It was a woman. He lashed the horse, bent, and scooped her across his saddle. She fought like a man, silently, her fists thudding on his mail and his face. He bent his head and wrapped his arm around her. He veered the horse into the deep woods. The horse was in a full gallop. The girl cried out suddenly.

He caught her right wrist and twisted it behind her back. The branches swiped at them. He bent down, bending her with him. He reined the horse in suddenly.

Her face was bright with pain. He eased her arm a little. Her eyes stared scornfully at him.

"Ugly little bitch," he said.

She spat at him and struck awkwardly with her free hand. He wrenched her right arm. She gasped and bit her lip and the tears streamed from her eyes.

He felt blood on her hand. She had cut her hand on the edge of his helmet. He struck her on the side of the face. She slacked against him. He held her across the saddle and rode into the woods. He rode away from where his men would gather. The trees were thick. He held her easily, waiting for her to wake up. He found a hollow where two hills came steeply together, where the trees grew far apart and the grass was tall. He dismounted, dropped his reins, and put her down.

She wore a man's clothes and a loose heavy cloak. The bones of her face were broad and heavy like a man's. She was ugly. He laid her head on his knee and shook her. "Wake up."

She came awake like a baby cat. Now she fought like a woman, squealing and scratching. He held her by the shoulders and shook her wildly. Her hair flew loose around them. She stopped fighting. Her breath whistled through her teeth.

"Be quiet," he said. "I'll hit you again."

"Then hit me."

He raised his fist.

She looked at his fist, in the heavy glove studded with brass. She looked back at him. "No," she said.

He laughed. It was getting light; he could see her face and the eyes blazing. She was not afraid of him. The eyes were full of that. They were wide-spaced, intelligent eyes.

He lowered his fist and sat down. He took off his helmet and tossed it aside. He looked at the horse, browsing in the high seeding grass.

"I hate you, Norman," she said.

"I'm not a Norman."

"You are."

"Irish. I fight for the Duke of Normandy."

"Why?"

"He pays me."

"He pays you. He pays you."

He looked at her. He laughed. "I dreamed of you."

"How could you?"

"I did."

He looked at her. Her teeth were crooked and her nose was long. But her eyes blazed in her face like the fire through the trees. He wanted this woman; as if he had never had a woman before, he wanted her.

"Do you live in that village?"

"No. I live in the castle."

"Castle. You call that a castle. What were you doing in the village?"

"There was a sick man there."

"You Saxons. You have hearts like mud."

"Who else would have tended him?"

"Do you serve the lord?"

"I am his daughter."

"And you tend these . . . sheep?"

"Who else? I'm ugly—no man will marry me for love, and I'll die old and without children, and I have to do something."

"What's your name?"

"Does a man ask the name of a woman he intends to rape?"

"This man might."

He looked back at the horse. She said, "You want me to run away, don't you?"

"It would . . . make things easier."

He pulled off his boots and wiped the dirt from the spurs. He put the boots down neatly.

"Does your wife take your boots off for you?"

"Sometimes."

He laughed at her. She frowned. "I won't run."

"I didn't think you would."

"Did you dream that I was ugly?"

"I dreamed you were a witch. Tell me your name."

"Why?"

"That I might woo you with kind words."

"What is your name?"

"Laeghaire."

"Laeghaire."

He turned. He looked at the sky. It was almost light. He took off his gloves and went to find his helmet. He found the helmet and put the gloves in it and rested the helmet against a tree bole. He unbuckled his sword belt and tossed it by the helmet. He undid the mail shirt and pulled it and the surcoat over his head.

As soon as he had it over his head she was running. She ran straight for the heavy brush. He saw that she would have to swerve and he ran to cut her off. She veered, and he caught her in two steps, and they fell together and rolled and came to rest, interlocked in each other's arms, facing each other. She stared at him and her eyes flashed dully, like fire on armor. He straightened her hair under his fingers. Suddenly her hands flew up and locked behind his head and she drew his head down, awkwardly, and kissed him, and he kissed her. He reached up and undid her fingers and moved her hands down to hold him by the waist. He kissed her eyes, holding her face between his hands. Her hands moved clumsily at his waist. He undid the laces of the man's shirt she wore and drew it over her head. She shivered in the cool. He held her close to him. He felt her flesh under his hands and bent to kiss her and stripped her naked while he kissed her. Her knees parted. He moved over her. The tears sprang from her eyes but she never cried out.

He was tired and she exhausted him. He took her back to the horse and lay down with her, wrapped up in his cloak. She was silent. He dozed. Now and then he woke, when her hands on his body trembled. The day passed slowly over him. He woke up in the late afternoon and took her again. After that they lay silently together.

"Don't be afraid," he said.

"I'm not afraid."

He put his hand on her cheek and turned her face toward his. He kissed her. Her cheeks were red and rough from his beard.

Toward dark the horse suddenly raised his head and snorted. Laeghaire sat up. "Get dressed," he said. "Hurry." He went and put on his clothes and stood by the tree where his sword leaned, stamping his feet into his boots.

He heard a dim shout and went to the horse and held its muzzle. She came to him.

"That's my father."

"I know."

She looked away. She was very close to him. He put his arm around her and drew her against him.

"Will they know?"

"Will you tell them?"

"I—"

"Be quiet. Listen to me. I have never wanted a woman before the way I want you."

She turned her head to look at him. He stepped away, picked up his helmet and sword belt, and mounted. He put on the gloves and the helmet. He reined the horse away and spurred him up the opposite hill. He never looked back. The shouts grew fainter and fainter.

He found his men by noon. They woke up and watched him ride in. He was very tired. His face felt tight. He tethered the horse and rolled himself into his cloak and slept.

He had not slept very long before the shouting woke him up. He whirled up, throwing away his cloak, and saw the men running toward him. His Normans were grabbing up their swords and jumping to make a ring around the camp. The horses trampled and snorted by the little stream. The fires jumped and boomed. Laeghaire snatched up his sword and ran to join the ring. He shouted to the Normans to brace. The Saxons called out to one another and yelled war cries. They collided with the Norman ring. The fighting was wild. Laeghaire spread his feet and whipped his sword around him.

He would never be uprooted. The blade smashed against flesh and bone and stuck and he hauled it free with a twist of his wrists. A body fell against his hip and he struck at it, but it was already dead. He whirled to avoid an ax. The great edge sheared through the air around his head. He saw bright eyes, a small curled mouth in a tangle of beard; he brought his sword around in a lifting arc and saw the eyes glaze and the mouth dampen. That man fell, and he was leaping away from another sword before the corpse struck the earth. Now they were falling back, those Saxons. He hacked at them, howled at them to stand and fight; they began to run, turning their backs and running, and he ran after them. He was suddenly aware that his Normans were on all sides, and he shouted for them to run down these coward Saxons.

They chased them through the trees until there were no more Saxons before them. Laeghaire stopped and his men stopped. Laeghaire waved his arm. "Let's go back. They're gone."

They went back and cleared the camp of the dead and wounded. There were many dead Saxons and several wounded. Laeghaire stood by watching while they were tended and bound. He thought that he would let them go. He poked idly at the torn ground with the tip of his sword. One of them might be her father or brother.

The swelling voices of his men, triumphant, were all

around him. He dug up the earth. He heard, abruptly, "God's Sacred Heart, they call him right. He is a devil."

And another voice: "Shut up, you fool. He's right over there."

Laeghaire straightened. "I heard, and I'm a little sick of the epithet." He sheathed his sword and went off to sleep again.

The next night they came on a great field of corn, unharvested. Laeghaire sent men to see if there were sentries, and they waited; they made torches and lit them. The riders came back and said that there was a village and a great walled manor not far away, but no people in sight.

They galloped into the overripe corn and hardly had to lean from their saddles to set it on fire. They rode in a single long line, jumping the ditches that marked off each individual strip from its neighbor. The fire caught on and built behind them. The corn burned like tinder. It flared and howled and the wind came stronger and harried it after the Normans. They bolted from the field and Laeghaire turned and saw the flames reaching halfway to the sky, huge and curling and snapping sparks into the air. Like men, like warriors, the flames moved, like men with great supple arms, galloping over the field. His own men were little black shadows racing before it. He fought the black horse with one hand and watched the flames. The horse half reared. A family of field mice ran squeaking under the striking hoofs.

"Let's go."

They turned, wheeling all at once like dancers, laughing and shouting. He knew they laughed and shouted, but the flames' roaring drowned out all the noise, and even drowned its own noise, and the noise was like a vast silence. They raced away, whooping. The farther they rode from the fire, the more their voices came back. They galloped close to the village and the manor house, and flung their torches into the empty village square.

That night he had them set Byrth free. Byrth walked straight out of the camp, headed north. Laeghaire followed him carefully. Outside the camp, Byrth turned to the east and began to jog. He jogged across an open stretch of meadow. The moonlight flooded the meadow. Byrth ran with his shoulders raised and his head down, like an ox. Laeghaire stood in the dark trees, watching. It was cold. He waited until Byrth was out of sight. He sat down and wriggled his fingers inside his gloves.

Murrough, he thought, and was very sad. He stripped the bark from a drooping twig and shredded the bark. His hair fell into his eyes. He took off his right glove and fisted his hand and tucked it into his armpit, to warm his fingers. The glove, empty, collapsed and lay on his knee like a crushed hand. The studs were chipped and scratched.

The wind blew down the tall dry grass in the meadow; here he was protected against the wind. He watched the wind make rippling in the grass. The grass moved and a stag came from the trees, slowly, his head raised and his big ears wide. His antlers were shiny in the moonlight. He was trying to get to the water, to the stream that Laeghaire's men were camped by. They must have camped right over this stag's usual trail. He stood a long time, sniffing the wind and listening. He started across the meadow, his eyes wide. He was intent on the trees Laeghaire sat among, the trees that shielded the Norman camp. After him came two does. They moved uneasily across the meadow, quick, beautifully awkward with their long legs and their long slim necks and small heads.

They disappeared into the trees on the other side. Laeghaire took his hand from his armpit and put on the
glove. The shreds of the bark lay in a heap by his feet,
and the peeled twig was bright as a badge.

Rolf took the horse. Hilde smiled at him. "I'm glad you're back," she said. She put her hand on his arm. He kissed her.

"What did you do?" she said.

He thought of the woman. "Nothing. We just raided. Burned a few villages and fields." If he looked at her, she would know. He went into the hut. Rolf brought in his shield. Hilde told him what had happened while he was gone. Her voice was uncertain. She knows anyhow.

"Is William here?"

"Yes," she said. "Laeghaire, is anything wrong?"

"No." He took her by the shoulders and kissed her. She sighed. That made it all right for her. He went outside again, and she came up right behind him.

"He said you were to come and see him when you came," she said. She put her hand flat on his back, and he felt with his back her five fingers spread out. She pushed him gently. "Will you be back soon?"

"Yes." She was not angry with him. He turned and smiled at her. He went on foot down the shore, near the water, watching the breakers come in. The waves were softened by the harbor's shape. He found William's place. The guard in front of it saluted him. He went in and saw Guy sitting cross-legged on the floor.

"How did your raiding go?" William asked.

"I hardly lost a man. We burned everything between here and London."

Guy rose. "I'm going," he said. He went by Laeghaire in a rush. Laeghaire stepped aside to let him by. William stared after him.

"What's the matter with him?" Laeghaire said.

"His own problem. I have no reason to keep you. You look tired."

"Yes, my lord."

"Good work, Laeghaire."

He went outside again. It was overcast now. He went slowly back toward his hut. William always made him feel pleasant. He saw Guy, ahead of him, talking to Hilde by the door of the hut. He lengthened his stride a little.

They turned toward him. He approached them quickly, without saying anything. Guy looked off at the sea but Hilde smiled and reached out for Laeghaire's hand. She took Laeghaire's hand and led him into the hut. Laeghaire held back a little, passing Guy, and looked down at Guy's bowed dark head.

"Ho, ho," he said, going inside the hut.

"What?" Hilde said.

"Nothing. I'm hungry. Get me something to eat."

She left, and Guy came in immediately and sat down.

"It isn't what you think," Guy said.

Laeghaire moved idly around the hut, shedding his cloak and his surcoat. He took a cup and filled it with water from the bucket. "What do I think?"

"She has nothing to do with it."

"With what?"

"Don't play with me, you carrion-eating dog."

"So you have the nerve to curse me, serf? What the devil do I care if you have a longing for my woman?"

Guy frowned. Laeghaire drank the water. He laughed at Guy. "You fool," he said. "You damned stupid fool."

"She—"

"I don't care what she did or is doing."

Guy got to his feet. "You black-hearted—"

Hilde came in. "What are you arguing about? I could hear you shouting all the way to the well, Guy."

She put meat on the spit and cut bread. Laeghaire sat on his heels and began to eat. She poured him wine and sat next to him. Laeghaire sat chewing meat and looked over at Guy. He swallowed the meat and laughed at

Guy. Guy turned on his heel and went out.

"What's the matter?" Hilde said.

"Guy wants one of my horses. He's taken a great affection for one of them."

"Guy wouldn't take anything of yours."

"I was just teasing him. He could have it if he wanted it, but he's too honorable to take it."

She shrugged. "I don't understand."

"That's all right." He slapped her rump. "Neither does he. Where's Rolf?"

He went out to find Rolf. He spent a little time telling him to clean up his shield and sword, and went off to check his horses. He laughed, watching the horses graze on the scanty grass by the sea.

He did not sleep that night. He lay in the bed, watching the moon through the window over them. Hilde lay beside him, curled up. Her hair was tossed around. He slid out of the bed and walked around the hut. He went outside into the cold moonlight. The stars were all out. The moon was a sickle. He went down to the harbor. The water lapped against the shore. It raked and pulled the pebbles. He sat down cross-legged and watched the waves sweep in. The boat's dark hulls edged back and forth in the harbor. Off by the end of the land he saw the torches of sentries.

Like a slab-sided dog Guy jogged down the beach, crunching pebbles underfoot. He paused and looked at Laeghaire; he stood on one foot and rubbed the other foot against his shin. Suddenly he slithered down and sat by Laeghaire, his knees drawn up and his arms around them. He laid his cheek against his knee.

Laeghaire studied him. Nights like this, he thought, dogs howl and the devilish things of the world go walking. The water smelled like dead men. Guy seemed to

shiver under his tunic. The hair on his neck curled. Laeghaire felt tired. He remembered riding alone in the forest of Germany. It was gone. He would never have it
again. Now he would be a lord and live like a lord with a
lord's duties. Everybody has to grow up.

Guy never said anything. They sat together and never
said anything. Guy was sad. Laeghaire could feel it. He
looked at the moon on the water and watched the boats
moving.

The bell in the church began to ring. Guy started up.
Laeghaire caught his arm. They turned and ran to the
marketplace. Laeghaire had slept. The moon was down.
It was still dark. It was getting light on the eastern hill.
They ran. Laeghaire's chest burned. The marketplace
was filled up, crowded. The bell stopped ringing suddenly. No use alarming the enemy. They were here. It
was time.

William appeared on the well, standing on the edge.
He clung to the crossbar with one hand and waved the
other. The marketplace was crammed. The noise stopped
suddenly.

"Get ready," William said. "We leave as soon as you
are ready."

No need to say anything more. Running. They made
little noise. The horses galloped herded in through the
marketplace. Squires clung to their lead ropes. The
horses reared and played and kicked out. No neighing.
Too quick for noise. Saddles flung over their backs and
girthed and the bits, chilly from the night, forced in between their teeth. The brown stallion squatted his
haunches clenched with muscle, and Laeghaire cursed
him under his breath, buckled on the bridle, and twisted
his ear to keep him quiet. The stallion blew fog through
both nostrils and his eyes rolled. Rolf danced around
with the lead rope in one hand and Laeghaire's mail
thrown over the other arm. Laeghaire grabbed the rope,

made a slipknot in it, and tightened the loop over the stallion's upper lip. The stallion was wild with excitement and anger. Rolf held him down with the twitch.

Laeghaire put on his mail and surcoat in the hut. Hilde sat still on the bed.

"Be careful."

"I will."

Shield, lance, sword. He buckled the belt. The tongue slid into the worn hole. It rested around his hips, settling into ruts it had made over years. Ruts in his body. He took his helmet. She charged into his arms. He kissed her. He thought of the Saxon woman. She stood away from him. He turned and went out. He mounted the brown stallion and Rolf took off the twitch. The stallion fought madly. He twisted and kicked and reared. Laeghaire bent out of the saddle and snatched the rope from Rolf. He beat the stallion with it and spurred him. He beat him solidly over the shoulders and barrel. The stallion stood stock-still. His ears lay back against his poll. Laeghaire gave him rein. The horse shook his head and stayed standing. Laeghaire flung back his head and laughed. He tossed away the rope and turned the stallion and galloped down to the marketplace. The street rang with his passage.

It seemed to move so slowly. The sun came up. The marketplace was clogged with knights and men on foot. They struggled to get into some kind of order. William watched them somberly. He sent men off to direct the masses here and there. There was little noise. Laeghaire saw Tailleford, the jongleur, riding a mule by the well, singing songs.

Slowly, gathering, straightening out into lines and files. The sun lifted away from the hills. They began to move. Now there was noise. Horses and men marching. They moved out of Hastings. The Saxons who had been there all the time came to stand on the wall and watch the Normans go.

Tailleford rode in front of the Duke, singing the old song about Roland and the massacre at Roncevalles. He tossed his ax into the air and caught it tumbling down. He sang in a good deep voice, like an Irish ollamh. Laeghaire turned in the saddle to look back. The men behind him were all arrayed in bright colors, all marching to the time of the song, the foot soldiers first on their palfreys, the knights behind them, and the archers all around. Behind everybody else, the camp-followers came, but he did not see them. He saw nothing but the glinting of the armor and the bobbing of helmets.

They made a long train. He wished he could ride off so that he could see it. Many men, and all of them polished and on their war-horses, all bright in their surcoats, all chanting the refrain to Tailleford's verses. Beside him rode William, who would be King of England if he had his way. William rode his big gray gelding; he rode head and shoulders above Fitz-Osbern on his right and a head taller than Laeghaire on his left. Laeghaire thought he looked like a prophet from the Bible. He looked at William's face, half hidden by the helmet. William's hand on the rein looked strong enough to break Laeghaire's wrist.

The brown stallion shook his head. Laeghaire leaned forward and slapped at a late fly, sucking on the stallion's neck. The land unfolded around them. He wondered if Roland had felt this way, riding to fight the pagans. But Roland had died. Tailleford was singing the death song now. He felt his heart jump, hearing the old song.

He could hear Tailleford's voice and the answering voices of the men behind him, and the hoofs of the horses and the feet of the unmounted men, pounding on the land. He looked again at William's great fist.

"How many battles have you fought?" William said suddenly.

"I don't know."

"Are you ever afraid now?"

"No."

"Do you suppose that Roland was afraid?" Fitz-Osbern said.

"No." Laeghaire said. "Roland could hardly have been; he'd told the Emperor that he would prefer to die in the vanguard than live by flight, and anyhow, he had a chance to call up help and he refused."

"Would you have sounded that horn?" William said.

Laeghaire grinned. "Yes, by God. I'm thirsty. Where's wine?"

Fitz-Osbern called for one of the squires riding nearby and sent him for wine.

"It was a betrayal, though," Fitz-Osbern said. "Not an ordinary case."

"It makes no difference. I would have blown that horn until my chest burst."

William laughed.

"There are finer songs in Ireland, though," Laeghaire said. "None of this mess with honor and to blow a horn or not."

"Sing us one."

"It's in Gaelic. You wouldn't understand it."

"What is it about?"

"Cuchulain, the greatest hero in Ireland, except for Fionn MacCumhail, and I always preferred Cuchulain."

"What else?"

"Cuchulain had curses against him, because he had killed the hound of the smith Culain—that's how he got his name. He couldn't eat dog, but he had to accept food when it was offered—"

"Why?"

"Because those were the terms."

"I like Roland better," Fitz-Osbern said.

"What happened to Cuchulain?" William said.

"He finally had to eat dog because of this curse, and he died in battle. He tied himself to a stone column with his belt so that he would die standing on his feet."

"You mean the curse killed him?"

"The curse weakened him. He couldn't pass a fire where food was cooking without eating of it, and three witches cooked dog over a fire by the road he had to pass along, so that he would lose some of his strength."

"Sing it in Gaelic, now that we understand," William said.

"I would rather listen to Tailleford, my lord."

But he sang the song to himself, reciting the Gaelic, and did not listen to Tailleford.

They came to the place where the Saxons were drawn up, even while Tailleford was singing the last few verses. Tailleford sang of the old, old Emperor lying asleep, and the Normans gathered, facing the Saxons. The Saxons were still moving into place. Tailleford sang of the angel coming to the Emperor in his sleep, and the Saxons raised their shields before them and made that great unbreakable wall, and their standards went up; while the Emperor wept into his long beard and lamented that God had called him out again to fight.

They were all silent. They stood there, on that hill at the other end of the valley, those Saxons, and Laeghaire saw the housekarls in the middle and the fyrd on either side, ranged on the top of the hill and protected by the ranging of the trees. The standards curled and uncurled above them. Harold's banner and the Wessex Dragon. Harold's banner was of gold, and it snapped in the wind. The gray clouds raced above it and the wind rippled through it. He could hardly hear William's instructions. They were waiting. One of them was waiting for him.

One of them was going to kill him. Kill him, Laeghaire, Laeghaire of the Long Road, all to end here, and he felt his heart gather and ice. The field was long and green and brown before them, all the way to the opposite hill and the shield wall. Now the archers jogged up, to take a place off to the left, off on a little bit of a rise. The shield wall was closed and hard, like the back of a turtle. The standard curled and uncurled above it. There was no sun. The sun had gone in. That was what the dream meant, the dream of the wolf and the witch: dying.

The horns blared. Laeghaire rode by William, down along the field, and the whole heated press of the Normans was all around him. Not one man here speaks my born tongue, not one man here knows my home. He gripped the lance and raised it a little. All my life come to this. Perhaps it's better. Yes.

William sent Fitz-Osbern up to call out Harold the Saxon and declaim against him. Fitz-Osbern rode alone over the plain on his gay, draped horse. The sound of the horse came clearly back to him. Laeghaire turned and looked at the banner, borne close by William, the torn blue banner blessed by the Pope. He spat into the dust. His mouth was dry.

Fitz-Osbern spoke some words, and the Saxon spoke some words. Fitz-Osbern turned and rode back. His horse grew larger and larger, cantering back across the valley. The sound grew bigger. Fitz-Osbern leaned out, saluting William. His horse reached the Norman lines. The horns blasted. They charged.

The foot soldiers ran in first, with half the archers. The arrows of the archers dropped harmlessly against the shield wall. The foot soldiers closed the gap rapidly. William held back the knights, watching. Laeghaire trembled all over. The stallion plunged and curved his neck. The foot soldiers seemed puny. Suddenly the defenders on the hill loosed a rain of missiles on them.

Many of the foot soldiers fell. Laeghaire swore under his breath. He glanced at William. William stared down at the shield wall. His eyes never blinked. Laeghaire could feel his mind working. The noise from the battle up there was tremendous. William moved his hand and the motion was gigantic.

The knights galloped down, threading through the retreating foot soldiers. Laeghaire galloped beside William. The stallion was faster than the gray gelding but Laeghaire held him back. They struck the shield wall. It clanged like a sword on a sword. A fence of axes rose before them. Laeghaire hurled his lance and drew his sword. The stallion reared, clawing at the wall. Laeghaire bent down and slashed awkwardly at a helmeted head. The head swung back when he struck it. An ax reached for him. He thrust it away with his sword. He felt a tight binding in his chest. He felt the heat rising in his chest. He shouted and took the sword in both hands and smashed at the housekarl below him. Suddenly the man vanished.

The rest of the knights were backing away. Laeghaire wrenched the stallion around. From the corner of his eye he saw a Saxon, shield advanced, running in toward his back. He swung around and wheeled the sword backhanded. The blade took the Saxon across the shoulder and toppled him.

He turned and galloped after the other Normans. He was the last man away from the shield wall. He heard a cheer behind him and swung his shield around to cover his back. He saw part of the fyrd break the line and come running after them, cheering and waving their weapons.

The Normans were all in a wild flight. Laeghaire shouted. He veered the stallion. He saw the gray gelding leap around, and a horn blew. Knights swerved around all over the field. They flew down on the isolated little band of Saxons, cut them apart from the shield wall, and turned in on them. They rushed together and for a moment struck and butchered, and rushed back, cantering off. Behind them Laeghaire saw the tangled, mauled bodies of the little band of Saxons.

He rode back with William to their hill and watched the Normans slowly regrouping. They sat silent on their horses. The shield wall was unbroken. Their Norman dead lay on the slope, and that litle patch of Saxons. The banner flew wildly over the wall. The Saxons cheered again, and Laeghaire called for water and dampened his lips and sat motionless, breathing.

"Is there a chance that we could encircle them?" Fitz-Osbern said to William.

"Take us all day to ride around. Lose the advantage."

"What advantage?" Fitz-Osbern said, and bit his lip. "They are slaughtering us."

"He just reached this place last night. His men are tired. And he hasn't got all his men here yet. You wait and see."

Laeghaire walked the brown stallion back and forth. He passed William and Fitz-Osbern every few moments and heard bits of what they said. He hardly cared. He looked up at that wall and at the dead men and horses on the slope. It seemed straight as a church aisle, straight from him to the men he would kill and who would kill him. For this day he had been born, to sit his saddle on this day and see all the events of his life in the pattern that took him to this straight line that lay between his life and his death.

The horns blew and they reassembled. The greatest mass of the foot soldiers was on the right flank now. The archers were all up on the end of the hill to the left. William had moved his fingers and everybody had scurried into place.

The archers cocked their bows and leaned back and

aimed and fired, and on the whining of the flying shafts they charged.

William beside him seemed to brace; they struck the shield wall and the horses smashed against it. The axes and the swords and the Welsh hooks reached for them. The brown stallion stumbled and Laeghaire snatched for the pommel of the saddle. Something crashed against his shield. The stallion struggled up. Laeghaire was half out of the saddle. He lashed out blindly with the shield and felt the edge strike another shield and crush it in. The stallion lunged. Laeghaire was over the cantle of the saddle. He hauled himself back into the seat. He was in the middle of the Saxons. They turned on him like devils. The wall was behind him; he was alone. He lashed out around him. The shield was half wrenched from his arm. He cleaved a Saxon from shoulder to waist and the blood showered over him. A sword crossed his and he whipped it free. He caught an ax blow on the edge of the shield and heard the iron ring. He wheeled the horse and spurred him, dropping the rein. A man leaped for him and caught his wrist. He swept the Saxon away with his sword. The stallion reared and bolted. Laeghaire caught a blow on his right fist and struck back by reflex. The swing struck nothing until the very end and caught bone and flesh. He clubbed down a housekarl with the flat of the sword, and the stallion jumped. Laeghaire caught at the pommel of the saddle and the rein. The stallion galloped down the slope, full speed.

He rode back to where William sat his horse and talked. It was hot, as if the lowering clouds penned all the heat under them like a forge.

"I never thought I'd see you back again, Irish," William said.

"There was a moment when I wasn't too sure of it," Laeghaire said.

He dismounted and looked at the stallion. William sent someone to call a truce so that they could look for wounded. The stallion was cut over both knees and breathing hard. Laeghaire washed the blood from the horse's knees. The stallion was covered with blood, but most of it was Saxon.

Laeghaire took off his glove. His thumb was smashed. A piece of white bone thrust up through the torn skin. The thumb was shapeless.

He took a piece from his surcoat and wrapped up the thumb. William rode over. "If that's all you're wounded, you'll survive."

"I need it to hold my sword." He put the glove back on and curled his fingers. "Unh. That's all right."

William smiled. "Are you ever afraid, Irish?"

"Would it make any difference? I think I'm going to get it today."

William was silent for a while.

"It's as good a place as any to end my life, isn't it?" Laeghaire said.

"No," William said. "It isn't."

Laeghaire looked up at him.

"Mount up," William said. He looked angry. He had not been angry all through the battle.

He mounted. He could see the sun faintly, through the clouds, and the men coming back, with the wounded carried on their saddles. Jehan passed him, borne between two men. They laid him down. His back was smashed. His head turned slowly from side to side. His mouth was so drawn up with pain that it seemed to slit his head in half.

"Let's go," William said. He looked over at the archers, shooting in regular volleys, now that the field was cleared, and the arrows sliding through the sky and down past the wall, past the standard rippling like a snake.

They rolled in on the shield wall and the whole line hacked and struck at it and at the Saxons behind it. A few Normans broke through and were cut down before they could widen the gap or hold it, and the wall closed up behind them. Laeghaire saw the twisted mouths of the Saxons, saw them swear and wince and scream, and his arm was independent of his body, launching the sword against them. Only the sharp pain in his thumb reminded him that that arm was part of him. He took half a dozen murderous blows on his shield, turning them off, his arm numbed. He felt the stallion shy once at a Welsh hook and come up against William's horse. They withdrew again in disorder and the fyrd came down after them and desperately the Normans turned and hacked them to pieces, hating them.

"We won't break them," Fitz-Osbern said. "They are like iron."

"We'll break them," William said.

Laeghaire raised his head. He took off his helmet. The cool air touched his sweaty hair and he felt better.

"They've lost a lot of men," William said. "We'll take them."

It was midafternoon now. The sun was gone again. The clouds pressed down on them. The standard of the Saxons waved and fluttered before them. Suddenly it was small, who won or lost here, who lived or died. All the great plans, they sounded good and wise and huge when we talk about them, Laeghaire thought, they sound like the actions of God, but when I come up to them they are nothing but little men on little horses playing war.

He looked at William, doubting, and William's face was calm and steady, the mouth not smiling, not frowning, thinking, the eyes thinking. He never stopped thinking.

"Mount up. Mount up."

His body screamed that he could not mount up again

and ride down there. He mounted. They were very much fewer. Jehan was gone; he must have died.

They rode straight for the wall. The stallion was tired and would not race. The horses labored and the foam splashed over them. Laeghaire knew from the way the horse shifted his weight that they had reached the base of the slope up to the shield wall. They came against the wall and were stopped and they fought across the shields. The swords glittered in the air; the air was full of iron. The Saxons seemed to lean forward to claw at them, the shield wall folded in on them.

William's horse reared straight up and fell. Laeghaire bent the stallion around. The gray was thrashing on the ground. The Saxons broke to surround them. Laeghaire flung out his shield to cover William. He smashed at the grinning, clawing enemy Saxons. He wanted to destroy them all; he wanted to hurt them, to pound them into pulp. He could not see. His eyes were in his sword, and he moved his sword with his whole body. He stood in his stirrups and crushed the Saxons under his sword and ground them down. Their heads cracked under his sword like bugs. Their faces split and their grinning mouths grew all around their heads, and their chests fountained blood. The blood sprayed over him and he was covered with it and the horse slipped and stumbled. He flogged them with his sword. William was up behind him. He spurred the stallion away. They retreated wildly, and once again the fyrd charged after them, and once again the Normans wheeled to cut them off and slaughtered them, but the housekarls stayed on their hill and would not come down and be slaughtered too.

He reined up. William slid to the ground and walked a few steps away. He sat down on the ground. Laeghaire said, "Are you hurt?" He dismounted. The stallion had a cut on his foreleg. Laeghaire bound it up.

"No."

The Normans had regrouped, but they were shouting. Laeghaire raised his head. He listened to them. William stood up. "Give me your horse," he said. He mounted the brown stallion.

"They think you are dead," Fitz-Osbern said. His face was black with blood and dirt. "They think you are dead."

William pulled off his helmet. He turned and rode out in front of the Normans. They quieted. He rode along before them and a cheer began and followed him. It grew up like a storm and followed him. Laeghaire sat and heard them and bent his head.

He could have died, he thought. He might have died. Oh, God, if he had died—

William rode back. He called for another horse. Laeghaire looked up at him. He thought he had never seen that face before. Calm as a priest's and savage, and huge; he thought this man much bigger than any other man he had ever seen. He shook, looking at William. The eyes stared glittering out, seeing farther and seeing greater than the eyes of a man. He thought he looked at a mask, and behind the shields of the eyes burned all the fires of the world in arms.

Laeghaire glanced at Fitz-Osbern. He wondered if he looked as Fitz-Osbern looked, seeing William. He got up and mounted the brown stallion.

"Thank you," William said. He mounted a bay horse. He gathered the reins into his hands. He clapped Laeghaire on the shoulder. "Once more, Irish."

He looked down the long ride to the shield wall and saw that they had cut down the wall's length. The Saxons had lost men, too. Laeghaire flexed his thumb and bit his lip against the pain. He curled it around his sword and rested the flat of the sword on his other wrist. William's new horse was fresh and restless. It shied and kicked out.

"Once more."

They charged under the horns and they ripped at the shield wall and were flung back. It was almost sundown. The sky in the west was red when they drew up. The field was slick with blood.

"This is the last one," William said. "Rest for it. This is the last one. We'll camp here tonight and try again tomorrow if this one doesn't work."

The archers bent their bows and raised the arrows and let fly. Laeghaire watched the arrows whisper into the ground and glance off the shield wall. He knew that he would not come back from this charge.

"I'll be disappointed if I don't die today," he said.

William laughed. The laugh was big and thundering.

No, we will never break them. The arrows slid by the Saxons. They pierced the standard of gold that whipped in the wind.

"Charge."

The horse moved forward, sluggish, and Laeghaire bent to ease him. He saw the bay horse moving easily beside them. The bay horse, that capered, while they moved with such pain.

Up there, the golden standard fell.

The Normans went a little way before they saw and realized it. They cheered. Laeghaire pulled the dirty air into his lungs and cheered. He felt the horse leap forward.

"Get them. Get them. This time—"

The brown stallion hurtled into the wall and it collapsed. The Saxons fell back step by step, and all along the wall the line broke. Laeghaire leaned forward and chopped over the stallion's shoulder, clawing at them. He saw their startled faces, filthy too, and they fought up at him. Suddenly they turned and ran, and the Normans cheered again and chased them. Laeghaire spurred the stallion. The horse took three strides and fell. He fell over his head and somersaulted. Laeghaire thudded against the ground, ten feet from the horse.

He got to his feet, dazed, and a great black bear of a Saxon dove at him. They fell and wrestled on the ground. Laeghaire drove his fists into the man's face. He gasped for breath. The man had him around the waist. He snatched out his dagger and stabbed the man in the back. The Saxon reared up and threw him down. Laeghaire's head struck the ground and he was stunned. The Saxon hulked over him. The Saxon drew a dagger. Laeghaire twisted away from him, flinging himself sideways. The dagger leaped for his face. The dagger slashed him, sliding over his helmet and driving into his face. He could not see; his eyes were full of blood. He lashed out. He flung the man off and staggered to his feet. "You've killed me—" He lunged against the man and felt the arms embrace him again and crush the life out of him. He stabbed again into the man. The flesh yielded like water. He stabbed and stabbed and stabbed. They were on the ground, rolling. He felt his last breath whistle through his teeth. He felt himself dying. They came to rest. The Saxon was still on top of him. The arms embraced him. He felt no more life in him to fight. He lay still.

In the darkness he opened his eyes and saw nothing. He turned his head. The face of the man he had killed stared back at him. The eyes were dead stones.

He moved. He pushed the man away and came to his knees. His head burst with a terrible ache. He swayed. It was dark. It was black night.

Far down the field he saw fires. He climbed to his feet. He took two steps and stopped. He was alive. He could barely move. He was alive.

I am alive. He took a step for each word: I am alive.

The fires came closer. He saw men on the field, looking among the dead. The dead lay everywhere. He went down to the fires. They were spread out in a wide circle.

"Who goes?"

Sentry, off to his right. He stopped and lifted his head. The torchlight flooded over him. The sentry stared at him.

"My lord." The sentry took a step forward. "My lord. We thought you were dead. We thought—"

The sentry turned and shouted, "Hi, you bloody Normans, the Irishman's come back."

Laeghaire went by him. His horses were standing there, just past these fires. There was a lot of shouting. They were shouting his name. He stopped. They gathered around him. They did not touch him. They began to cheer. His name rose up out of their voices like a wave out of the sea. They shouted his name like a battle cry.

Guy came shoving through them, beating them aside, and came up to him, with his head down like a penitent.

"She's looking for you," he said.

He put his hand on Laeghaire's arm. Laeghaire jerked. "Take your hand off me," he said.

Guy looked up at him. The Normans were still all

around, cheering him and shouting. His name hung in the air.

"She said you weren't dead," Guy said. "She said nobody could kill you."

Laeghaire shook his head. "Well . . ."

He started toward his tent. He looked up over the heads of the men who surged around him and saw William. William sat his fine bay horse there behind them all and watched. He wheeled the horse suddenly and galloped off.

Laeghaire tasted blood in his mouth. He looked after William and laughed. He went down to his tent.

"Laeghaire. Laeghaire."

She caught him by the arms and turned him. She put up a hand and touched his face. He felt the wound again, all down the side of his face. She sobbed and embraced him. She turned and crying led him back, led him by the hand like a child. She took him to her fire and sat him down like a child and got water and washed his face. He saw the firelight leap over her face and the tears and her hair and eyes. She gave him food and he ate.

"Your face. Your poor face."

He could not see from that eye. Perhaps he never would. He finished eating. She wept. She held him in her arms and wept. After a while he pushed her away. He went to the black horse, tethered by the fire, and pulled the rope loose. He mounted the horse bareback. She stood by the fire. Her hair was a halo from the firelight. He rode off, just a little way, to a tree, and dismounted and sat under the tree, with his back to the fires.

He remembered the child in the vault where the giant and the giantess were buried. He remembered the body of the child in the vault. But he was alive.

It began to rain. He thought of the child and sat still. The rain soaked into him and washed down his face.

"Irish."

"Well," Laeghaire said. "Behold. The King of England."

William said nothing.

"And now are you happy?" Laeghaire said.

"They love you, Irish. They shouted your name like some hero's."

"So they did. I heard them."

"If you hadn't been there today, I might not be alive now."

"I accept your gracious thanks, my lord. Accept your life out of my hands, if you wish it. But it's all in a day's work, my lord. You need not thank me." Laeghaire squirmed a little against the tree, getting comfortable. "As for me, I will always say that I have known the King of England." He put his head back against the tree and looked at the branches. "And that the King of England knows my name."

"Laeghaire from Tralee. Laeghaire of the Long Road."

The wind came up and blew the rain into Laeghaire's face. William's horse lowered his head and snuffled the grass. Laeghaire grinned. The silence drew out like a web between them. He could feel William testing it, uneasy of his way. The rain was cool.

"What do you want, Irish?"

"Why, what can you give me, King of England?"

"Damn you."

William swung his horse and rode off.

Laeghaire sat under the tree and listened to the rain. He felt it in his eyes. He thought of Murrough, of his dead son Murrough.

He got up and went down again to the fire. Rolf and Hilde and Guy had put up the tent. He went into it. Rolf and Guy left at once. Laeghaire sat down and Hilde came over to him and bandaged his face. She wound the white linen over his face, careful to give him one eye to see by.

"Laeghaire," she said.

"Yes."

"You're leaving, aren't you?"

"Yes."

"I'm not going with you."

"No."

"Would you stay if I told you I was pregnant again?"

"No."

She fastened the linen. She was not crying. "You ought never to have brought me here. You ought to have left me in Germany."

"You'll be happy here with Guy."

"I don't love Guy."

"Why, I don't love you, either. Leave me alone."

"Why can't you love me?"

"Leave me alone."

"When are you going?"

"Tomorrow."

"Where are you going?"

"I don't know."

"Oh, God, that sounds terrible. That's horrible."

He laughed. He got up and went away from her. He felt stronger now. He laughed again. "Go be a countess, little one. But leave me alone. The King of England, may God bless him, will give you what you want for the mention of my name. Speak of me now and then to him, will you?"

He went to the door and looked out. It was cool. The rain was chilly. He touched the bandage. Well, tomorrow, he thought. Tomorrow I will go.

Cecelia Holland

Cecelia Holland was born on New Year's Eve,
1943, in Henderson, Nevada, and was raised in
Metuchen, New Jersey, and Woodbridge, Connecticut. She is a graduate of Connecticut College,
and is currently studying toward a doctorate at
Columbia University.